D1501237

Breeding LIKE RABBITS

Ardyce C. Whalen

iUniverse

BREEDING LIKE RABBITS

iUniverse books may be ordered through booksellers or by contacting:

iUniverse
1663 Liberty Drive
Bloomington, IN 47403
www.iuniverse.com
1-800-Authors (1-800-288-4677)

Because of the dynamic nature of the Internet, any web addresses or links contained in this book may have changed since publication and may no longer be valid. The views expressed in this work are solely those of the author and do not necessarily reflect the views of the publisher, and the publisher hereby disclaims any responsibility for them.

Any people depicted in stock imagery provided by Thinkstock are models, and such images are being used for illustrative purposes only. Certain stock imagery © Thinkstock.

ISBN: 978-1-5320-2415-3 (sc)
ISBN: 978-1-5320-2416-0 (e)

Library of Congress Control Number: 2017909791

Print information available on the last page.

iUniverse rev. date: 07/03/2017

O God, give us the serenity to accept
what cannot be changed,
the courage to change what can be changed,
and the wisdom to know the one from the other.

—Reinhold Niebuhr

ACKNOWLEDGMENTS

I am thankful to my two good friends and readers, Carolee Mock and Judie Kelly, for their honesty and helpful criticism.

INTRODUCTION

The name of my book, *Breeding like Rabbits*, is derived from Pope Francis's press conference with journalists on the plane back to Rome from the Philippines on January 19, 2015. During the conference, he stated that Catholics do not have to "breed like rabbits" and should instead practice responsible parenting, adding that there were "many" church-approved ways to regulate births. (Abstinence and the rhythm method are the only two approved ways.)

He firmly defended the 1968 encyclical *Humanae Vitae* (*Human Life*), which prohibits the use of contraception, "any action which, either in anticipation of the conjugal act [sexual intercourse], or in its accomplishment, or in the development of its natural consequences, proposes, whether as an end or as a means, to render procreation impossible" (*Humanae Vitae* 14). Such an action is a mortal sin, putting the soul in danger of death.

"Human weakness" was given as a reason for this constraint, especially the weakness of young men who must be encouraged to be faithful to moral law. "It is also feared that the man, growing used to the employment of anti-conceptive practices, may finally lose respect for the woman and, no longer caring for her physical and psychological equilibrium, may come to the point of considering her as a mere instrument of selfish enjoyment, and no longer as his respected and beloved companion" (*HV* 17).

Notice that it is *male* weakness that the pope understands, but the conjugal act also involves a female who brings an egg to the act—no small thing. The female, who provides the egg; who nourishes the embryo, should conception take place, with her own life's blood; and who raises the resulting child, had no say or thought given to her in the formulation of the encyclical.

The act of sexual intercourse has two persons inextricably related in an active manner that makes both persons involved responsible for the act; it takes two to tango. To make church law about such a situation without considering both persons equally is unconscionable and results in a flawed law.

Perhaps the pope and those around him realized that they could not understand the female perspective; after all, they were all unmarried men.

Britt, the protagonist in my book, realizes that her marriage is unraveling—the rhythm method does not work for her and Andy. She decides to do what she must to save her marriage and her sanity. She and her husband would be "responsible parents."

Today we have serious problems: world population is more than 7 billion, and of that number, the Vatican figures 1.2 billion are Catholic (40 percent live in Latin America). The biggest growth spurt of Catholics is in some parts of Africa, where brother fights against brother and fathers against sons for enough land to support their families—and the Zika virus is spreading.

This is not acceptable. I'm not so naive to think that I can change the encyclical, but if enough people decide that "responsible parenting" is their moral duty, they will change what they cannot accept, as Britt does in my novel. (Perhaps the church can reason its way into needed change and into the twenty-first century.)

CHAPTER

1

A lone figure made her way down a dark street of a small town in northern Minnesota. It was two in the morning. Her boss had let her go an hour early from her job as a carhop at the only drive-in hamburger place in town. It wasn't easy getting Jackie to let her go early, but when she volunteered to help with cutting whole chickens into pieces for the Chicken-in-the-Baskets next Saturday, Jackie agreed. Britt just couldn't miss the coming-home party for the boys back from the summer harvest brigade. This was Andy's second year of being a combine driver with Mel Olson's fleet of combines. In May, they trucked their combines to Oklahoma and became part of the great custom combining operation. They worked their way up and across the Great Plains, harvesting the ripened fields of wheat, earning eight dollars an acre. In September, when there were no more wheat fields to harvest, they headed back home to Minnesota.

Britt had missed Andy a lot. She picked up her pace, eager to get to the party at Andy's parents' home. She could hear the music, and her tiredness vanished. "I've Got a Lovely Bunch of Coconuts," not Britt's favorite tune by a long shot, blared out into the night—someone had probably piled a whole stack of 45 rpms on the record player. She hoped they'd play "Buttons and Bows"—she liked the rhythm. Someone let out a loud belly laugh—that was Luke, Andy's brother. He was, as usual, the life of the party.

Britt opened the door in time to see Luke weaving toward her, balancing a large platter of sliced ham. *Too many beers in that boy,* she thought. Her eyes opened wide, and her mouth gaped as the ham started to slide off the platter, slice by slice—*splat*—onto the floor. *Oh no.*

She picked up the ham slices and put them into a large bowl. "Here, Luke. You dropped them; you deal with them." How he dealt with them, she didn't care, but as the girlfriend of a returning combine driver, in whose home this party was held, it was probably up to her to clean the grease off the floor—someone might slip in it and get hurt. She'd have to get down on her hands and knees in order to scrub the cracked linoleum. Thank goodness it was a small kitchen. Britt went into the closet off the kitchen and found the scrub bucket, filled it half full of water, and poured in some Pine Sol. She then grabbed the scrub brush and scrub rag and set to work.

Job done—no one would slip on ham grease now. She stood, put her hands to the small of her back, and stretched to get the kinks out. Luke was making some kind of speech.

"Lishin up, guys! You're at this party, firs' 'cause the parents are out of town, secon' 'cause Andy is back home and he bought a keg ..." Luke paused until the cheers and whistles died down. "An' third cause Andy joined the navy! I kid you not, he's gonna be swabbin' a deck in a cute sailor suit for four years!"

Britt felt sick. He'd just come home, and now he was going again. She had no idea he was planning such a thing. Some of the partiers started singing "Anchors Aweigh," others were thumping Andy on the back, and someone yelled, "A girl in every port!" Britt headed for the back door.

She plopped herself down on the splintery bench in back of the house. Coming to the party after seven hours of work at the drive-in, having to get down on her hands and knees to scrub ham grease off a floor, and then hearing that Andy had enlisted in the US Navy was just too much. Brit was exhausted. Her mind was awhirl, and in the whirl, she found an old nursery rhyme that her mother used to read to her and her sister:

> Bobby Shaftoe's gone to sea,
> Silver buckles on his knee:
> He'll come back and marry me,
> Pretty Bobby Shaftoe!

But maybe he won't come back. His ship might be bombed. Or maybe he'll come home with a war bride.

The back screen door slammed. A guy came out and walked to the back of the house. It was Andy. He saw Britt sitting on the old bench.

"Scoot over." He sat down and tried to hug her.

Britt pushed him away. "How could you? How could you sign your life away for four years and not tell me first?"

"You're making too much of it. I enlisted so I wouldn't be drafted. I didn't want to take a chance on that and end up living in a foxhole somewhere in Korea."

"When do you go?"

"In two weeks."

"So soon? What for? And just where is that anyway?"

"It's for basic training, or boot camp, and it's at the Great Lakes Naval Training Center in North Chicago."

"And I had to find it out from Luke at this party, at the

same time everyone found out." Britt crossed her arms across her chest to avoid hitting him. "You're chicken. You thought that with all those people around I wouldn't get mad, didn't you? Well, I'm mad."

Andy leaned back on the bench, resting his head against the white clapboard of the house. He didn't know what to say, so he looked up. He tried to think but was distracted by the night's beauty. The town was too small for any streetlights to interfere with starlight. The stars twinkled, and in Technicolor yet: some slightly pink, and there was a pale blue one. Maybe his eyes were playing tricks on him. How would the stars look out at sea with the whole sky in view? He wanted to get away. Winter was coming, and if he stayed around, he'd be stuck in a dark, dank potato warehouse, sorting potatoes for shipment. A mole, that's what he'd be.

Britt broke the silence. "You'll be gone four *years*. What am I supposed to do? Sit and wait? You know I don't like waiting; I'm not an 'absence makes the heart grow fonder' kind of person."

"You're in college, so study!" His head left the clapboard siding, and he sat erect and looked right at her. "Get your degree."

"But I haven't even chosen a major yet! Dad doesn't want me to be a nurse. A couple of his sisters were nurses, and he says it's a dog's life, whatever that means—after all, some dogs have it pretty darn good. I could be a teacher, but I'd just die if I had to stand up in front of a class—everyone looking at me—and then I'd have to talk."

"You'll think of something." He leaned back to rest his head on the clapboard siding once more and closed his eyes.

"We could get married. If a girl doesn't want to be a nurse, teacher, or secretary, all that's left is to get married. We've been dating for four years, after all—we know each other. I want to know your intentions. That's all."

"Yeah, you just want to go out with other guys. That's all."

"I don't want to be dangling on a string, or as you sailors would say, dangling on a lanyard, not knowing where we stand. I want some certainty."

What *would* she do while he was gone? She'd completed two years at the university but had not yet chosen a major. She'd started out in home economics, but being sure she was not cut out to be a teacher, she switched to nutrition—she'd be able to wear a white coat and work in a lab—but she found the required organic chemistry course to be tedious, so she dropped it and the nutrition idea. She was now taking a business course. She really didn't know what to do, but she knew she didn't want to *not* know where their relationship was heading during the four years Andy would be gone. Was she going to lose her best friend or not?

Andy turned and faced her. "Okay. Let's get married."

Britt was stunned. She thought for sure he'd say something like, "Okay, let's cool it and decide later when I get mustered out." Had she wanted him to turn her down? Did she love him enough to actually *marry* him? She'd never gone steady with anyone else. Oh, there was Jesse. He'd sat behind her in one of her classes last semester, but they'd only gone out twice. She liked him.

But marriage to Andy was what she needed to consider now. She was comfortable with him—she trusted him. He liked people and could talk to anyone, so unlike her. He was her icebreaker. How could she face the world on her own?

She sat, her arms wrapped around her in a hug, more to comfort and protect than to ward off the slight chill of the early morning. She was too tired to think.

"Andy, I can't answer you right now. I need time to think. I need sleep."

"Well, think about this: I'll have my service pay. We can make it." He gave her shoulder a little squeeze. "You can come with me no matter where the navy sends me. It'll be great."

After a few kisses and a big hug, they said good night.

Britt walked to the house where she'd rented a room for the summer—not a long walk in a town of fewer than eight hundred people. Her parental home was ten miles out in the country, an unacceptable commute, especially since on weekends carhops worked until nearly sunup. She'd have a hard time sleeping tonight—so much to think about.

Lying awake in bed, Britt wondered if Andy was right when he said they could manage to make it as a married couple and that she could travel with him. But *marriage*? That was serious—that was forever. She could practically hear doors—doors of other choices, other opportunities—slamming shut. It was frightening, but the thought of losing Andy was more frightening, and he must have felt the same way when he suggested marriage.

Did she really want to drop out of college? She'd have earned no degree. What would her parents say? They'd feel they'd wasted money on her, just thrown it away. But she was so lonely! She'd made no *real* friends in the two years she'd been attending the U. The classes were easy, but when not in class, she felt out of place. The girls in the dorm seemed so sophisticated, so worldly; in comparison, she was a baby. Britt was afraid that if she opened up to any of them, they would treat her as she was treated in high school. She didn't want to go through anything like that again. Britt rolled over, sat up, and gave her pillow a couple of hard punches. Lying down again, she thought about those bad old days.

High school! Her first year there was a disaster. She didn't know how to act after coming from a country school that never had more than a dozen students—relatives and neighbor kids. Around strangers, she lacked social skills.

Small talk, what's that? Britt was especially uncomfortable talking to boys. She blamed her cousin, a town kid, for most of her freshman problems, because she told everyone that Britt had showed her how one of her growing breasts was bigger than the other. When Britt came to class, she was greeted with, "Here comes Britt the Tit!"

She wanted to die. Just thinking about it made her face flame—she could feel the heat—embarrassment? Rage? Idiots. One day it got so bad that she left school and just walked around town until it was time to get on the bus for home. She didn't realize that the powers that be would call her parents. Britt got the third degree when she got home. She cried and pleaded with them to let her quit school. They wouldn't hear of it. When her sister, Hannah, two years younger than she, started high school, it was better. They'd wave to each other when passing in the halls, and by that time, she'd made a friend of her own—she wasn't as lonely anymore.

Britt couldn't just drop out of school and go home; life would be awful. She'd spend her days arguing religion with her mother, who'd remind her that her Pentecostal preacher grandfather had fled Norway and come to America to avoid persecution, which was much worse than any problems Britt might have. Her mother would say, "You can get over your shyness if you just practice talking to people; push yourself. In time, you'll have lots of friends; I know it. If at first you don't succeed, try, try again!"

Her mother didn't understand that Britt did not want "lots of friends"—one or two would be great, three would be almost too many. More than hating to argue with her mother, she hated disappointing her father. He wanted his daughter to be a college graduate and get a job that paid well. He had always wanted more schooling. After one year of high school, the near death of his father from Spanish flu had forced him to quit and come home and farm. Marriage seemed the only way out for Britt.

Marriage would give her an instant identity: "Mrs. Andrew Hughes." After all, wasn't that the main reason girls went to college? They were there to get their "Mrs." She'd heard that sad joke countless times. She had wondered earlier if she loved him enough to marry him, but did she love him at all? What is "love"? She never felt the earth move, nor did she hear bells when they kissed—such reactions may only be propaganda spread by mushy romance novels. But she certainly *liked* him, and he was kind. Last year when he returned from the harvest brigade, the first thing he bought was a Sunbeam mixer for his mother. Britt wanted a man like that—one that would put her first and who'd be kind. It didn't hurt either that Andy was very handsome, with black, wavy hair, brown eyes, and the body of a natural athlete, which he was.

It would be an adventure! "Join the navy and see the world!" In her case, it'd be, "Marry a sailor and see the world with him." Britt wanted out of small-town rural America. Getting married meant that she no longer had to figure out who she really was and what she really wanted. She'd be a wife, with a husband who also was her best friend. But was she just using Andy as an escape hatch? Perhaps, but she could help him make the marriage work. She was taking a business course now, and she was a good typist. If she dropped out of the university and went to a business school, she could be certified as a secretary by the time Andy finished basic training. A good secretary could get a job anywhere.

But marriage was scary. She rolled to her other side. Darn! Now she was all tangled up in the sheet. She freed her legs, and her mind again snapped back to thoughts of marriage. Andy's parents didn't have a particularly happy marriage. His father took construction jobs in other states, and when he came home, he read books and drank. His mother worked as a clerk at Ace Hardware part-time, and she took in washing and ironing for other people. Her income was the only steady one, the one that fed the family. Britt had been over there several times, but never did she see any show of mutual affection, nor did she hear them talking, really talking, to each other.

Britt's parents wouldn't win a happy marriage contest either. A silent father who avoided affection in both word and deed was a hard man to live with. Her mother was just the opposite; she craved affection, was starved for it, and suffered when it was not forthcoming. The only time either one laughed and seemed to enjoy life was when they were with others: her mom with the quilt club or chatting up the hired "girl," and her dad out in the fields yakking it up with his hired hands. Many times, Britt wondered how those two ever made it to the altar. She'd heard that her father had been engaged to another and that the woman had run away with his cousin. They married, and seven months later, the woman gave birth to a premature baby. It must have hurt her father a lot if it were true. She never dared ask.

The question was, could Andy and she have a good marriage with those role models? Losing him, however, terrified her—and love conquers all, right?

Yes, she would be a navy wife. And with that decision, Admiral Farragut's words appropriately popped into her head just before sleep descended: damn the torpedoes and full speed ahead!

CHAPTER

2

On Britt's last day of work, she planned to tell her boss, Jackie, a sturdy woman with a my-way-or-the-highway attitude, that she was going to be married to Andy Hughes early next year. While waiting for Jackie to finish totaling up the day's proceeds, Britt took a good look around.

It wasn't a big place, but the location was great—right off the highway that ran north to the Canadian border and south to the Twin Cities of Minneapolis and St. Paul. It had all the usual equipment needed by a fast-food place that served hamburgers and french fries. You knew it was a drive-in though, because of the long, eighteen-inch-wide shelf right below the two large front windows. The windows slid open when an order was ready. The carhop put the order on a tray, the kind that attaches to a partially rolled down window, and brought it to the person or persons who had put in the order. The only tricky thing about this was making sure that the tray was secure and in no danger of falling and dumping the food on the ground.

My first real job—will I miss it? I don't think so. I loved french fries when I first started here. Jackie let me eat as many as I wanted. After gaining ten pounds and struggling into my clothes, I quit eating them. I can't even stand the smell of a deep-fat fryer anymore. One weekend I had to lock up. I thought I'd done a good, responsible job, but Jackie didn't. She said I'd left grease in the corners of the grill. "Didn't your mother teach you how to clean things properly?" *I left the grease, and now she's attacking my mother? Here she comes. I wonder how she'll take my news.*

"Jackie, I'm marrying Andy Hughes as soon as he finishes basic training at the Great Lakes Naval Training Center." Britt swallowed hard when she saw the scowl on Jackie's face. "I won't be working here anymore."

"It'll never last. Not only are you of different religions, but your father is one of the biggest farmers in the county, while his father has never had a steady job and they have a hard time making it." She folded her arms under her big breasts.

Britt's hands clenched into fists at her sides, and she wished her nails were shorter. "Andy is not his father. He's a hard worker and he's good to me, but most important, we love each other."

"Love—at your age? I doubt it. It's just lust, and lust wears off. What do your folks say?"

"I'm going to tell them tomorrow."

"Ah." Jackie's eyebrows lifted so high they almost disappeared. "Now is when it hits the fan. No more college money—no money at all. You'll change your tune pretty quick when you can't depend on Daddy's checkbook."

"We can make it. We've got it all figured out. Andy will get extra pay when he marries—I'll be his dependent but not really, because I can work too."

"Oh, yeah, doing what? Don't try getting a job cleaning— you have a few things to learn about that. Go to college, get a degree, and *then* you can look for a good job. Use your head, girl."

Britt studied her shoes, afraid that tears would spill over and fall onto them. She was glad that this was her last day at the drive-in. She'd given her notice two weeks ago. Jackie thought she'd be going back to college for the fall semester, and she'd been okay with that. The drive-in closed in late fall and didn't open again until the spring.

"I *am* going to college, secretarial college in Minneapolis. I'm a good typist, and I know some shorthand. By the time Andy finishes boot camp, I'll have my secretarial license. I'll be able to get a good job." Britt squared her jaw, lips pressed together, and looked Jackie straight in the eye.

Jackie looked back, her jaw as set as Britt's. "It'll never last. You're both too young."

Britt picked up her last paycheck and left.

The next day, she packed up all her belongings and cleaned her apartment. She called home and was pleased when her father answered. "Dad, I'm all done with work—got my last paycheck today, eighty-nine dollars and twenty-five cents for one month. Seventy-five cents an hour really adds up. I want to come home. Will you come and get me?"

The ten-mile ride back to the farm with her loving yet silent father gave Britt time to think. It'd be a long time before she'd see the farm again. She grew up on a much smaller farm, one that had cows, pigs, chickens, and horses— her father loved horses, but he sold them when he realized how much more land he could cultivate with tractors. Now her father farmed over two thousand acres—crops of wheat, barley, potatoes, and sugar beets. He was a good farmer, and WWII had proved profitable for most farmers in the fertile Red River Valley of Minnesota.

Carrying and heating water for clothes and people

washing was a must during Britt's childhood. They didn't get running water on the farm until she was thirteen. They had to wait until the Rural Electric Association made it out to their way—running water needs an electric pump. All farm water, including water for the stock, was pumped by hand. Their well pump sat on a concrete base about thirty inches high, and wood planks covered the top on which the pump was bolted. An end plank was hinged so that it could be lifted up, giving access to the cold water below. A rope hung from a rod, and Britt's mother used to put food into a pail and lower it down into the well to keep butter, vegetables, and other food stuffs fresh in summer's hot weather (in the winter, they just put perishables upstairs). The old red pump was still on the farm, but it was rarely used. Paint was peeling off, and rust spots took the place of the peeled paint. No longer did a dipper hang from the pump to give thirsty people a cool drink of water. Sad, but oh the wonder, the ecstasy, of running water when it finally came: priceless.

Britt would always miss the big red barn with its hay loft where she used to hide to read in peace when it wasn't too hot or too cold. It was the one place where she didn't have to fear being startled by her mother yelling, "Get your nose out of that book. Look around. You can see what has to be done—do it." But during one bad storm when Britt was eight, the barn was hit by lightning and burned to the ground. Her spotted baby 4-H calf was too small to leap over the half door, and he died in the fire. Her father didn't rebuild. Instead, he set a Quonset hut on top of the old concrete floor and halved it. One part held a cow or two for milking, and the other half stored hay and feed.

Yes, the big barn was physically gone, but in her mind she could still see it. Tomato red—her father kept it painted—with a cupola on top. A kid could crawl up inside the cupola and look out over the prairie; on a clear day, one could see for ten miles. Atop the cupola was a weather vane—a horse, telling you the direction of the wind. Hannah now had that horse.

Britt thought of the house last, because the original house held sadness. It was a small white clapboard house with wood shingles. A story and a half, they called it—three rooms and a space for a future bathroom downstairs; a steep stairway led to a loft where Britt and Hannah slept under a mountain of quilts in the winter and where they roasted during the hot summers. The sadness came from the accident that occurred when the house was moved from a low spot to a higher, healthier place on the farm so it would be ready for the soon-to-be-wed couple, Britt's future parents.

The day of the move was cloudy with threatening rain. Grandpa Anderson was helping his son with the move. The cellar had been dug, and with the help of jacks, the house would be set over the cellar. It started to drizzle. Grandpa decided a jack had to be adjusted. In the process, the jack collapsed, and the corner of the house fell on Grandpa Anderson and crushed his chest. It took three painful days for him to die.

They pulled into the yard, and Britt looked at the house. It looked nothing like the house of her childhood, though the sad core of it was still the original house. It was twice as big and sported gleaming white siding with green trim around windows and doors and green shingles. It was not a bit player anymore, for the house dominated the farmstead. It had three bedrooms and a sewing room upstairs. Besides her parents' bedroom downstairs, where it had always been, there was a large living room on the west side—the old living room was now the dining room. A modern kitchen and bath were the stars of the downstairs.

Britt looked to the left where two new and very large Quonsets sat in the southwest part of the farmstead. These

Quonsets were machine shops for repairing and storing all the farm equipment and machinery that kept the farm running. Also in the southwest part of the farmstead was a large gasoline storage tank. The tank sat on a sturdy seven- to eight-foot-high scaffold. Gravity allowed the gas to fill empty tanks.

The farm of her childhood with all its animals was gone. The Anderson farm was now an agricultural industrial complex. *There is no place like home anymore.* Britt felt an ache, an emptiness, in her stomach.

After dinner, she and her parents sat around the table enjoying a fresh apple pie and making small talk. Britt chose this time to tell her parents about Andy's and her decision to marry.

She took a deep breath. "Andy has enlisted in the US Navy, and we're going to get married."

Ingrid shoved her chair back from the table so hard it almost fell. She stood up. "You can't marry a Catholic, Britt. You just can't!" She grabbed her apron, tying it around her waist with angry jerks, and started clearing the table. A plate hit the floor, and tears threatened."You're being foolish— halfway through college, and you want to quit! Are you pregnant?" She drilled Britt with her eyes.

Britt's face flushed, but she returned her mother's look. "No."

"Will he become a Lutheran?" This from her father.

"No. I've been studying the religion in school, and I've decided to turn Catholic."

"You're going to worship Mary? Now I've heard everything." Ingrid clamped her lips together and folded her arms in front of her.

"Mother, Catholics don't *worship* Mary; they don't believe she's God—they revere her and respect her."

Ingrid grabbed her chair and sat down, her face a frozen mask, her eyes tear-filled.

Britt's father cleared his throat. "Did you even *ask* him to become a Lutheran?"

"Yes, but he can't be anything but a Catholic." The "yes" was a lie, but Britt knew that the rest was true.

Her father was quiet, thinking over all that his daughter had said. "How are you going to live?"

"We won't marry until he finishes boot camp, and while he's in North Chicago doing that, I'll be going to secretarial school in Minneapolis. I saved enough from my job at the university and this summer at the drive-in to go to business school in the Cities. I'll finish school about the same time he finishes basic training. I'll be able to get a job no matter where we live—we'll both be making money."

Her mother roused herself and said, "Finish college. I could have gone to nurse's training in Canada, stayed with relatives there, but I married instead. I've had my regrets ..."

Father and daughter looked at each other for a long moment. Britt then broke the silence. "Dad, I've been going to school, but I don't know what I want to be—two years, and I haven't chosen a major. If I went back, you'd be wasting your money. Andy will be gone *four* years. I'm afraid I might lose him ..."

They were all tired of talking. Britt helped with the rest of the dishes, and they retired for the night. Britt had wanted to hug her parents before she went upstairs to bed, but she couldn't breach the wall of their deep disappointment.

It was a soggy, rainy fall day when Britt left for school in Minneapolis. The acrid smell of wet cottonwood leaves filled her nostrils; a wonderful smell—the smell that meant her favorite time of year was near—potato harvest with all the workers. Most commuted from their homes, but three or four lived in the bunk house, taking their meals with the family, until all the potatoes were picked. Britt loved the way her father reacted to the hustle and bustle of it all. He, who was usually so introspective, came alive. He talked and joked with his workers, told them where to find gunnysacks and potato baskets, and said that lunch would be brought out to them at ten in the morning. It was his world, and he ruled.

Ernie, her cousin, who had business in Minneapolis, was driving back there, and Britt's mother insisted that he let Britt ride with him. Britt had no place to stay, but Ernie drove around until he spotted a YWCA, and he dropped Britt off there.

The Y, a clean, Lysol-smelling, sterile place was her home for a few days. It was a world of white: walls were white, the bedspreads in the rooms were white, and windows had white pull-down shades. The one-inch by one-inch tiles in the bathrooms and on the main floor were also white—strong and easy to clean. Girls, all older than eighteen—some much older—ran here and there. Britt didn't dare ask anyone anything—she knew no one. The good thing about it was that it was only a few blocks from the school, and it didn't cost much.

Early the next morning, Britt walked down the street to enroll at the business school. She marveled at the height of the buildings—the highest building in her hometown was the three-story hotel, if you didn't count a couple of grain elevators. She craned her neck to see to the top of the building she was near—it had to have at least five or six floors to it. She looked at the large, arched doors over which she read "Dayton's." *Oh, I've heard of you.* She peered in the windows, marveling at the mannequins dressed in the latest fashion. She saw dresses with tight bodices and free-flowing skirts. A beautiful brown chiffon dress in polka dots with a ruffle around the neck, with one ruffled end extending down to the brown four-inch belt, almost made her drool. Slip on a pair of heels, short brown or white gloves, a matching hat with handbag, and she'd look like a movie star. Not all the skirts were full. She spied a red suit with a slim skirt and a cropped jacket. *Now that's what I'd wear to the office, with heels of course, and always, always a girdle. I don't have time now, but on my way home, I'm going to go into this store. I hear they have an escalator—I've never ridden on one. Does it go up or down? Must be up, considering the name. How do they get down again? Stairs, probably. This is like another world.*

Britt enrolled, and then she took advantage of the school's employment office and applied for a part-time job as a live-in nanny. The Y was okay, but she needed to make some money. The next day, a Mrs. Kelly called, and they met that afternoon for an interview.

The school had a small interview room with a table, two chairs, and a two-seater sofa upholstered in dark brown leather, over which hung a beautiful print of Winslow Homer's oil painting *Breezing Up*. On one side of the sofa was a stack of old magazines, a lamp, and an ashtray.

Britt sat on the sofa, reading a magazine when a tall, well-dressed, and attractive, dark-haired woman entered. She was slender but also obviously pregnant.

"I'm Mrs. Kelly. You must be Britt. Let's sit down and talk." They sat down across from each other at the table.

Mrs. Kelly placed a sheet of paper with several items written on it in front of her. She took out a pen and began: "I need someone to help with the evening meal and cleanup afterward. I also want the bathrooms and the fireplace cleaned on Saturdays, and the noon meal prepared—usually hot dogs and soup. It would be for my husband and two boys. I write for a fashion magazine, and I have to go into the city and meet with my magazine's editor on Saturdays. One more thing—Mr. Kelly and I sometimes go out at night. You'll then babysit. Do you think you could handle all that?" She had checked the items off on the sheet of paper as she talked. She looked up, eyebrows raised.

"Yes, Mrs. Kelly. I'm through with school at three each day. I should be able to get to your home on time if there's a bus going out that way."

"There's a streetcar stop only a block from our house. You can ride it in the morning to go to school and to come back here in the afternoon. We'll pay your streetcar fare. By the way, where are you from?"

"A small town in Minnesota, Great Prairie, not far from the Canadian border—you've probably never heard of it."

"No, I haven't. Does your family use a horse and buggy to go church on Sunday?"

"Oh, no ... we have cars."

"I'm sorry. I hope I haven't offended you. I come from Boston. I think we have a different idea about how people live in the Midwest. We also believe Midwesterners are hardworking and honest."

Britt got the job. She left the Y and moved in with the Kelly family. Mr. Kelly was a lawyer, and he and his wife had two sons—Ian, aged five, and Sean, aged two, with a third child on the way. She definitely needed help. Britt would be paid a dollar an hour for fourteen hours a week, an extra dollar an hour if she had to babysit. She wouldn't have to walk to school anymore. She could take the streetcar—much better for someone having to wear high heels; the school made all female students wear high heels to school every day. She used her time on the streetcar to study shorthand and bookkeeping.

Christmas was coming, and Britt dreaded it. She'd written her parents and told them where she was living, but they didn't write back. She didn't want to spend Christmas wandering around uptown, nor did she want to intrude on the Kellys' Christmas. She'd window-shop and go to a movie, and on both Saturday, Christmas Day, and Sunday, her day off, she would go to church.

A letter arrived from Andy. He'd just learned that his leave time started on Friday, December 24, and ended on Sunday, December 26—they could spend Christmas together. Would she be able to come to North Chicago? He missed her a lot. Would she! She had Friday off, so she could leave Friday morning and be in North Chicago before four in the afternoon. Andy could meet her and take her to the hotel where she'd reserve a room in her name for two nights. Sunday morning, she'd again board the train and get back to the Kellys' in the afternoon. Britt wrote Andy, telling him she was coming and when he should come and pick her up at the train station. She also gave him the Kellys' phone number in case he needed to make any changes.

Britt packed on Thursday night. She wanted to look her best for Andy. Green and red plaid skirt and red sweater— what could be more in tune with the season than that? What a shame she had to cover it with her navy blue storm coat—at least the coat had a nice fur collar. She threw in her pajamas, underwear, and three pair of nylons (just in case). No need to bring a girdle; she'd be wearing that. The navy blue jumper with the light blue tailored shirt always looked nice—she'd wear that on the train, both coming and going, but she better pack an extra shirt. Her black dress shoes would go with everything—no need to bring an extra pair of shoes. Now to put in some makeup, and she'd be all set, and it all fit into her small suitcase.

Friday morning, Britt was on her way to North Chicago. She brought a book with her, *A Tree Grows in Brooklyn* by Betty Smith, but was too excited to concentrate on reading.

She debated whether she should eat something at noon in the dining car but decided against it. She didn't want to spend the money, and she was too excited to eat anyway.

Why was it taking so long? Maybe her watch had stopped. She lifted her arm up toward her ear. No, it was ticking. She tried reading again, but her mind kept drifting off, thinking of Andy. Right on time, the train pulled into the North Chicago station. Britt looked out the window and saw a sea of sailors all in their navy blue dress uniforms. She'd never find Andy. In a panic, she got off the train and just stood there and then decided that that's what she should do. Andy could find her more easily than she could find him—and he did. He grabbed her and hugged her, they kissed, and he took her small suitcase with one hand and cupped her elbow with the other. He guided her to the waiting cab.

After he settled her into her hotel room, they took a cab out to Mary's Pizza Place. It was close to the Navy Training Center—Andy wanted to show off his future wife to his buddies at this favorite eating place. Britt was very hungry. She hadn't eaten since breakfast, and she was also curious to find out how a "pizza pie," the kind Dean Martin sang about in "That's Amore," tasted.

Britt met a couple of Andy's friends, and then they sat down to eat their pizza—she liked it. They talked and talked—catching up on news. Luke was a medic on the island of Okinawa. Hannah had broken up with her boyfriend and was concentrating on bringing up her grades so that she could go to the college she had her eye on. Wedding plans made up the bulk of their conversation. Britt told him that the banns in his hometown church were going to be read and that she'd buy the license. They exchanged Christmas presents. Britt had had a gold ID bracelet engraved with Andy's name on the front, and in the back was engraved "All My Love"—their song. Andy pulled out a small package and handed it to Britt. With shaking hands, she unwrapped—an engagement ring!

"I didn't want you wandering around Minneapolis free as a bird. I want people to know that you're spoken for." He got up, pulled her to her feet, and enfolded her in a big hug. He then planted a big smooch on her lips. Neither one heard the cheers and whistles of Mary's Pizza customers.

Britt breakfasted alone Saturday morning. She was glad she'd brought a good book. Only having a book to read made eating alone tolerable. Andy picked her up at nine thirty. The first thing they did was take a cab out to Lake Michigan. Britt wanted to see the lakeshore, but the day was cloudy, windy, and cold. Even cuddling close did not stop their shivering. Enough of that. They went back to the hotel and the restaurant and ordered hot coffee to warm up. What now? They had only this day together, and they wanted to make the most of it. They decided to go to a movie at a theater nearby. It was showing *White Christmas*, starring Bing Crosby, Danny Kaye, Rosemary Clooney, and Vera Ellen—dancers and singers. Way up in the balcony, they could watch the movie, and if it wasn't very good, they could spend the time necking. They did both.

After the movie, they walked back to the hotel for dinner. Britt noticed one old guy sneaking looks at them. Midnight Mass, a Hughes Christmas tradition, was next on the agenda. The incense, the flowers, the singing of Christmas carols were uplifting, filling both of them with reverence at this holy time. Andy walked Britt back to her hotel, kissed her good night, a long, passionate kiss, but that was all. The aura of holiness still clung to them, preventing them from doing what they'd soon be doing with God's blessing.

Britt woke up to a sunny day, but inside she was not sunny. She'd be leaving today—she wouldn't even see Andy.

He was stuck on base. She dressed, packed, and went down to breakfast, bringing her book. Scrambled eggs, toast, and coffee should hold her until she was back in Minneapolis.

While she was waiting for the cab she'd called to take her to the train station, the old guy who'd been eyeing them last night at dinner came up to her.

"Young lady, I saw you at dinner last night with your sailor boy—an attractive couple. You looked especially fetching in your red sweater."

Not knowing what to say and not wanting to be rude, Britt said, "Thank you."

"I book acts for a vaudeville and burlesque theater in the Twin Cities. If you're ever looking for a job, honey, look me up. It's good pay." He handed her his business card.

"Uh, well, I'm marrying that sailor boy in March. I don't think he wants me to work." She pocketed the card and said, "There's my cab. I have to go." *Was that a compliment or an insult?* On the train, Britt shredded the card into little bits.

There'd be no more leaves for Andy until he finished his training the end of February, but they'd write—that was enough for now. Britt was busy with school and with the planning of a small wedding. Not much to it, the main thing being that she and Andy show up at the appointed time at the church with two witnesses, but she did buy a packet of twenty-five invitations. She sent one to her aunt Stella, who lived in a Minneapolis suburb, and a few to school friends of hers and Andy's, and to Andy's parents—though she knew they wouldn't come because of the cost. Britt also sent an invitation to her parents, though she knew they would not attend a Catholic wedding. The banns were read. She mustn't forget to buy the marriage license—Andy would owe her for that—and she had a dress to buy. She wished her mother were there to help her find one.

In her mind's eye, Britt stood in the middle of her room, admiring it. It was 1951. She'd miss this room when she graduated in June. She'd decorated it herself. She'd taken out the old linoleum and painted the floor gray and added a red area rug. Her bed was built into the alcove below the slanted ceiling. She'd chosen red and yellow as her colors. Her three-quarter-size bed was lined with pillows—she loved pillows. Someone told her once that she must not have had enough time at her mother's breast, and that's why she loved pillows so much. Maybe. She'd made ruffled pillow tops for them, and then she'd curtained the alcove with floor-to-ceiling draperies, using tiebacks to secure them in swags to the two walls. Cozy.

Half of a round kitchen table became her vanity. She'd skirted it in yellow, gathered material, and then she'd padded a stool top with red to form the seat for her vanity (an apt name, that's for sure). A wardrobe and a chest of drawers, both painted white, were the walls of her built-in desk to the left of the door. In the southwest corner of the room was a red armchair with a good reading light. She would miss this room very much.

It was in this room that she'd learned about her mother's pregnancy. Ingrid had tapped on Britt's door and entered, wearing an old shirt of her husband's. Mother and daughter stood, facing each other.

"Britt, I have something to tell you. I'm pregnant."

"What? You're too old. And we were finally becoming friends."

"I know, but it's true. You'll be going off to college in the fall anyway."

"I'll leave sooner than that. I have a job for the summer at the drive-in—I'm going to rent a room in town. I need money for school clothes, and this way I won't have to babysit. Hannah will be glad to. She loves babies—look how she treats her stuffed animals. She kisses all of them good night. Sickening."

"She's younger than you. It's okay if she feels tenderness even if it is toward stuffed animals. I don't want her to grow up too fast and leave."

"You worry about being lonely, but don't. Maybe you'll have the boy you always wanted. If you do, it's too bad Grandma Anderson isn't around to know it. She thought it was awful that you didn't pop out sons to help your husband, her favorite son, with farm chores."

"Britt, that's enough." Ingrid turned and left.

Saturday at the Kelly home, Britt was preparing noon lunch when Mr. Kelly handed her a letter. It was from her mother.

> *Dear Britt,*
> *I need to be part of your wedding even if I don't approve of your marrying a Catholic. I want to come to the Cities and help you find a nice wedding dress. I'll only be there for two days, but I need to do this.*
>
> *Love,*
> *Mother*

Britt shared the letter with Mrs. Kelly but did not share with her the last conversation she'd had with her mother right before she'd left for business school. It was a conversation she'd never forget.

"Mother, when I was at the university, I took a religion course. I told you that, but I didn't tell you that it was Catholic Marriage and Family Life or that I was baptized a Catholic."

"What do you mean, you were *baptized a Catholic*? You are a baptized Lutheran; you've been confirmed!"

"I know. And the priest said my Lutheran baptism was good. He just wanted to make sure and so he baptized me again. It's okay."

"Wanted to make *sure*! Did the pope make him do that? Don't you have any free will anymore?"

"Mother, I know you're upset, and I probably shouldn't tell you this, but Andy and I had sex once; at least I think we did."

"*Think* you did? That doesn't make sense."

"Remember the time Andy and I borrowed his dad's car and went to his aunt and uncle's place in Lebrun for their fiftieth wedding anniversary? Well, on the way home, he went by the cemetery where his grandma and grandpa are buried. He found their graves. He cared a lot for them; they lived with Andy's family until they died. He knelt and prayed a while, then came back to the car, quite emotional."

"So?"

"Andy opened the door to the backseat and motioned for me to get in, 'Just for a little while.' I thought he just wanted some comfort—to be held and maybe a few kisses—but he, well, he put his hand on my thigh and slid it upward, pulling up my dress at the same time. I couldn't wiggle free; he was leaning on my chest. He unzipped his pants and was tugging at my panties and shaking. I-I helped him. I was curious! It was over in seconds, whatever 'it' was—I didn't feel anything. Honest! But I think we did it, as least he did. Some sticky stuff that smelled like bleach was on my dress—I threw the dress away. If we did do it, the Bible says we have to marry: 'If a man entice a maid that is not betrothed, and lie with her, he shall surely endow her to be his wife.' You remember that verse, Mother; it's in Exodus."

"Oh, Britt, Britt, why are you always so curious? Curiosity killed the cat. You know that saying. Now you've gone and ruined your life. I guess you better marry him. There'll never be anyone else for you."

Ingrid took the train from their small home town to Minneapolis a week before the wedding. Mrs. Kelly allowed her to stay with Britt, sleeping in her room.

They went shopping in secondhand shops for a wedding dress and found one: ecru lace over satin with long sleeves and a V-neck. Britt did not care for the veil at all—a circle of fake pearls with a veil attached that smashed her hair— but the price was right: seventy-nine dollars. Britt's mother would go back to her three-year-old twin boys, William and Owen, knowing that she'd done something to show Britt she still cared for her, even if she couldn't support her wedding.

That night, as Britt and her mother shared the double bed at the Kellys', Britt lay on her right side, back to back with her mother, pretending to be asleep. When she heard her mom's soft snore, she turned and opened her eyes and looked at the back of her mother's head. It was tightly pin-curled, covered with bobby pin crosses, the top bobby pin securing the bottom one, so that no curl could unfurl. *So typical: she wanted things to be right and nailed down, and my wedding was none of the above.*

Ingrid would board the northbound train in the morning. Britt wished that she could get on a train and go far, far away. At that very moment, Britt heard a train go by and imagined that she was on it. Where it was going didn't matter, as long as it was away. What had she gotten herself into? License bought, invitations sent, banns proclaimed, a wedding dress purchased—it was simply too late to back out now. Her train had left the station. Exhausted, she fell asleep.

Britt and Andy became husband and wife on March 20, 1954. They were married in the Catholic church Britt had attended ever since she'd moved into the Kelly home. She wore her wedding dress with its ugly veil. Andy wore his navy blue sailor's uniform. Britt said, "I do," and Andy said it too. They exchanged rings, and they kissed.

A couple of Britt's business school friends and several of Andy's high school classmates, along with Britt's sister, Hannah, came to the wedding. One of Andy's classmates, John Kraal, was his best man and witness. Andy's sister, Mary, stood at Britt's side as bridesmaid and was the other witness. She scolded Andy for not buying Britt any flowers.

An unexpected and very welcome wedding guest was Stella, Britt's father's sister, eight months pregnant. Britt thanked and embraced her with tears in her eyes.

Janet, a business school friend of Britt's, invited the wedding party of six to come to the house that she and three roommates rented. She wanted Britt to have a wedding dinner, if pizza, the new baked dish from Italy, and beer could be called a wedding dinner. Janet did her best to make it more formal. The dining room table's four leaves expanded so that it could seat twelve. A white tablecloth, napkins, and a centerpiece of white carnations with a tall white candle on each side of it did add a touch of elegance.

Ten people, including Janet's three roommates, sat around that table, enjoying the pizza and beer. The bridal couple, who hadn't eaten since the night before their wedding, would have happily dined on bread and water. The inevitable then happened, and it was just as annoying as the tapping of a spoon on a glass of champagne—someone rapped his pizza fork on his beer bottle. Andy and Britt had to stand up and kiss—again and again.

Let the toasts begin! Andy's best man, John, was the first to toast the couple, and he did it with the Irish marriage blessing:

May God be with you and bless you;
May you see your children's children.
May you be poor in misfortune,
Rich in blessings,
May you know nothing but happiness
From this day forward.

A couple more toasts followed, but the last toast, Hannah's, left everyone laughing: "Today when Britt married, I gained a brother. More than that, her bedroom can now be my sitting room. Britt may have married her sweetie, but I got a bedroom suite."

No bridal suite for the newlyweds. They spent the night in the St. Anthony Hotel, one of the older hotels in Minneapolis. Mr. and Mrs. Hughes were not only tired after the long day, but they were also a little tipsy from the beer. It seems that they'd ended the wedding dinner with a game of quarters. Once in their room, Britt took a shower but failed to notice that the shower curtain was on the *outside*. Water flowed out and all over the bathroom floor.

Andy had collapsed onto the bed. Wondering if Britt was done with her shower, he opened the bathroom door, and there she was, down on her knees, sopping up water with a bath towel.

"What are you doing down there?"

"Uh, I got water all over the floor. I'm wiping it up."

"Well, hurry up and come to bed."

"In a minute. I'm almost done." She wrung out the soaked towel, letting the water fall into the toilet bowl, and bent to continue mopping.

Five minutes later, she was done, but by then, Andy was asleep. Britt, trying not to make a sound, in spite of her chattering teeth, inched herself into the bed and fell asleep.

Toward morning, Andy, half-asleep, rolled over and soon

realized he was not alone. He reached for his wife. She turned toward him, and he kissed her, a long, slow kiss. It woke him up all the way, and he shifted into fifth gear. His hands sped over her body, trying to touch everything at once. Did he think he was a NASCAR racer and her body the race track? It was disconcerting.

They did it, for sure this time. It hurt a little, but it didn't last long. Britt got up to wash herself, making sure that the shower curtain was on the *inside*. When she got back to bed, Andy was fast asleep.

CHAPTER

3

From Minneapolis, they headed north, back to the cold country where they were born. Though March, winter was still king. Britt and Andy rode with two of Andy's classmates, wedding guests. One was a cousin on his father's side—the one who, Andy had told her, often got him into trouble. In fact, this cousin had insisted on stopping in Stillwater to visit a relative who was an inmate at the Minnesota State Correctional Facility, leaving Britt to wonder if he was an admirer of behavior that landed one in prison. He went in alone, leaving the others to sit and shiver in the cold car. Fifteen minutes later, he came out, and they were on the road again.

Great Prairie, hometown but a strange house—Andy's parents' house would be their home until Andy's leave was over. Only Andy's parents lived there now. His sister, Mary, one of the witnesses at their marriage, was away teaching school in another town. His brother, who had spilled the platter of ham at Andy's going away party, was now a corpsman with the marines, stationed on some island. Britt was glad it wasn't crowded. She liked Andy's mother, Josette. She was even-tempered, even stoical, a bit like Britt's dad. Andy's dad, Phil for Phillip, was the opposite; he was often depressed and drank too much. Andy had told her that he used his belt to discipline Andy and his brother when they misbehaved. Their misbehavior was usually in the form of fighting with each other. When their father told them he drank because they fought, he and his brother quit fighting for a whole year. It was a lie; he drank because he drank. Britt did not like her father-in-law and had as little to do with him as possible.

Marriage surprised her. She really didn't know what to expect. When she was thirteen, her mother handed her a book titled, *Strictly Confidential.* It told all about the human reproductive system, male and female, and about menstruation—correct and scientific with black-and-white drawings. It showed how men were built; she didn't know a penis looked like that—so fleshy. She also found out that her equipment "down there" was not called what her mother called it, an "apparatus," but that it needed three terms for proper definition, none of which was her mother's term. The book said nothing about love or how intercourse between a man and a woman was accomplished or how it was supposed to feel.

In the early 1940s, a gale had roared through the county, overturning small buildings and trees. On the Anderson farm, two huge, partially uprooted cottonwood trees had snapped off about fifteen or twenty feet from the ground. They leaned to the east at a twenty-five-degree angle, five feet apart and parallel. Britt and her sister, Hannah, slapped some burlap bags on them for saddles, and near their snapped-off tops, they added a bridle made of rag strips, and voilà! They had two high-spirited, western riding horses that went up and down as they bounced—galloped—along. They whooped and hollered as they galloped into the sunset; no, that's not right. The trees faced east, so they galloped into the *sunrise*. No matter: it was fun, and they were pretty proud of themselves for creating such fine saddle horses. Their mother came out to see what all the hollering was about. She took one look at what Britt and Hannah were doing and said, "Girls, if that starts to feel good, *stop!*"

Britt didn't know what she was talking about—she was, after all, only seven. Her sister didn't know either, and they didn't dare ask. They figured it must have something to do with "down there," but the only *feel good* that Britt or Hannah got out of it was the feeling that they were cowgirls riding their broncos, rounding up cattle!

Now Britt realized that her mother must have been talking about sex. And Andy seemed obsessed with it. He thought of her as a sex toy, and he was always in the mood to play. She was getting sore in more ways than one. She couldn't understand why he was like that, especially in his parents' house! When they'd come downstairs in the morning, she could barely look his parents in the eye, she was so embarrassed. Her mother had told her only two things about marriage: (1) men were more needy when it came to sex (that information was right on) and (2) making love was a wifely duty, and a good wife never said no to her husband. Was her father ever like Andy? Britt would never dare ask her mother something so personal.

In one week, Andy had to report back to Newport Navy Base, but before that, he wanted to meet his cousin's new husband, a former classmate, and say goodbye to both of them. They lived in Daville, fifty miles away. They left Great Prairie on a Saturday afternoon. They chose Saturday because both would be home that day. It was very cold, twenty degrees below zero, but the sun was shining on flat, snowy prairie, turning it into fields of sparkling diamonds too bright to look at without sunglasses—a glorious day.

They rode along in the car Andy had purchased as soon as he came home from boot camp; a married man needed a car! It was a '48 Ford, the weird model that some called the suicide model. Its back doors opened toward the front. If a wind caught those back doors, they'd be blown right off, and maybe a passenger would tumble out. They felt great. They were on their own, starting a life together, and everything seemed possible. Andy's cousin and her husband felt the same way: life was good. The four of them had laughed and joked, catching up on all the news—who was going with whom, and was anyone pregnant. They then played some pinochle, snacked on chips and nuts, and had a couple of brews—things like that, just an all-around good time.

The good time ended when the windows began to rattle. A good, old Minnesota blizzard had blown in, creating a white-out condition. They should have tuned into the weather news before they left, but they hadn't. Andy's cousin and her husband had a hide-a-bed, and they slept on that. In the morning, the weather report said the storm would abate by ten in the morning. Not wanting to outwear their welcome too much by staying for lunch, they left for Great Prairie at eleven thirty.

The sun reflecting off the snow created a world so bright and so white it hurt to look at it. Here and there, a few groves of trees, indicating farmsteads, dotted the all-white landscape. The roads weren't bad; the storm had blown the snow across the roads, diagonally, creating finger drifts.

Britt heard Andy say, "I hope he stops!" She leaned forward to fiddle with the radio, trying to find some music they both liked. Andy liked country western, and Britt was more into pop. Then the unthinkable happened: something big slammed into the side of their car and sent them flying. Later they found out that they'd been struck by a snowplow clearing a side road. It was a huge machine, with a wide V-shaped blade in front. They hit the left side of the blade, careened up its side, and off into the air.

Airborne, in silent slow motion, the car rolled over and over. In slow motion, Britt's body moved with each roll. She floated up, and her head touched the roof of the car. Then her feet settled on the floor mat, and she sank into a crouch. She drifted against the car door and slid down to rest against Andy, who slumped, motionless, in the driver's seat. Britt glanced out the passenger side window. Snow blocked the view except for one small upper corner where a bit of blue sky was visible. Wait! She heard voices and something else—the sound of digging. What was going on? What happened?

Questions, questions—five days ago, she stood in front of a priest in Minneapolis as he said, "Do you, Britt Lucy Anderson, take Andy Sean Hughes to be your wedded husband, to ... be faithful only to him so long as you both shall live?" And she said, "I do," but now she had no answers. All Britt knew was that a pleasant visit with friends in Daville, before Andy returned to navy duty, had ended in a crash.

Andy's side of the car was not as deeply stuck in the snow-filled ditch as Britt's, so they pulled him out first. Finally, they opened her door, and hands lifted her out. Two men tried to stand Britt on her feet. She looked down and saw that she was wearing her navy blue knit suit, her honeymoon traveling suit, the one with the pearls around the neckline—her favorite. It took Britt over a month of part-time work to earn the money to pay for it. About then, she realized that her legs weren't cooperating. Britt crumpled down onto the snow.

The men picked her up and put her in a car. Britt didn't

know who they were—one was probably the driver of the snowplow that had slammed into them. The other must have been the Good Samaritan who had stopped to help. Andy was in the car. He was awake and seemed only to have a bump on his head and a sore arm. For that, Britt was thankful—from wife to widow in only five days would have been just too cruel. Andy glanced at his watch. The crystal was smashed, the hands frozen at ten minutes to one. The date was March 28.

Andy wasn't even hospitalized, though he did throw up once in the hospital. In fact, he was again airborne two days later, flying back to duty aboard the US Navy destroyer, the *Dortch*, harbored at Newport, Rhode Island.

Britt wasn't so lucky. Seat belts didn't exist back then, so when a car rolled and bounced, so did its passengers. As a result, Britt's pelvis was broken and a hip socket cracked—no wonder she couldn't stand up. Doctors can't put a cast on breaks like that, so Brit spent two months in a hospital bed with her rear end in a sling, dangling in the air, a bit above the mattress.

Tough break, but she will never forget the comfort and joy of dozing in the sun's warmth as it streamed in through the east window and right onto her hospital bed. Its warmth enveloped and soothed her. Britt loved the sun.

Sunday afternoon, and the new Lutheran pastor, Pastor Thomas, was a lunch guest at the Anderson farm. His black hair and brown eyes made him stand out in the mostly blond and blue- or green-eyed, Scandinavian parish. And he was a looker, quite a contrast to old Rev. Samuelson, the recent retiree.

Eight-year-old Britt walked through the grove of trees, swinging the old garden basket. She was on her way to the garden, just beyond the trees, to pick lettuce. Pastor Thomas was their lunch guest, and her mother wanted lettuce for a salad. It didn't take Britt long to fill the basket. She started back to the house and came face-to-face with Pastor Thomas. What was he doing out there? He grabbed her hands and saw that her nails were painted a hot pink.

"Britt! What's that on your fingernails? Paint? Don't you know that's from the devil? Only bad girls paint their nails and wear lipstick. You don't want to be a bad girl, do you?

"No."

"What did you say? I can't hear you."

"No!"

"Don't ever paint your nails again." He released her hands, and Britt raced to the house, gripping the handle of the lettuce basket and trying to figure out what had just happened. She knew she was *not* a bad girl and didn't want to be one. What did hot pink nails have to do with anything? It was just a color, a pretty color, and God used lots of pretty colors, and if all things came from God, then so did pink nail polish.

Later that summer, she lay in bed, experiencing that twilight stage between waking and sleeping. It was a Saturday morning—no school. She was alone; Hannah had already gotten up. Britt snuggled down deeper into her bed and then realized that the blankets didn't cover her anymore. She was, instead, cocooned in a substance that looked like pink cotton candy but was oh-so-soft and not at all sticky. She was cuddled in softness, warmth, and an orangey pink glow. No edges existed between the cocoon and her body. They were one. It was glorious, and she basked in overwhelming love and security, knowing that she belonged. Britt stayed as still as possible, hardly breathing for fear she'd break the spell. It didn't last long, but while it did, she was in heaven.

Britt didn't expect her parents to visit her in the hospital. She knew she had disappointed them very much by becoming a Catholic and marrying Andy. They lived thirty miles away, and one never knew what the weather would be like in March. In 1941, March 15 and 16, a terrible blizzard with winds reaching 85 mph blew into the area, causing thirty-two deaths ("Beware the Ides of March"). But many other people did visit. She had visitors every day but one. Andy's cousin, John, came often, bringing Britt books and Dairy Queens. One of the nurses, impressive in her white uniform and starched white cap, said, "You watch it, or you'll get big as a horse eating all that ice cream with no exercise." Brit didn't though—a couple pounds, yes, but not horse size.

Pastor Thomas came to visit out of what he no doubt considered his Christian duty. He was the one who had scolded her for wearing nail polish when she was eight years old. No longer the slim, handsome, young pastor, he was almost fat, but that did not stop the black-suited figure from storming into Britt's hospital room, his face red and contorted above his pastoral collar. With his right arm outstretched, he pointed his finger at her and roared, "You are going to hell for marrying a Catholic; this is just the start of your punishments!"

He told Britt that he would pray for her. It frightened Britt to see him like that, and her heart beat fast, but she stiffened her backbone as much as that's possible when you're lying flat out in a bed with your rear in a sling. "I will pray for you too, Pastor Thomas."

Without another word, he turned on his heel and left. He did not come back.

Every two weeks or so, Britt was rolled to x-ray to see how her bones were healing, and finally the doctor said, "Get up and practice walking with a walker." What a wonderful day! After a few days of that, Britt was released, and that was another wonderful day, as her dad came and took her home. She found out later that he had paid her hospital bill: six hundred dollars and a few cents.

CHAPTER

4

Britt stayed at her parents' house for a week; it didn't feel like her home any longer. She wasn't theirs anymore; she had a husband. They tiptoed around each other, feeling out their new relationship. It made for long, painful pauses, but then they weren't a family that talked to each other very much anyway. Britt would soon take the train to Connecticut to stay with Andy's aunt until he got a leave. He would then come and get her, and they'd go back to Newport, Rhode Island, and find an apartment to rent. But before she left, she wanted to look around, to revisit all that had meant so much to her as she was growing up.

Britt walked to the country school she had attended for eight years—it was only an eighth of a mile away. She had walked alone to school her first two years, but when Hannah started first grade, the sisters walked together. One day when she was in third grade and Hannah in first, their dad gave them a ride to school. The weather was bad; it was fifteen degrees below zero with blowing snow. Their Dad harnessed up the horses, hitched them to a sleigh, lifted in Britt and

Hannah, covered them with an old, stinky buffalo robe, and away they went! Britt had wished the horses were wearing jingle bells.

During the eight years Britt attended the country school, she was taught by four different teachers. Her fourth-grade teacher, Miss Turner, was very pretty, a sweet face set off by curly brown hair, and she had a trim figure—a twenty-three-inch waist. She only taught one year because she married in the summer, but while she was still teaching, she'd sometimes come over to Britt and Hannah's house and have coffee with their mother.

Britt and Hannah hovered in the background, eavesdropping and sneaking peeks while Miss Turner and their mother sipped coffee and enjoyed a raspberry jelly roll.

"Britt's a good student—learns fast—she's a pretty girl, though she is something of a scatterbrain." Miss Turner broke off a piece of jellyroll and popped it in her mouth.

Ingrid put down her cup of coffee. "Don't ever tell her she's pretty. She'll get a big head. It's not good for a child." She paused, letting her words sink in, and then picked up her cup again.

Why had her mother felt that way? Britt walked on, kicking a stone out of her path. *Why is being a good student okay, but being pretty is not?* Sometimes it was hard to understand her mother. She had reached the school. It looked blind and old. The dirty windows, tall, blank rectangles, lacked life. The school's white clapboard siding had peeled, and now it looked almost gray. Britt climbed the three rickety steps, crossed the porch, and entered the school. A musty smell wrinkled her nose, and she sneezed. Britt looked to the left. The green, two-burner kerosene stove was no longer on the counter. *We used to cook our lunch potatoes on that stove.* Also gone was the water pail and dipper. The two oldest students had to take the water pail each morning and go over to the neighbor's pump, seventy yards away, and fill it up and carry it back to school. Now the counter held bags of superphosphate fertilizer.

She bypassed the cloakroom to her right, fearing what she might find in there, and entered the main room, the classroom. Britt's feet encountered the floor heat register—a circle, four feet in diameter, that let the heat from the big old furnace in the basement enter the classroom. *We girls loved to stand on that circle. It blew up our skirts until it looked like we were wearing hoops skirts. We could pretend we were Southern belles. We fought to stand there. If a girl hogged the circle too long, someone would push her off—it's my turn!*

On the south wall, Britt saw the map rack with its four rolled-up maps. She walked over and pulled down the map of the United States and sneezed from the dust. *I blame you for my difficulty in knowing directions. I always think the top of a map is south because you're on the south wall. And east is to my right. Wrong!* Blackboards covered the entire wall from left to right, below the map rack, but to the right of the map rack hung the picture of President George Washington, the one that still appears on a one-dollar bill. Additional blackboards ran the entire length of the west wall. Above them hung the old school clock as usual, but time had stopped.

The bookcase, the school library, on the north wall was gone. Built of wood, stained walnut, it stood six feet tall and was four feet wide, with pull-down wood-framed glass doors to protect its contents. *I loved that bookcase. I wonder who has it now. I read all its books except the biography of Lincoln. The book had his picture on the cover, and I just couldn't get past his beard.*

No rows of ink-stained, wooden desks with inkwell holes and with names carved into them remained. The room was quite bare because whenever an election was held, the room contained portable voting booths, and voters milled around the center of the room, waiting their turn to register and vote.

She turned and took one last look toward the front of the room. Before Christmas, the entire front of the room was turned into a stage for the annual Christmas program. The Christmas program was, in the true meaning of the word, *awesome*. Students were freed from the Scandinavian command, "Don't show off!" They sang, recited pieces of poetry, showed off their artwork, and put on a one-act play, all to the applause of their proud parents and relatives.

Three weeks before Christmas, the teacher sent a note home with each student. The note asked for a spare bed sheet and a folding chair or two if possible. Parents were also asked to bring cookies and Kool-Aid for the big night. Coffee for the grown-ups was made in the school's makeshift kitchen.

The sheets were needed as curtains for their eight-foot by twelve-foot stage. A long, strong wire, supported by ceiling wires, stretched from one side of the twenty-two-foot-wide schoolroom to the other. Two other wires stretched from the cloakrooms to that long wire. On these wires, the sheets—white, no colored sheets in those days—were hung, using large safety pins as hangers, allowing the sheets to be drawn open and shut with ease. The east cloakroom served as their dressing room. Student performers would come out of it and wait in the space sheeted off from the main stage until they heard their cue to get out and do their thing. The folding chairs were for the overflow crowd, and there always was one.

I starred in the one-act play when I was in eighth grade. I had to kiss a boy. I hated the very thought of kissing. But it turned out to be worth it. On the way home, my dad turned to look at me sitting in the backseat of the car with Hannah, and he said, "You sure were good in the play, Britt." What a wonderful night!

Britt wandered outside to the old swing set with its attached teeter-totter. She touched one of the steel supporting legs. *I stuck out my tongue, and it stuck to this leg. It was a really cold day. I thought I'd never get my tongue back. I closed my eyes and pulled. I got my tongue back, minus some tongue skin. It hurt for over a week.*

We played during recess: Steal Sticks, Pum Pum Pull Away, Kick the Can and Kitten Ball, and Hide and Seek. I liked school a lot, but I loved recess.

Time to walk back home—she had a lot left to do. Britt entered the house the usual way, through the back door, and saw her parents sitting at the table having their morning lunch.

"Dad, what are you doing in the house at ten o'clock in the morning? Did you forget to take your lunch with you?" She walked to the back of her dad's chair and put her arms around his neck.

"I'm working out in the Quonset this morning—getting the potato digger all set up for work. I'm going to miss seeing you on the tractor seat while I ride the digger, making sure the vines don't get stuck on their way back to the field."

"It's been two years, Dad, since I've done that, but I miss it too."

Ingrid cut into the conversation. "Enough reminiscing, you two. I've got a job for you, Britt. You're leaving—don't know when we'll see you again. I'm going to move Hannah into your room and turn Hannah's bigger room into a room for the twins—they'll be four years old soon. You have some stuff in a cardboard box in the back of the closet. Go through it and throw out what you don't want. What you do want, take it with you."

"But she can have some lunch first." Carl Anderson reached over and pinched the skin on Britt's lower ribs. "No fat there—she's too skinny!"

"No, she'll do it now. If she doesn't, she might forget to do it. She can have her lunch later. She's not going anywhere today. Go on, Britt."

Not wanting to start any kind of disagreement—who knows when she'd see them again?—she headed off for the upstairs closet in what was still Hannah's room.

Britt sat on the floor with the opened box beside her. She found some old clothes, those she'd give away, and her old photo album. Her father had given her a camera when he visited her in the hospital after her appendix operation. She'd filled this album with pictures of the farm. She'd take that with her. A large manila envelope contained essays she'd written for English—only the good ones. She started to read the top one. It was titled "Potato-Picking Time."

> I shivered with the cold and with excitement as the old white truck ground to a halt on the edge of the potato field. Dad, Hannah, and I sat looking with squinted eyes at the potato field. A cloud had descended upon it, making it difficult to see. Out of the cloud, lumpy shapes emerged—potato pickers with folded sacks on their backs. The sun was burning away the cloud/fog. It was time to get out and get to work.
>
> This year I was working to earn money for a wristwatch. Last year I'd earned enough to buy a bicycle.
>
> Dad moved among the workers, doing a mental roll call of the hired pickers—twelve pairs. They always worked in pairs; counting Hannah and me, he'd have thirteen pairs, but

we worked only on Saturdays. Our parents would never let us skip school.

We made our way to the big sack pile. We'd each lay ten burlap (gunny) sacks lengthwise on the ground in a neat pile. We then would each fold one sack lengthwise into a three- or four-inch belt. This we'd put across the midpoint of our sacks on the ground. Folding the sack stack in half, we'd each hoist it to our waist and secure the belt around our middle with a five-inch nail—bent like a C. When we bent over to pick, we had to be careful not to fall on our heads from the weight of the sacks.

We each had our own row and our own potato basket. When our baskets were full, we'd meet in the middle. One person would pull a sack out of the pack on the other's back and hold it open between the two rows. The other person would empty the baskets into the sack. That made a bushel. We'd proudly stand our bushel up between the rows. For each bushel, our dad paid us ten cents.

Potato picking was one of the best times on the farm. During potato-picking time, a cook was hired, and the basement of the farm was turned into a big kitchen and mess hall. Canned goods on shelves lined the north wall— vegetables, fruits, and even jars of canned meat. Meat also filled the monstrous twelve-foot freezer that occupied the east wall. A stairway coming from the main floor's back entrance ended in the center of the basement. Come down, turn right, and against the west wall was the kitchen: stove, sink, and a counter with cabinets underneath (the only refrigerator was in the upstairs kitchen). The rest of the basement had two rows of tables with benches to feed the hired men. Not only did the men get three meals a day, but they also had two lunches, one at ten in the morning and the other at three in the afternoon. The cook made up the lunches, and Britt's mother drove out to the field with coffee and sandwiches for the men.

It truly was the best time on the farm, until Britt went and turned it into the worst by one "righteous" incident. She was going to fight evil, and she convinced Hannah to go along with her. She knew what she was planning was wrong and that they would be punished.

Britt closed her eyes and saw her nine-year-old self. Hannah was seven. The cook that year was a large woman in her fifties, named Helga. She came from upstate, close to the Canadian border. She was a great storyteller, and her stories held Britt and Hannah entranced. That is until the day Helga told them her favorite story. It was about a blue light that had shown her the way out of some woods after she'd lost her way driving one winter night. After that, it followed her and told her things: her personal little blue spy. It told her what to avoid so that she'd not fall into sin, and it told her what sins others were not avoiding. Hannah and Britt almost shook with fear; her stories invaded their dreams. What was the blue light telling her about them? They'd never heard such a thing before; it wasn't a Bible story. In church, the preacher never mentioned a blue light. The blue light must be from the devil. That would make the cook someone who listened to the devil!

Christians were supposed to fight the evil, and someone who listened to the devil was evil. She and Hannah would be Christian soldiers, as in the hymn "Onward Christian Soldiers" that they sang in church. They went into the woodshed, and Britt grabbed the ax. They would scare the cook away. Down the basement they went, and Britt handed the ax to Hannah. If their mother got angry, and Britt knew she would, she wanted Hannah to get the most blame.

"I carried it all the way down here," she said to her younger sister, "so now you have to take it. Hold it out in front of you and tell the cook to get out of here and off our farm!"

Hannah obeyed; she always obeyed Britt. She held the ax in front of her and shouted, "No more blue light or we'll kill you!"

The cook told on them, of course, and their mother was furious. She made them apologize and spanked them both in front of the cook. The basement was out of bounds for them until the end of potato picking.

Potato picking was never the same after that.

Britt walked out to her dog's grave. Spot was buried in the evergreen grove south of the main farm buildings. A stone marked her grave. Thoughts of Spot filled Britt's mind as she knelt beside the grave. *If there's a heaven for doggies, there's one thing I know ... Spot has a wonderful home.*

She got Spot, a black-and-white giveaway mutt, when the puppy was seven weeks old and Britt was seven years old. Britt loved Spot passionately from the moment she got a whiff of her sweet puppy smell and cuddly pudginess. For years, Spot was one of her best friends, second only to her sister, Hannah. Whenever Britt felt bad, she could count on the comfort of Spot's love and wet kisses. Spot was never judgmental. Her kind, brown eyes radiated unconditional love. (Perhaps that's why Britt always preferred brown eyes to blue, gray, or green.)

Britt loved her but also knew that she was not perfect. Spot had developed two bad habits: she learned how to get in the chicken house and suck the insides out of eggs—egg-sucking dogs were not myths—and she learned the thrilling sport of car chasing, a sport that would be the death of her.

Her front leg was broken in the sport one sad day. Britt's father made strips of wood from a peach crate and tied them securely to Spot's front leg to form a splint. At night, Britt slept with her in the shed that was their cookhouse during harvest time. With piles of burlap sacks for a mattress, it was actually quite comfortable. In time, Spot's leg healed perfectly.

For a while, it seemed that she really had learned her lesson, but the thrill of the chase was not to be denied. She went back to her old ways of chasing, nipping, and barking at car tires, until one day a driver swerved and ran her over. Britt figures he just couldn't take this irritation anymore. He's forgiven, but Britt would never forget him; nor would she ever forget her best friend, Spot. As Britt walked back to the house, she noticed that the two partly rooted- up trees that she and Hannah called their "broncs" were gone, but she could hear her mother saying, "Girls, if it starts to feel good, *stop!*"

Britt would miss her home, her parents, the known, but she was ready to live the life of a navy wife. But on the day before she was to board the train for the East Coast, Jesse's letter came.

CHAPTER

5

Jesse! She hadn't thought about him at all after Andy said, "Okay. Let's get married." She'd been stunned; she'd not expected that—they were so young! He accused her of not wanting to get married because she wanted to date other guys. Well, that was probably true. Andy was her best friend, and they'd dated for four years, but she never thought of him as her one and only. The two years she'd been in college, Andy was working, and she didn't see him very often. For one thing, he didn't have a car. So she had dated other guys once in a while, and one of them was Jesse, and now, a day before she is to take the train to Connecticut where Andy's aunt lives, she gets this letter from him!

Jesse. He was the boy who sat behind her in English Lit during her sophomore year, second semester, in college. The seating arrangement was no accident. When Britt had walked into class on the first day, looking for a seat near the front because she was a bit nearsighted, she saw him. He sat by the window, second seat in the row, and the sun was gleaming off his blond crew cut, turning it a strawberry blond. As she looked at him, her fingers ached to touch his bristly hair to see how it would feel to run the flat palm of her hand over it. No one occupied the seat in front of him, so she made a beeline to it before anyone else saw the empty seat. She sat down but didn't turn around; she didn't want to be too forward, too friendly. She knew from experience that that was a bad idea.

What was it about her and redheads anyway? Britt had a crush on a red-haired boy when she was in seventh grade. A family with two boys had moved into a farm up the road a ways. The oldest boy, Pat, was in the sixth grade; his brother in third. About his brother she remembered only that two fingers on each of his hands were webbed. Red-haired Pat was the one she had a short-lived crush on—short, because after two months, the family moved out of the area.

In high school, she was madly in love with another red-haired guy, Steve, a year older than she. When he came into study hall, her hand shook, and she had to stop writing. One day he asked her to go to the movies. This meant a lot of driving for him—ten miles out to her home, back into town for the movie, then he had to bring her home again, followed by his drive back to town where he lived. He must have really liked her to drive forty miles just because of her. She was excited and afraid, afraid she'd be boring. What would they talk about? He was coming Saturday night, so she spent part of Saturday reading the newspaper so she'd have something to say to him, and a couple of hours at least, deciding what to wear. Her parents were excited too. Steve's father was a wealthy farmer, and they were Lutheran—it could be a match made in heaven, or so her parents must have thought.

Steve—tall, red hair combed neatly, a sport coat and slacks, and smelling of Old Spice—knocked on the door.

Britt opened it and invited him in. She introduced him to her parents, and off they went to see the new western movie, *Shane*. Britt wasn't crazy about shoot-'em-up westerns, but she did like Alan Ladd.

The ten-mile drive into town seemed to take forever. *I have to say something—this silence is making me even more nervous.* "I like Alan Ladd, don't you?"

"He's okay. Did you know that if he has a tall leading lady, he has to stand on a box to kiss her?" Steve, who stands six foot one, laughed at the idea.

"No, I didn't know that. Interesting." *And I didn't need to know that, thank you very much.*

"Have you seen the movie *Johnny Belinda*? That's excellent. They had to change the Motion Picture Production Code to show it—it's based on a true story, and it's about rape." He looked over at Britt to see how she reacted to the word "rape."

She felt her face flush. "No, I haven't seen it. I don't think my parents would want me to see it."

"Do you always do what they want you to? Live a little. That's what I say."

"Would you mind if I turned up the volume on your radio a bit? I can barely hear the music."

"Sure, go ahead."

Britt reached over and turned up the volume. *Thank goodness. Now we can stop talking.*

The movie was good—the good guys won, or rather, Alan Ladd did, but he was wounded. Steve put his arm around her back and rested his hand on her shoulder. "Good movie, huh?" He waved to some friends and steered her in their direction for a little small talk. Steve looked at his watch. "Oh! Better go. I'm sure your parents have a curfew for you." He steered her to the car and opened her door.

The first thing Britt did was turn on the radio. Mel

Tormé, the Velvet Fog, was singing "Bewitched, Bothered, and Bewildered."

Britt really liked that song. "Isn't that song just the greatest?"

"I wouldn't say that. The guy just sounds mixed up. I like his singing, but his 'Blue Moon,' now there's a song."

"My sister, Hannah's, favorite is 'Harbor Lights.' I hope they play that next."

Listening to the disc jockey spin those 45s kept them entertained with a minimum of talk until they reached Britt's house. *I sure wasted my time reading the newspaper; those subjects would have fallen flat. I didn't read the sports page. That was probably a mistake.*

Thinking about her date with Steve, she decided that it wasn't too bad—they both liked the singing of Mel Tormé. They had something in common. Maybe they had something going, even if he didn't try to kiss her good night. Britt wrote him a note, telling him how much she liked the movie and how much she liked being with him and talking about music. She walked up to him in study hall and gave him the note. It must have scared him off. He never called her again.

She moped around the house for almost two weeks. Her father couldn't stand it. "If you're going to be so down in the dumps when you go out with someone other than Andy, just go with Andy!"

She felt a tap-tapping on her right shoulder. Britt turned around and looked into eyes bluer than any eyes she'd ever seen—bluer than her dad's.

With a shy smile, he said, "May I borrow a pencil?"

"Um, yeah." She smiled back at him and handed him a pencil while thanking her lucky stars that she had an extra one.

Class over, he smiled that smile again, the one that made her heart beat faster, and returned her pencil with a "Thank you."

Britt smiled back. "You're welcome." *He's polite; I like that in a man.*

Three weeks later, after class, he asked her to take in a movie with him.

"I'd love to." *What took you so long?*

They saw each other regularly after that. The night they went to a baseball game, he really opened up. His father was a judge, strict on the bench and strict at home. Whenever Jesse got in trouble, he went to his mother, who understood him. He broke his leg climbing over someone's fence to swim in their pool. He was hospitalized and almost became addicted to morphine. Jesse didn't know what his mother told his father, but it must have been good; he was not punished. Maybe his father thought that a broken leg was punishment enough. Out of the blue, he then asked Britt a strange question:

"How much do you weigh?"

Off guard, she said, "One hundred and twenty pounds. Why?" *Do I look fat or something? I thought I looked really nice tonight: my new red, short-sleeved, V-neck T-shirt, tight but not too tight, and my black jeans.*

"That's what my mother weighs!"

Alarm bells rang. *Is he a mama's boy? He looked so pleased that his mother and I were the same weight. I've heard that a man who loves and respects his mother will love and respect his wife: this is good. But could it be too good? Would he take his mother's side if we married and I disagreed with my mother-in-law? Not good.*

A week later, he took her aside after class and said he'd enlisted in the army and would leave as soon as the semester was over. She couldn't believe it! How could he leave just like that when they were having so much fun getting to know one another? She felt abandoned, thrown away.

And that's how she was still feeling when she left the drive-in after work to go to Andy's party. When Andy told her he had enlisted in the navy, she flipped out—she felt he was abandoning her too, just like Jesse had. It was too much. Britt opened the airmail envelope with trembling hands and pulled out the letter:

> Dear Britt,
>
> I'm sorry I sprang my enlistment on you like that without any explanation, and then I just left. It was a rotten thing to do, but I did have a reason. My father found out that I broke my leg trying to climb a fence to swim in a stranger's pool—it was a very nice pool. Four beers must have clouded my judgment. But what kind of father doesn't even ask his son how he broke his leg? It took him seven months to look into it—seven months! And he only did so because a man complained about a kid trying to climb his fence and swim in his pool, but the kid broke his leg when he fell. So now I'm "irresponsible and childish," and I need "to learn how to be a man by supporting myself." Until I prove I'm a "man," he will not pay for my college education. What better way to prove you're a man than by being a soldier? And I'd get a place to stay and food to eat. So I enlisted. I didn't think they'd call me up so soon.
>
> I was angry at my father, and I acted in haste. I'm sorry I left just when we were getting to know each other. If I close my eyes, I can see you now—you're so beautiful. And I'm so lonely. I wish I were sitting

in back of you in class right now. I'd tap you on the shoulder so you'd turn around, and I'd look into your green eyes, and then I'd notice your full red lips. I think I'd kiss you right there in class.

Please write to me. Take some time out of your studies and write to me. We can continue to get to know each other by mail. Many couples have done that when apart. Please.

I miss you,
Jesse

He thought she'd gone back to school! He didn't know she was married. Tears started to form; she wiped them away. *I thought he didn't care for me, that he'd enlisted as an easy way of breaking up with me. By marrying Andy, I've slammed the door on any opportunity to ever again be with Jesse.* She blinked back the tears—she didn't want her mother to see them. Britt then carefully inserted the letter back into the envelope.

"Who's the letter from, Britt? You seem upset."

"Just a college friend who thought I'd be back in class by now. It's a friend I'll miss." Britt reached under the kitchen sink and pulled out the trash basket, dropping her letter in it. "Mom, I'm going out to burn the trash." *But not all in the basket is trash. I'll remember your letter, Jesse, forever.*

The next day, Britt boarded the train for the East Coast. She took along yarns in her favorite colors and her crochet hook, all stashed in a carry-on with toiletries and a couple of books, *The President's Lady* and *The Cather in the Rye.* Her black trunk, carrying some personal things as well as household items, could be sent when her parents had an address for her and Andy.

CHAPTER

6

Britt had plenty of time to brood over the letter, for the next day she was on her way out east, and train travel can be tedious. She'd brought a good book but found it hard to concentrate—why didn't Jesse write her sooner? Now it was too late. She took out her crochet hook and began the center of a granny square for a throw pillow cover. The thing about crocheting was that she was good at it and really didn't have to think much while doing it—she could probably crochet with her eyes shut—so she had time to think about Jesse, his letter, and about Andy.

Britt knew that she was too impulsive. Her mother always said, "Look before you leap," but she seldom did. She had expected Andy to break up with her when she said she didn't want to *not* know where their relationship was headed during his four-year enlistment. He suggested that she just wanted to go out with other guys and followed that statement with a totally out of the blue suggestion: *marriage!* Maybe Jackie, her old boss, was right when she said they were too young—too young to know what love was, let alone marriage. Britt knew that she liked Andy and that he liked her—they wouldn't have gone together for four years if that were not true. Is "liking" strong enough to build a marriage on? Because if loving someone means putting the welfare and desires of the other person above your own, maybe she didn't love Andy. Was she only thinking of herself when she agreed to marry him? Marriage would free *her* from having to find out who she was and what she wanted to do with her life. Had she been not only cowardly but selfish?

Britt couldn't stand thinking anymore. She left her coach car seat and made her way to the dome car of the train. She needed distraction, and from what she had read about dome cars, you climbed up some steps to reach the domed section, and from there you could see in every direction. It was true— no matter which way she looked, she saw a landscape rolling by. Britt felt the swaying of the train whenever they rounded a curve. She was surprised she could see so far. She looked out the back—how fast those tracks were receding! It was alarming—they must be traveling at over a hundred miles an hour. She wished she could sort out her problems, her tangled emotions at that speed.

The dome car was exciting for about an hour and a half— time to head back to coach and try to think things out again. Jesse's letter—it had rocked her. She was just getting to know him. She liked him, and he liked her, but she wondered if he really did. Maybe he liked her because she weighed the same as his mother. She didn't *know* him well enough; now she never would. She couldn't stand the thought that she may have missed out because she'd been too impulsive—that she'd messed up. Jesse was a Lutheran. That would have pleased her parents, but she'd already become a Catholic even before she started going out with him. Britt never told him this. With her last name "Anderson," she was sure he would have assumed she was Protestant. She was not only a Catholic now; she was a *married* Catholic.

I will be a good wife. I promised before God to be a good wife. I take promises seriously—if you make a promise, you keep it. When I was thirteen and had just had my appendix removed, Mother promised me that I could get a dog. She promised but did not keep her promise. I was disappointed. Of course I was disappointed that I couldn't get a dog, but I was more disappointed in her. She'd broken a promise. People say, "I promise," too often and without thinking. I don't. I will keep my promise to Andy, to love him until death, and when children come, I will be the best mother I can be. Mother—that's an identity for you. But couldn't the results have been the same had Jesse and I married? Something I'll never know. Something I do know: I'm starving.

Britt found the dining car. One end of it was split into a galley, or kitchen, off limits to passengers. A corridor ran parallel to the galley and opened to the main part of the car, which held tables and chairs. The whole thing was one long restaurant, tastefully decorated in the art deco style, traditional mixed with bright splashes of color. It cheered her, and she needed that. Britt ordered a grilled cheese sandwich with bean soup, comfort food. She ate her lunch and listened to the hypnotic clickety-clack of the train as it sped across the country.

Soon she would be in Bridgeport, Connecticut, where Andy's aunt and uncle lived. Britt would stay with them until Andy's leave, at which time he'd drive to Bridgeport, visit with his aunt and uncle, and then take Britt back to Newport with him. They had a car again! Their '48 Ford was totaled when they'd been hit by the snowplow. He'd been so proud to be the owner of a car. All those years of growing up and having to beg other people for rides made having his own car one of Andy's top priorities. She was happy that he'd bought another, and if he was going overseas soon, she would not have to beg for rides either.

Before this train ride ended, Britt decided to check out the lounge car; she'd heard it was luxurious. It was. It was beautiful too, with bright-colored fabrics in geometric designs. The walls were stainless steel with a few art deco wall decorations. Public seating—benches or swiveling armchairs—invited people to relax. It also boasted a small bar. The best thing was the space; people could move around, talk, eat, drink, and enjoy the scenery. Britt didn't stay in the lounge car very long. She was alone, and all the people socializing just made her feel lonely.

It took her two full days and nights to reach Bridgeport, Connecticut. Her sore muscles and aching head were minor compared to her bone tiredness. She could have slept in a sleeping car, or Pullman, but it was too expensive. She managed to take short naps in coach by scrunching herself into a fetal position when she felt her eyes getting heavy and strained from too much crocheting and reading. What she needed most was a bath and then at least twelve hours of sleep.

Uncle Fritz, a large, bearded man, met her train. "Britt?"

"Yes. You must be Andy's uncle!"

He gave her a bear hug and picked up her suitcase. On the drive to their apartment, he filled her in on what to expect.

"Jean, your aunt Jean, is a nurse, and she won't be home yet. She works the 3:00 to 11:00 p.m. shift at the hospital. You'll meet her tomorrow. Our daughter, Ellen, is home. You'll share her bedroom while you're here.

"We own the apartment building. We used to live on the first floor, but Jean thought everything got too dusty down there—she hates dusting—so we moved to the second floor, and she was right. The place stays cleaner now."

When they entered the foyer, Britt was surprised to see that the building had an elevator. Here she'd been thinking that they'd feel differently about living on the second floor when they got older, but if they had an elevator? Maybe not.

They stepped off the elevator and entered the living room of the two-bedroom, two-bath apartment. It was lovely. A three-seat, overstuffed, sea-green sofa dominated the far wall. Over it hung a large, framed mirror. Throw pillows, in lavender and peach, casually placed on the sofa, added to the feeling of ease and hospitality. An overstuffed chair, slipcovered in a peach and sea-green floral print, filled the space to the right of the sofa. A rust-colored area rug covered the oak hardwood floor. Light peach walls combined with limed oak woodwork and a cabinet radio, also in limed oak, gave a cozy yet airy feeling to the room.

"Ellen! Come and meet your cousin, Andy's wife!"

Twelve-year-old Ellen, with a mop of curly black hair, ran into the living room, ducked her head, eyes looking up, and checked out the newcomer. "Hello. I'm almost as big as you are. Would you like to hear some music?"

Britt smiled. "Maybe later, but now I'm just too tired. Your dad said that we'll be roommates. Thank you so much for letting me share your room, Ellen."

Britt peeked into the master bedroom as they passed it on the way to Ellen's room where she'd be sleeping. White chenille bedspreads covered twin beds separated by a night table. The room was painted a light aqua. *Andy and I will not sleep in twin beds; we'll have a double bed. It was good enough for my parents and for his; it will be great for us.* They entered Ellen's room. It too had twin beds. This time, the matching chenille spreads sported flowers—roses with green leaves against a white background.

Fritz lowered Britt's suitcases to the floor. "Your home away from home. You'll be comfortable here, and Ellen's used to sharing her room. Because she's an only child, we encourage her to have friends sleep over on weekends. They listen to music and talk. She likes the new music. Rock and roll, they call it. We've held off getting a television because we don't want her to neglect her schoolwork. We want her to get into a good college when she graduates."

Britt yawned. "Thank you, Uncle Fritz. If you don't mind, I'll unpack a bit and just lie down for a while. I'm pretty tired." Stuffed animals covered half the surface of one bed. *Just like Hannah's bed.* Britt chose the other one and began to unpack a few things.

Britt stayed with Andy's aunt and uncle for a week. During that time, she and Ellen would head for the beach right after breakfast. They put their swimsuits on before they left, covering them with shorts and a top. Britt packed a light lunch of snacks for them before they caught the bus to the beach for swimming and sunbathing. Britt's Swedish skin got sunburned, and she had to go braless for a couple of days. Noxema helped heal and cool her down. Luckily, she'd brought a shirt with two pockets in just the right places, so she could go braless and still be decent. Ellen, with her olive skin and brown eyes, browned beautifully and looked like a gorgeous Indian princess.

Aunt Jean slept until almost ten in the morning. When Ellen and Britt returned from the beach at about twelve thirty, she and Aunt Jean would talk, woman to woman. "How did you and Andy start dating?" was Aunt Jean's first question.

"We met at the roller-skating rink. He was so cute in his white stocking cap. When he asked me to be his skating partner, I couldn't resist. My father would drive into town Friday nights to check on things at his potato house and play a few hands of Smear at the pool hall. He'd bring Hannah and me along and drop us off at the skating rink. It was great fun skating to the music with so many others."

"Fritz and I met at the World's Fair in Chicago, in the beer garden. It was love at first sight. We married after three weeks and have never been sorry. We say the Lord's Prayer together on our knees every night—maybe that's the secret to a happy marriage."

Britt wasn't sure about that, but it couldn't hurt if she and Andy picked up the habit. "You were Catholic, and he was German Lutheran. Did your parents get upset when you switched your religion?"

"Not really. They probably wished that I hadn't, but two of my brothers had changed religion before me. Both had married Lutheran women—they paved the way for me. Here, Britt, have a cookie. You should always eat something with your coffee; it dilutes the acid and is better for your stomach."

"You and Uncle Fritz get along so well. I can see that you like each other as well as love each other. Don't you ever fight?"

"Oh yes but not very often. I remember when I wanted to go back to work after Ellen was born. I'm a registered nurse, and I just couldn't see why I should waste my education. He didn't want me to work at all. He thought any man that let his wife work was telling the world that he wasn't a good provider. It was pretty quiet around here for a while, broken by some yelling, but we finally compromised. I'd stay home until Ellen started school, and then I'd go to work. It was the best way."

"You disagreed, but you were able to find a compromise. Perhaps that's another secret for a happy marriage."

Because her aunt worked the late shift at the hospital and slept in, Britt started making breakfast for her uncle and Ellen. She and Hannah used to cook for the family when their mother suffered a migraine, so she knew her way around a kitchen. This kitchen had the same red Formica-topped table with the chrome legs as the one in her mom's kitchen. She wished her mother had a pantry like Aunt Jean's though: everything within easy reach. A large white sink with its attached drainage board made washing dishes a breeze. Of course there was a refrigerator—white with rounded shoulders, and the red-and-white linoleum looked like a checkerboard and brought to mind cheerful thoughts of playing checkers with her dad. Someday she'd like a kitchen just like this. Right now, however, she'd settle for an apartment with Andy.

Andy called. He had a seventy-two-hour leave, and he was coming to get Britt, starting out from Newport right then. He'd be there in less than three hours. After a day and a night with his aunt and uncle, they would have to leave the next day, early, for the drive back to Newport. He had a dental appointment at eleven, and after that they'd go apartment hunting. Britt could hardly wait—it'd been four months since she'd seen him. She was so nervous she put water in the percolator but forgot to put in the coffee grounds; coffee drinkers had to settle for the hot water poured on a tea bag. She kept running to the window to see if he was coming, but how could she know? She didn't even know what kind of car he'd be driving. Britt caught herself chewing the ends of her hair; she hadn't done that since taking college exams. Finally a gray car slowed and then stopped, and a handsome sailor stepped out.

Britt raced to the elevator and pushed the "down" button. *Come on, come on! Finally.* She stepped in and, with shaking hands, pushed the "ground level" button. *Everything's taking so long!*

The door opened, and she dashed out. "Andy!" She flew

into his arms. "Andy, I missed you so much—you're burning up!" Britt removed her arms from around Andy's neck and raised her right hand to feel his forehead. "You have a fever."

Aunt Jean showed up just then. "What's this I hear? My nephew has a fever?" She walked over to him and put her hand on his forehead. "Well, I guess so! How do you feel? Are you in pain?"

Andy gave his aunt a quick hug. "I had an abscessed tooth and had a root canal done, but it hurts more now than it did before. Every time my heart beats, I can feel it throbbing in my tooth. I have another appointment with the dentist tomorrow—that's why we have to leave early in the morning."

"I'll give you something for the pain, but be sure to keep that appointment."

"Yeah, I will." Andy put his arm around her. "You're lookin' good, Aunt Jean."

"So are you, in spite of your swollen top lip. You sure favor your mother—those French eyebrows. How is my sister these days?"

"We stayed with my folks when we returned home after the wedding—she was fine. Still working part-time at Ace Hardware."

"And your father?"

"Not working, but he makes a great split-pea soup."

They all trooped back into the house and made a beeline for the kitchen, where Aunt Jean made a fresh pot of coffee, and unlike Britt, she did not forget to put in coffee grounds. While it was perking, she went into the bathroom and came back with a bottle of pills. "Take two of these now, Andy, and two more every four hours—your pain should be a lot less. And don't eat or drink anything that is hot or cold. You stick to warm food and drink. I'll pour you one half cup of coffee. Add milk to make it a full cup." She handed Andy the bottle of pills.

Uncle Fritz had been watching and listening while he filled his pipe and tamped down the tobacco in the bowl. He lit it, took a puff, and said, "Andy, why did you join the navy?"

"I didn't want to get drafted into the army and end up digging foxholes. I wanted a job where I didn't have to get my hands dirty. That's what the navy offers, plus a clean place to sleep and regular meals. When I get out, I can get the GI Bill. I'll use it for more education and to buy a house for my wife and me." Andy put his arm around Britt and drew her close to his side. "In fact, I've been accepted into cooking school. Britt and I will be together for a few months before I have to go on any cruise."

Ellen perked up at this. "Learn to make brownies and birthday cakes."

"I will—the school teaches cooking and baking." Andy poured milk into his coffee and took a sip. "You're right, Aunt Jean—warm is good."

"Mom, do you have any more cookies? I finished the last one."

"I put some in the fridge. Ellen, take this empty plate and fill it up. We've got a lot of talking to do."

Britt, overjoyed to see Andy again, was sorry that he was in pain. In a way, she was relieved too. She was near the end of her period. She hadn't told Andy because she didn't want to disappoint him; it was a sin, maybe even a mortal one, to have intercourse with a woman who was menstruating. But if he was sick, he wouldn't want to do it anyway. They'd be sleeping in Ellen's room—Ellen on the sofa in the living room. They'd have privacy, but she was still relieved that she had an excuse not to do it in Andy's aunt and uncle's house.

Britt told Andy about her condition at bedtime when they were choosing, separate beds or together? They chose to sleep together in one bed. So what if they couldn't have relations; they could be next to each other. Britt, as usual, lay on her left side. Andy did too, putting his right arm around her waist. They fell asleep, nestled together like two spoons in a drawer.

CHAPTER

7

Newport was an island city in 1954, reached only by going over the Narragansett Bay by way of a long bridge or by flying in. A port city, it smelled of the sea—sometimes but not always, a good thing. Thames Street, Newport's oldest street, was paved with cobblestones—a surprise to Britt, as she'd never seen streets like that before. In their exploration, they drove down Purgatory Road, and one of the shops along the route made tombstones! They stopped at a cemetery off Spring Street and were amazed to see death dates in the 1700s. So old and all fenced in with wrought-iron fences and gates. They took Ocean Drive, a must for anyone coming to Newport. The drive follows close to the seashore and is exhilarating, especially when waves race in, smash up against rocks, and spray you with drops of the Atlantic Ocean—a blessing.

Newport was a sailor's town—all about the navy. It was the home of the United States Naval War College, the Navy Undersea Warfare Center, and a major United States Navy training center. Sailors in their dress blues and their cooler whites were everywhere, coming out of bars, stepping out of stores with a package or two, walking into the post office, and always and everywhere, snapping off salutes to anyone who outranked them.

It was the morning of Andy's dental appointment, but they had time to eat a light breakfast and visit the Traveler's Aid Center. They wanted help in looking for an apartment. The woman behind the counter, a volunteer, told them that not much was available. "Many of Newport's residents," she said, "did not like or trust sailors, especially enlisted men." Right now the only vacancy was a small house out by Easton's Beach. "You can go out and look at it if you want to."

"A house on Easton's Beach—that sounds wonderful! Let's go, Andy."

"Okay, after I see the dentist."

The woman at the desk spun her Rolodex until she found the homeowner's card. "I'll see if he'll open up the place for you. Give me a call just before you go out there to be sure it'll be open." She wrote the Traveler's Aid phone number on a slip of paper and handed it to Andy. "If it doesn't work out, check with me again tomorrow. That's when the new listings come in."

While waiting at the dentist's office for Andy, Britt thought about what the volunteer at Traveler's Aid had said about residents not wanting to rent to enlisted men. *Did the community believe that old saw that sailors had a girl in every port? Did they look at a sailor suit and think of it as a suit of immorality?* Andy walked out into the waiting room, a smile on his face.

"Hey, you're smiling—that didn't take long."

"When he did the root canal, he put in a 'sleeve' to drain the abscess. Somehow it got plugged up, and that's why my tooth hurt so much. He unplugged it and gave me a penicillin shot. I have another appointment next week. He'll probably give me another shot, and after the infection is all gone, he'll finish fixing my tooth." He took her by the hand and pulled her up. "Come on, Mrs. Hughes. Let's find us a place to live."

The house out by Easton's Beach was small, but it had two bedrooms and a bath—their own bathroom! It wasn't close to the beach. It was set back into the woods, and the road to it was crumbling. Britt would be lonely out there when Andy was gone—it was, in fact, scary.

"Britt, this is too far from the center of Newport. We have to find something in town."

Britt agreed; this would be private, too private. They drove back to Newport, had a good meal—Andy's first good meal in two days—and, exhausted, checked into a hotel.

An old man with a fringe of white hair circling his large bald spot looked at them, one eyebrow raised and a smirk on his face as they signed the hotel register, "Mr. and Mrs. Andrew Hughes."

Britt wished she could stop her thoughts, but she just knew he was thinking: *Well, what have we here? A couple of randy kids coming in for a quick roll in the hay. They can't fool me with "Mr. and Mrs." I've been around the block; I know what's what.* In a way, Britt didn't blame him. They did look young. In the hospital when she was recovering from their car accident, one nurse swore she was only fourteen. It was her round, baby face that fooled them.

Their room was upstairs. As they climbed, Britt was careful not to snag her heels on the worn carpet. She wouldn't want to land on a carpet that looked so in need of a good cleaning. At the head of the stairs, they turned left, and there it was, room 210. Andy fumbled with the key, and the door squeaked open, treating them to the smell of mold and cigarettes. He made as if to carry her over the threshold, but Britt shook her head.

"Not here. This place is not a home; it's just a needed stopover. Let's get some sleep, but first I want to take a shower." *I want to wash off the dirt I feel after the look we got at the hotel register. I hope this shower isn't like the one we had in our room the day we married; I'm too tired to mop the floor tonight.*

Showers refreshed them, and they went to bed. Andy put his hand on her breast, and they kissed. His other hand moved up her thigh, but it was not demanding. They hadn't made love at his aunt and uncle's house because Britt was not yet completely through with her period—besides, Andy was afraid. He worried that Britt's pelvis and hip joint injuries from their car accident in March may not yet be strong enough. Britt was afraid too but not that she'd break; she was afraid the man at the register would hear them and get off on imagining what those "kids" were doing.

Crack! The bed gave way and their mattress landed on the floor. They were too tired to do anything about it. What could they do anyway? They said their prayers together, kissed good night again, and this time they meant it. Andy fell asleep almost right away, but Britt lay looking up at the yellowed ceiling and all the brown water stains. She tried to see pictures in the stains the way people do when they lie on their backs and look up at moving clouds. She could see a four-leafed clover—a good sign. Sleep then claimed her.

They checked out early and headed back to Traveler's Aid and its list of available places to rent. It was a short list, only two new listings, but they were both close to downtown, a good thing. When Andy shipped out, Britt intended to look for a job, so that meant something not too far away from Thames, the main street in Newport. They drove to the Webster Street house first. It was a 712-square-foot rental with one bedroom and one bathroom. And that's all. The "kitchen" was in the bedroom: a plug-in, two-burner hot plate; a small refrigerator; and a table for two with two bent-wood chairs. The kitchen cupboard was an old armoire with shelves built into it. It held mismatched dishes and two dishpans. This would not do at all.

The second listing was on Front Street. Andy knocked on the door, and a frowzy, gray-haired woman opened it, her left hand gripping a cane. She wore run-down slippers, and a far-from-clean apron covered her faded floral print housedress.

"We're here about your room for rent."

"It's right in front. Come this way," She shuffled down the hall for about eight feet and then opened the door to her left. "It's not much, but it has a good mattress. You'll be sharing the kitchen with me and the couple in the back room. I have the kitchen from nine to ten in the morning, one to two in the afternoon, and seven to eight at night. I don't want to see any crumbs or dirty dishes lying around after you leave. Work out your kitchen time with the other couple. Do the same with the bathroom time. You won't have to share with me there; I have my own bathroom. Oh, and your refrigerator shelf is the middle one—the one down from yours belongs to the other couple. Any food that gets put on my shelf, I'll eat. Understand?"

It was plain to see that she really didn't want them there. They found out later that she was a widow and did need the money. They took the room, fearing that if they didn't, someone else would, and then they might not find anything else. They paid the rent for two months, and she gave them a receipt and the apartment key.

Andy opened the door to their apartment, turned around, bent down, and scooped Britt up in his arms and carried her over the threshold. That night they celebrated by eating out—clam chowder and beer—at the White Horse Tavern just one block over from Thames Street.

The couple in the apartment on the other end of the house must have gone out too, for they had the bathroom all to themselves when they returned. Not once did anyone pound on the door and yell, "Hurry up in there!"

Squeaky clean and relaxed, they returned to their apartment and prepared for bed. Andy turned the radio on with the volume down low, and the romantic strains of Irving Berlin's "Always" sung by Frank Sinatra wafted through the air.

In bed, they held hands and said the Lord's Prayer together. Andy would not let go of her hand—he pulled her to him and started kissing her neck and moved on to plant a light kiss on her lips. He stroked her face with his fingertips, moving from cheek to chin. Britt put her fingers on his lips, and he kissed them. She moved her fingers down the bridge of his nose and touched the bump there. It was a reminder of when he broke his nose in a rough game of basketball. Britt gently slid her hands over his muscular shoulders and upper arms and into the tender hollows of his elbows. She pulled his shirt over his head. She felt him slide her silky nightie up and off her body. They held each other, skin against skin, hearts pounding, until they could breathe again.

He cupped her breasts, kissed them, and ran his tongue over her nipples. He kissed the curve of her hip bone. He took her hand and guided it down to help him remove his shorts. He then reached his hand between her legs. She bent her knees and opened them, urging him on further. One finger slipped inside of her and found her center, moist and plump. She felt his hard penis on her inner thigh—he started to shiver. She spread her legs like wings, inviting him. He accepted the invitation, and she helped guide his penis into the moist warmth. Andy began to move—increasing in power and speed as he felt her tighten around him. He crushed her to him and exploded.

Exhausted, they lay across the bed, his penis still within her, but it was shrinking, retreating. Their gasps became gentle and regular breaths. *Never have I felt so close to anyone before. We were one. What is that song I hear? "Unforgettable"—it really was.*

Andy stirred, sat up, and reached for a cigarette.

Andy had applied for Navy Cooking School, a nine-week program, in order to spend more time in Newport with Britt. After he graduated, he would leave Newport aboard a destroyer and spend the next six months at sea. Andy had school five days a week, starting at 0800 hours and ending at 1600 hours. Britt interviewed for a job at a law office on Thames Street and was hired as a member of the "steno" pool. Knowing their time together was limited, they made the most of it by doing the things tourists do on the weekends that Andy had off.

Newport had a lot to offer, and as they'd never had a honeymoon, they made every possible weekend until Andy shipped out a mini-honeymoon. The first weekend they visited the Breakers. The Vanderbilt's summer "cottage," a seventy-room Italian Renaissance villa that opened to the public in 1948, was high on most visitors' lists. Income from visitors went to support the Preservation Society of Newport County.

Andy and Britt didn't see all seventy rooms, but they saw the ones that were important to them. The library impressed Britt the most. Its ceiling was painted with dolphins, symbolic of the sea and hospitality. A wide border of walnut paneling right below the ceiling was impressed with gold leaf, making it look like a horizontal row of leather-bound books. Book shelves and gold-leafed paneling dominated the room. A large fireplace bore the inscription "I laugh at great wealth, and never miss it; nothing but wisdom matters in the end." A large, patterned area carpet in reds, whites, and blues covered the floor in front of the fireplace, and on this carpet, arranged in a semicircle, were comfortable upholstered chairs in soft greens. No chance to sit: the area was roped off.

The kitchen drew Andy's interest, not surprising since he'd just started cooking school. All those copper pots and pans—more than thirty!—hanging overhead drew his gaze: stunning. Andy admired a work counter of beautiful dark wood, at least twelve feet long, with a single row of drawers under its zinc-covered top. It combined practicality with beauty. Ingredients were crushed by a marble mortar in front of this counter. Light and airy, the kitchen was located on the first floor—preventing cooking smells from migrating into the main house.

They didn't think anything could ever eclipse that beautiful mansion, unless it was Easton's Beach, their destination the next weekend. It was within walking distance, but they wanted to wear their swimming suits and bring some things—blanket, sunscreen, towels, and dry clothes—so they drove. Parking was free. Soft white sand, a cool breeze off the ocean, and lobster rolls for lunch, purchased at the snack bar, made this mini-honeymoon just as wonderful, though very different, from the Breakers of last weekend.

Britt and Andy loved the beach so much they decided to visit another: Fort Adams Beach. Here they were able to watch sailboats pass. Most enjoyable was a walk along the rocky coastline. If they'd had the time and money, they would have signed up for scuba diving. Maybe someday.

On several weekends they went to the Enlisted Men's Club, or "EM." Often there'd be special entertainment. Britt, who loved to dance, would never forget dancing to the music of Guy Lombardo—live! On another unforgettable night, Connie Francis sang "Who's Sorry Now?" and when she was done, the place exploded with applause and whistles that just went on and on. Andy's favorite, Joni James, sang "Your Cheating Heart," and that too was another unforgettable performance—some of the sailors had tears in their eyes, and as it was for Connie Francis, the applause was deafening.

Victor Borge, the Clown Prince of Denmark, gave a unique and memorable performance—a classic pianist and a comedian, what a combination! When he played Debussy's "Clair de Lune," Britt knew that she'd love that music forever. He later explained his punctuation invention, using different noises to enhance oral words, "Phonetic pronunciation." Then he read a story illustrating what he meant: hilarious. As a pianist, he was superb; as a comedian, intelligent and oh so funny.

The Annual Jazz Festival began in 1954, and Britt and Andy were there. So many greats performed: Billie Holiday, Pee Wee Russell, the Dizzy Gillespie Quintet, Gene Krupa Trio, and Ella Fitzgerald. More performed, but these were Brit and Andy's favorites.

Thinking over and discussing all they'd seen and experienced on the weekends while Andy went to school, they concluded that they couldn't choose Newport's most outstanding offering, as they were incomparable because of their variety. They had no trouble deciding that they'd had the best mini-honeymoon possible.

In September, Andy sailed away as the apprentice cook on a Navy destroyer. He'd be gone for six months.

CHAPTER

8

Britt dragged herself to work the day after Andy left. She didn't know how she could stand living in this place without him. Thank goodness she had a job to go to, something to do rather than pining for Andy, and she was making friends. Most of the girls in the steno pool were navy wives, just like her. Jan, a lively redhead with a big smile, lived only a block from where Britt lived. Jan was pregnant and just starting to show. Carmela lived in Jamestown, a town of just over two thousand people on the island of Conanicut, yet still a part of Rhode Island. She took the ferry in to work in the morning and then took it back home when the work day ended. This cut out any after-work socializing with Carmela, but they took their lunch breaks together. Krista, another friend, lived on the third floor of the building in which Jan lived.

A couple of months after Andy's departure, Britt was coping just fine, but she wasn't feeling all that well. The mornings, in particular, were a problem. She loved coffee, but now it seemed she couldn't even stand the smell of it! Dry toast was about all she could keep down for breakfast.

That wasn't like her. She'd been brought up to believe that breakfast was the most important meal of the day, and here she was just eating a piece of toast. Maybe that's why sometimes she even felt woozy.

About the same time that she was having these strange physical feelings, a weird thing happened, one that caused some emotional unease. Britt washed her clothes at the Laundromat at the end of the block and across the street and then took them home and hung them on her landlady's clothesline—she had permission to do this. One day, she hung her clothes out on the line before going to work, only to come home from work and find that all of her underwear was missing from the clothesline! Her landlady wouldn't have done it—none of Britt's underthings would fit her. And just her underwear? Weird.

Britt couldn't do anything about her underwear, except notify the police, which she did, hoping they'd keep an eye out for any suspicious characters in the area. She, however, could do something about her strange physical feelings. She made an appointment with a doctor at the Navy Hospital. He did the usual blood pressure, temperature, pelvic exam, and then said, "You are about two months pregnant."

Britt was ecstatic. "Really? Are you sure?" *If I'm pregnant, I'm not alone, and I'll never be alone again. I'm growing a baby, a friend, a family!*

"I'm sure. You'll have to watch your weight now. If you gain more than two pounds a month, we'll put you in the hospital until you lose the extra weight."

But Britt couldn't stop smiling. She and Andy would no longer be a couple; they'd be a family.

When Britt told her landlady the good news, it went over like a lead balloon.

"I'll not have a crying baby in this house." She clamped

her jaws together, and her lips formed a thin line—the look in her eyes would have curdled milk.

"It'll be a good baby. I just know it will."

Her landlady was like a stone. Not only did she say that Britt would have to move if she had the baby; she also gave Britt advice on how she might get rid of it. "Fill the tub with water as hot as you can take. Soak in that water until you're all wrinkled. That may cause a miscarriage."

Britt paled, and her mouth opened, though no words came out at first. Then, "I'd never do that. I want this baby more than anything." She could feel her stomach roiling with rage. She didn't want to say anything she'd later regret, so she turned and ran to her room, slammed the door, threw herself across the bed, and sobbed.

At work the next day, she poured out her troubles to Jan—her confrontation with her landlady, and then she threw in the weirdness about her missing underwear. After a big hug, Jan said, "You're in luck! A second-floor apartment just became available where I live. You'd be happier with your own place, your own kitchen, your own bathroom, and you can hang your clothes on the second-floor balcony in the back."

Britt didn't need any more convincing. Right after work, she went to see Jan's landlord, a Mr. Veroni who ran the first-floor delicatessen in Jan's building. He was happy to rent again so soon. Then she told her landlady that she was moving. She wanted to be among friends while Andy was gone. *Andy!* What would he say? She'd have to tell him as soon as she got settled.

Jan and Krista helped Britt move her things to the second floor of Veroni's Delicatessen. The shotgun apartment had a bathroom to the left of the front door, and the other rooms followed in a straight line: kitchen, bedroom, and living room. The bathroom's miniscule window on the far wall let in just enough light during the day to highlight the claw-footed tub. In the far left corner was an ancient gas water heater. It was used to heat water for bathing. A strange-looking thing, it had to be lit about thirty minutes before you wanted to bathe. If she left the burner on too long, would the water heater blow up? The thought scared her. Britt set her little kitchen timer for exactly thirty minutes each time she heated bath water. The toilet sat to the left of this contraption. There was no sink.

In the kitchen, a large sink with drain board was fastened securely on the left wall. Next to it was an apartment-sized gas stove. To the back wall of the kitchen and in the left-hand corner was a standard sized window. A seven-foot-long counter, made of boards covered with linoleum, took up most of the back wall. It had board shelves beneath it, but nothing covered the shelves, and there were no top cupboards. The right-hand wall, to the left of the door to the bedroom, was occupied by a large, white, round-shouldered refrigerator. A red Formica-topped table with three chairs stood in the space between the front door and the bedroom door.

Only two pieces of furniture occupied the bedroom: a bed and a three-foot by four-and-a-half-foot dark brown dresser. The last room, the living room, held an old hide-a-bed. But on the wall facing the street, a glorious bay window let in the light. Britt would stand there and watch people coming and going on the street below. This room held the only closet in the entire apartment, a three-foot by four-foot built-in tucked into the left hand corner of the back wall. All rooms had an overhead light fixture, consisting of a naked bulb with a pull-down string hanging from it. The apartment, however, was clean and newly painted—white—and all the floors had fairly new linoleum on them.

Britt would have to do something about getting cupboards for dishes, but that would have to wait. Now she had to sit down and write to Andy.

Dear Andy,

I have some great news: we're going to be a family of three! No, I didn't get a dog. I'm pregnant. How I wish you were here. I miss you so much, but I have part of you growing within me; I am not alone.

And that reminds me of what else I have to tell you. When I told our landlady about the baby, she was not happy. She doesn't want any kids around, and if we had one, we'd have to move. Then she proceeded to give me advice on how I might cause myself to miscarry. I hated her at that moment. I could not bear to stay there, so I moved.

Jan, my first friend here, told me that a second-floor apartment was available in her building on her same floor. It has three rooms, and we have our own bathroom and our own kitchen—no more sharing. It's on Spring Street; remember the street that crosses ours at the bottom of the hill? It's less than a block away. The apartment is above Veroni's Delicatessen where we bought those Rueben sandwiches. Jan and Krista, who live on the third floor, helped me move. Jan and Krista are both navy wives, and Jan is pregnant too.

This place needs some fixing up, but that will give me something to do until you get home. And just think, Andy, you're going to be a daddy!

All my love,
Britt

Dear Britt,

I can understand why you moved, but I sure wish you'd consulted me first. Couldn't you have waited until I got home? I'll be home before the baby comes. You shouldn't be carrying things when you're pregnant. You have to be careful. I can't even picture you living anywhere now!

Three rooms—how much does that place cost? We're not rich you know. An enlisted man doesn't make much money, and now we have a baby coming!

Be sure you eat enough; remember you are eating for two. Do you like the name "Anthony"? I miss you too, very much. I'm still seasick. This ship bobs around like a cork. I can't wait to stand on solid ground and to have my arms around you, though you should have told me you wanted to move.

Eat your vegetables and stay safe.

All my love,
Andy

From what he wrote, Britt didn't know if he was hurt or angry because she moved on her own—both probably. But she had to think of her own feelings, especially at this time, and she was looking forward to making this place a real home.

Mr. Veroni let Britt have two orange crates. She wetted down the labels on the ends until she was able to peel or scrape them off. She then painted the crates white and stood them vertically, side by side, on the long counter against the far wall—cupboards for her dishes. Britt did not like the look of the bottom shelves without any doors, so she bought some dark green fabric and rings for café curtains—only twenty-five cents a yard. She also bought a used Featherweight Singer sewing machine to sew and hem the curtains. She then screwed some cup hooks into the underside of the counter and hung up the curtains: much better.

The living room needed some color. Britt went to a craft store and bought two paint-by-number kits: one, when finished, would show a Mexican man with a sombrero and a serape made of blue, magenta, and orange wool yarns; the other was of a Mexican woman, wearing an aqua and lilac shawl and making a vase on a pottery wheel. Britt's mother had made her a zigzag, or ripple, afghan of magenta, aqua, white, and lilac yarns, and she'd packed it in the trunk that Britt now had in Newport. When the pictures were finished and framed, Britt hung them above the sofa bed and then casually arranged the afghan to cover the left two-thirds of the sofa. Lovely. One more thing: her throw pillows covered with the sewn-together granny squares she'd crocheted on the train, she tossed into the other end. Wow! Now she had all the color she craved. No one could stay depressed in this room.

With the apartment looking more homey, it was time to get out her little sewing machine and stitch up some maternity clothes to wear to work. Pattern books showed easily made maternity smocks. The skirts were straight with either a short slit up from the hem about seven inches in back, or a pleat of that length. In order to keep the skirt from riding up as your belly grew bigger, the waist line in front was cut down in a half circle, almost to the pubic area, and then up again to the waist. The diameter of this semicircle was about ten inches. Sewn at the center point at the bottom of the circle was a one-inch-wide strap with a loop at the top. The strap had to be long enough to reach the waist, where two ties were waiting. One tie was inserted into the loop, and then both ties were tied together at the waist. When a breeze blew, you didn't try to hold down your skirt; you reached for your smock and held it down so that the world would not see your bare belly. Her favorite outfit was a smock top, black cotton fabric with blue flowers complete with green stems and leaves. She put in some extra color by attaching a red bow at the bottom of the V-neck. She paired the smock with a black skirt. Dressy and cute. She also sewed a blue and white striped robe of cotton seersucker. She wanted something attractive yet concealing to wear when Andy returned. Sitting at her machine, she blessed her high school home economics teacher for being such an excellent sewing instructor.

Britt spent Christmas alone. She called her parents on Christmas Eve. She didn't talk to her father, he didn't like to talk on the phone, but she talked to her mother and had to hang up when she broke down crying. That was the only real bad time she had while Andy was gone. For the most part, she kept busy, and as her mother used to say, "Busy hands are happy hands." Work was going well, and she was putting some money away. Evenings she'd play Canasta with Jan and Krista, who were also alone and waiting for husbands to return. She and Krista had an ongoing cockroach battle. Living above a delicatessen just invited cockroaches. When Mr. Veroni sprayed, they went up to Britt's apartment. When Britt sprayed, they went to Krista's place on third floor, and when she sprayed, down they came ... it was a never-ending battle. Britt hated them. One night she felt something crawling in her pajamas. She jumped up, pulled off her bottoms, and saw a cockroach! She screamed as she slapped at it. It dropped and sped across the floor. Britt shuddered yet marveled: *How could something shaped like that run so fast!*

Britt welcomed in the new year on a happier note than

that experienced at Christmas. Jan, Krista, and she were invited by Carmela to a New Year's Day lunch at her home in Jamestown. Jamestown was on an island, so they had the fun of taking the ferry to the island where Carmela would be waiting to take them to her home. During the ride over, they happened to sit by an elderly couple who delighted in telling them about Jamestown.

They found out that ferries had been going between Conanicut Island and Newport since 1675, and that in 1678 Conanicut Island was incorporated as the town of Jamestown, named after James, duke of York who would become King James II in 1685. At the time of incorporation, only one hundred and fifty people lived on the Island. Britt was astonished. Almost four hundred years ago. She knew of nothing in Minnesota that was that old. Minnesota had become a state less than one hundred years ago. Her love of history prompted her to ask for more. "What else do you know about Jamestown?"

The two Jamestown "historians" beamed. "Well, let's see ... in 1775, two hundred British and Hessian troops—Germans hired by England were called Hessians—landed on the Island. They burned the ferry house, destroyed buildings and homes. Many people here had to flee to the mainland. A year later, also in December, a British fleet came and occupied Newport. They stayed for almost three years. They destroyed the Quaker Meetinghouse and the Jamestown Windmill."

"Oh, no," said Jan. "I love a windmill, but why did they need one on the island? There's water all around."

"The windmill was important as it provided the wind power to grind corn. You're right about there being a lot of water, but no source of running water to turn a waterwheel, and then," continued the elderly woman, "as the British left Narragansett Bay in October 1779, they destroyed the places they'd occupied and burned down the Beavertail Lighthouse.

The lighthouse was back in operation by 1784. About the windmill, Jan, you'll be happy to know that it *and* the Quaker Meetinghouse were rebuilt by 1787."

"Time to go ashore. We've hit Jamestown. I see Carmela waving. She's waiting for us," said Britt as she, Jan, and Krista thanked the couple for the interesting history lesson and rushed off to hug Carmela.

Lunch with Carmela and her parents, Anna and Tony Nicoletti, was like no New Year's lunch Britt had ever eaten before. They wanted to give these "landlubbers" a traditional Italian New Year's Day meal. The entrée was *cotechino*, best described as a pork sausage dish, with basil pasta and a salad. The simple meal had in mind the efforts of three pregnant young women to keep their weight down. Though champagne is a tradition on New Year's Eve, enough was left to toast the new year, a year that would be making mothers of three of the young women seated at the table.

They were quiet on the ferry going back to Newport. It *would* be quite a year for them. They sat and thought about how their lives would change when they became mothers. Would they be good mothers? They hoped for easy labors and easy babies.

Not long after that, Britt wanted to do something nice for Carmela for making New Year's Day a wonderful day instead of a very lonely day. She invited Carmela over for spaghetti. Carmela accepted and came over after work. They had fun talking about work and what the future might bring. As Carmela got ready to leave and catch the ferry for Jamestown, Britt asked, "Did you like the spaghetti? I made it because I thought that's what you'd like."

"Britt, don't ever make spaghetti for an Italian again." And Carmela was gone.

Britt was dumbfounded. *I don't think she liked the spaghetti at all. What did I do wrong? Did Carmela just insult me? I wonder what I'd think if she made lefse for me. She wouldn't be able to make it right—her hands would be covered with sticky potato and flour goo. It'd be a mess. It would probably go over with me the way my spaghetti with the store-bought sauce went over with her. My spaghetti tasted kind of starchy too. It's okay. We had a good time, and she gave me good advice.* Britt cleaned up the kitchen and got ready for bed.

Jan's husband came home at the end of April. One night when Britt was over there watching television with Jan and her husband, Bill, he looked at her and said, "You are a beautiful girl." It was perhaps a compliment, but Britt didn't like it. She was a married woman, and a pregnant one to boot, and Jan was one of her best friends. *Time for me to go home.*

"Thank you, I think, but I also think I better go home now. I'm pretty tired." She got up and went out their door and across the hall to her door. *My key! Where is my key? Oh, no, I've locked myself out.* She didn't want to go back, but she had to ask for help, though what they'd do, she didn't know.

"I can get it," this from Jan's husband. He hoisted himself, all six foot two of him, off the couch and went out in the hall and tried the door—no luck. He went back into the apartment, found a screwdriver, and took her door off the hinges. "There you are. Go in now, and I'll put your door back." And he did.

It was 1959, and the Hughes family was living in Minneapolis, Minnesota. Britt sat at the kitchen table drinking a cup of coffee and reading the *Minneapolis Tribune*. A caption on an inside page caught her eye: "Midwest man murders woman during baseball game." She read on, and the man named had the same name as Jan's husband. The murder occurred under the bleachers. According to the newspaper, the man had been dishonorably discharged from the US Navy.

CHAPTER

The phone rang; Britt almost tripped over her own feet in her hurry to answer it. It might be Andy!

Her hand trembled, and so did her voice as she answered the phone. "Hello."

"Britt, Britt, it's me, Andy. We just docked. I'll be home as soon as I can. How are you?"

"I'm—*we're* fine, Andy. I can't wait to see you."

Waiting was hard. She had to keep going to the bathroom. *What if they won't let him off the ship? They just had to.* She lit the gas burner under the hot water heater for a bath—she wanted to smell nice and look nice when he came in the door. She'd put on the striped, seersucker robe she'd made. She liked the style—long sleeves with ruffles at the cuffs and enough fullness in its front to almost completely hide her expanding belly. What would he think of her stomach? It looked like a big blister! The water was hot enough, and she couldn't wait any longer. She turned off the burner under the hot-water tank and ran water into the tub.

Ah, that feels so good, but I don't have time for a soak.

She grabbed a washcloth from the little stand near the tub, washed her face and rinsed it, and then scooted down a bit and turned over—she felt like a seal—to get wet. She soaped her body and rinsed by doing the "seal" duck-and-turn maneuver again. *Good enough!* Exiting the tub, hanging on to the edge until her feet were securely grounded, she toweled off and went to dress and "pretty up."

As she was trying to put on lipstick with shaking fingers, she heard knocking on the door and a voice: "Britt, Britt honey, open up! I don't have a key. I've never seen this place, remember?"

Andy! Throwing the lipstick tube down, Britt ran to open the door. There he stood, Andy, handsome as ever. They reached for each other, hugging and kissing; it'd been so long! The closeness wasn't the same. Something had come between them. Britt's belly, of course, kept their bodies a little further apart, but that wasn't all; Andy's belly was almost as prominent as Britt's! She pushed him away and looked at his midsection, "Wow! You must be a really good cook and baker."

"I know, I know. I've never been so heavy. When I first got on the ship, I was seasick—all I did was throw up and sleep. I wanted to die! I was so happy to feel hungry again that I guess I overdid it. It was those brownies—I make really good brownies, and when I missed you so much I could hardly bear it, I ate brownies! Now that we're together again, I won't be doing that."

Britt laughed. "Oh, Andy, I'm glad you missed me. I missed you too—so very much. We'll slim down together, me quite suddenly, but it might take you a little longer. Come in now." She shut the door and reached for him, hugged him as tight as possible, put her head on his shoulder, and cried. The long wait was over.

Not having to eat alone anymore was heaven; even

cooking was a pleasure. She had eaten good things when she was alone—fruits and vegetables, oatmeal—but she didn't bother to make what she'd been brought up to believe was a full meal; she mostly snacked. Maybe that was why she never gained more than the two pounds a month that the doctor insisted upon. Each month, after the weigh-in, she rewarded herself by buying a bag of burnt peanuts. She knew she should have bought something healthier, like green grapes, for example; they were only nineteen cents a pound, but she loved the sound and feel of the crunch when her teeth smashed the peanuts.

Going to St. Mary's church every Sunday, the church where John F. Kennedy and Jacqueline Bouvier were married in 1953, would be easier, pleasanter, with Andy by her side. Those questioning looks she'd encountered when she'd gone there alone, Sunday after Sunday, with her waistline expanding, would now be squelched. But by far, best of all, she now did not have to sleep alone every night; her partner, her love, was there, seven nights out of fourteen, to have and to hold. (Andy, being a cook, worked a rotation of two days one week and five the next. The days he worked, he had to remain on the ship overnight.)

Andy liked the place and what she'd done to make it homey. He was proud of her, so proud that he wanted to show off. He invited a shipmate over to dinner—their first guest as a married couple. The guest was Peter Lundstrom from Wisconsin. It was a delight for Britt to hear his Midwestern accent, though it did make her a bit homesick.

For dinner, Britt made scalloped potatoes and ham. She also made a green salad and finished off the meal with a serving of spumoni, an Italian ice cream consisting of three flavors—chocolate, pistachio, and cherry—plus fruit. Mr. Veroni of the delicatessen downstairs had introduced her to it, and it was delicious. The entire meal was delicious, as was the conversation. Britt knew that Peter was more than a little envious of Andy's situation because of the way he dragged his feet when it was time to go.

Peter pushed his chair back. "I should be getting back to the ship."

"It was so nice to have you as our guest—you're our first, Peter," said Britt as she rose from the table.

"Eating home-cooking, and you can really cook, Britt, nothing is better than that."

Andy was on his feet, moving toward the front door. "Don't compliment her too much; it'll go to her head."

"Peter, don't listen to him. Thanks for the compliment, and you'll have to come back after the baby's born so you can meet our little one."

Peter stood up, moved to the door, and said, "I'll look forward to it."

At the end of March, Britt quit her job. She wanted to spend more time with Andy, and she had to get things ready for the baby that was due on—who would believe it?— Mother's Day! She already had a layette. The Enlisted Men's Wives Club always gave a layette to the pregnant wife of an enlisted man. It was a small layette, and Britt knew that she'd have to add to it—diapers, for sure; receiving blankets (her mother said you could never have too many); baby lotion and some baby bottles. Britt planned to nurse, but she'd still need small bottles for water and juice. Then there was the question of the bed. Where would the baby sleep?

Walking by a pawn shop one afternoon, Britt and Andy saw a bassinet in the window. Their bedroom was small, but a bassinet would be able to fit in. They went in and came out with not only the bassinet but also a TV with a round twelve-inch screen. They carried home their precious purchases and tried them out.

The bassinet fit perfectly against the wall, and Britt decided she'd paint it white—a safe choice as they didn't know if the baby would be a girl or a boy. The TV was not as satisfying. The antenna, called "rabbit ears," was a tricky proposition. The two arms had to be positioned just right or the picture, which was none too clear in the first place, would start to roll. A person could get dizzy just looking at it rolling up or rolling down. The only way to stop it was to fiddle with the rabbit ears or give up and turn it off. Britt hoped that the baby wouldn't be as temperamental as this TV. However, on nights when *I Love Lucy* came in almost clearly, she was glad they'd bought the TV.

Bassinet painted white, Britt felt ready. Now it was up to Mother Nature.

Her back ached, but every time she'd had her period, her back had ached, so that was nothing new. She was down on her hands and knees, scrubbing the slightly cracked red and white kitchen linoleum when the ache had started. Then it turned into something a little different; the ache in her back came forward and clenched her abdomen, making it harden—a cramping spasm that soon loosed its hold. *Maybe I'm having those false labor pains—Braxton Hicks, I think they're called. I'd feel like a fool if I went in too early and then had to come home again.* She scrubbed on. Another ache, a clenching fist, radiated from her back to her abdomen and held on. Britt felt powerless against this onslaught; it would do what it would do, but she was not ready to give in yet. If she was in labor and soon hospital bound, she wanted to come home to a clean floor. Her mother washed the floor every single day. She couldn't stand a dirty floor, and Britt felt the same way.

How did her mother feel about labor pains? Britt had asked her that once, and her mother said God would not give anyone more pain than she could stand, and once a mother held her baby in her arms, she forgot about the pain. Britt believed this—her mother didn't lie—but she hated feeling so helpless. Her dad's favorite quote was from "Invictus" and he'd stand straight and proud while saying: "I am the master of my fate; I am the captain of my soul." No woman who had ever given birth could have written that poem.

Floor nice and clean, Britt went and got her bag—actually the suitcase her parents gave her when she graduated from high school—for the hospital and checked to be sure everything that she'd need was in there: pajamas that opened down the front for nursing; lotion, lipstick, and a comb; toothbrush and toothpaste; and for the baby, diapers, of course; an undershirt and a bellyband for the naval; a flannel receiving blanket; a little sweater and cap in white with pale green trim; pale green booties; and a warm, pale-green blanket trimmed with white satin. As to her clothing, she packed a couple of pairs of underwear and also a couple of sanitary napkins. She didn't pack a coming-home outfit. She'd wear home what she wore to the hospital because her friend, Jan, who'd had her baby two weeks ago—an eight-pound little girl she named Karen—told her that she'd still look about six weeks pregnant after the baby was delivered. "It takes time," said Jan, "to get back in shape." Oh! She mustn't forget to ask Andy how she could get ahold of him if he were on the ship. What if he couldn't take her to the hospital? What would she do? *Call a cab, I guess* ... She could feel another pain coming; this one was harder. Maybe she'd better start timing them.

As that thought crossed her mind, she heard the key turn in the lock. "Andy! I'm so glad you're home. I've been having some pains. They're about five minutes apart now. Do you think this is the real thing? If it is, we should go."

"Go where? What? You mean ..."

"Yes, the baby's coming. Maybe I really will be a mother on Mother's Day." Britt watched as Andy dashed about "like a chicken with its head cut off," her mother would say.

"Where are my keys? I just had them."

"On top of the dresser, like always. Grab my suitcase, will you, Andy?"

"Your suitcase! Are you leaving me?"

"Yes! But just to go to the hospital and have our baby. Let's go now!"

A nurse in a starched white uniform checked them in, got their information, and ordered a wheelchair for Britt. Then she sent Andy away saying, "You can't do anything here. Go home or go back to the ship." When Andy protested, she added, "You belong to the US Navy. If they had wanted you to have a wife, they would have issued you one. We'll call you when the baby gets here." She said all this without a trace of a smile.

Andy, not one to like being alone, went back to the ship.

The nurse wheeled Britt to a room with a white-sheeted gurney and helped her get on it. Enema time. *What! I'm in pain, and she's going to give me an enema? That's sick. I can't stand the pressure ...* The nurse helped her onto the toilet, and the enema did its job. She could rest now. But no, the nurse had another awful idea. "Into the shower. Wash yourself and then I'll get you into bed." *Yes, a bed. Get me a bed and leave me alone.*

But the fist of God would not let her alone; it just took over her body and squeezed it, hard, again and again. Her mother had said that God would not give anyone anything she could not stand. How did her mother know that? Her mother didn't even know her. A nurse entered and poked her gloved finger up her. *What is the matter with these people? Those are private parts!* Britt heard someone say something about "dilation," whatever that was. "Leave me alone!"

"No way, little girl," and two orderlies slid her onto a gurney and rolled her into a room with the brightest lights in the world. Masked, white-coated figures stood around, gloved hands raised. Was this the *Twilight Zone*? Before her mind could sort it out, she was rolled onto her side, and she felt the pain of a needle entering her lower back: the *Twilight Zone* receded into nothingness.

Britt woke sometime later. She was in a large room with six occupied beds; hers was one of them. A nurse came in, smiling (they could actually smile!) and handed her a pink bundle. "Here's your little girl!"

Britt held the bundle, hardly daring to breath. She pushed the blanket off the top of her head and gasped, "What's wrong with her head? It looks like a banana, and she has red marks on her cheeks!" *How could Andy and I have a baby with a head like this? Andy and I have nice-shaped heads.*

"It's because of the forceps. You have a narrow birth canal, and then there was that car accident when you broke your pelvis—it's on your chart. The doctor thought a forceps delivery would be best. Give her a couple of days, and she'll have a beautiful head. You just wait and see."

Well, I guess we won't be calling her "Tony." Britt undressed her little daughter to get a good look at all of her. She had all her parts, and if what the nurse said was true, she'd be perfect. Britt looked up as the nurse came in again, smiled, and took the baby away. "She'll be back in the morning to nurse, but you try and get some sleep now." Britt, exhausted, fell asleep almost immediately.

The nurse, true to her word, came in with the precious pink bundle at five in the morning and woke Britt up. Though groggy with sleep, Britt remembered what she wanted to ask. "What does she weigh and what time was she born?"

"Your baby was born at 1:13 a.m. and weighed in at six pounds, five ounces. You became a mother on Mother's Day. Your husband should never forget that date." The nurse handed Britt her baby, helped her sit up, unbuttoned her pajama top, and then showed her how to put the baby to her breast.

"Ow! It really hurts to sit. Is it always like that?"

"You had an episiotomy, which is common with a forceps delivery. The doctor made an incision between the vagina and anus—not a very deep one. While you're here, you'll have a Sitz bath every day, a bath in a tub with shallow, lukewarm water, just enough to cover your legs. You can do that at home too. Add some baking soda to the bath for added relief."

"How long will it take the incision to heal?"

"You do have stitches, so you don't want to lift anything heavy and take a chance on breaking them; that would set you back. Swelling will cause the stitches to pull. When you get home, continue with the ice packs that we're giving you now; it will ease the pain. A package of frozen peas makes a good ice pack. We'll give you cleaning materials to use after every urination and bowel movement now, and we'll send some home with you too. By the way, you should probably buy some stool softener."

"I was born at home with the help of a midwife, and I weighed just about the same as this baby," and Britt caressed her baby's downy head, "and my mother never mentioned anything about stitches."

"Maybe not, but we know *you* have stitches, and they need to heal. Keep clean, use ice packs, and no intercourse before your six-week checkup with the doctor and he tells you that you are healed."

"You mean I'll feel like this for *six weeks*!"

"No. You should feel better in two or three weeks if you take care of yourself. Some women find that a doughnut-shaped pillow makes sitting much more comfortable."

"One more question: as my baby's been nursing, my lower abdomen has felt funny; it's like a pulling together—a squeezing. Is something wrong?"

"Oh no, that's a good thing. Your baby's nursing is helping your insides get back in shape again." The nurse turned, looked back at Britt. "You two finish up here. I'll be back for the little one in twenty minutes."

Britt looked down at the nursing baby, but she wasn't nursing anymore; she was sound asleep yet making the cutest sucking motion with her lips. *What a darling! And her head is already getting more in shape.* Another thought struck her: *She's mine—my responsibility for the next eighteen years!* The reality of that thought literally took her breath away. *What have I gotten myself into?* Then the baby stretched and made little fussing noises, and Britt felt soft and mushy inside.

Another nurse came in, this one bearing a vase holding a large bouquet of white carnations. She put the flowers on Britt's night table. "Someone thinks a lot of you."

"My husband, Andy. They must have called him about the baby." Smiling, the nurse left, and who should walk in then but Andy.

"Andy! Come and look at the baby." But Andy was frozen in place, taking in the sight of his wife nursing his baby. He tiptoed over to the bed, white sailor hat in hand. He bent a knee as if to genuflect but stopped himself.

He kissed the top of Britt's head. "Britt, how are you? Was it very bad?"

"I'm okay. Mother was right, you do start to forget as soon

as you hold your little one, and the doctor gave me something called an epidural just when it was getting bad. It completely knocked me out for the hardest part."

Andy looked at the baby. "What's wrong with her head?" Britt told him what the nurse had said about a forceps delivery and that the head would get back to normal very soon. "In fact," she added, "it looks more rounded down already. Our problem now is to name this baby; calling her 'baby' takes away all her specialness. What about Josette after your mother? Or Esther after my grandma? Then there's Sara. I've always liked that name."

"Sara, let's call her Sara. A little name for our little number one."

"Sara does fit her, and it's biblical and modern at the same time." Britt looked down. "Sara, welcome to the world." At the sound of her name, Sara didn't even blink her tightly closed eyes. The nurse came in and carried her back to the nursery.

Andy and Britt were alone, not counting the five new mothers in the other five beds. "Andy, you are wonderful. Thank you so much for the flowers; I love carnations. They don't smell like funerals the way roses do, and they last longer. Thank you for remembering it's Mother's Day, and I'm a mother."

Andy looked at the flowers. He hadn't even noticed them. "I didn't send flowers, Britt—I wish I would have." He saw the tip of a little white envelope sticking out among the blooms, and he pulled it out and read the card out loud: "Congratulations!" And it was signed, "Peter Lundstrom."

"Britt, these are from Peter—he's the guy who came to dinner at our house. He was our first guest. I wish I hadn't told him that you'd gone into labor. I blabbed it around when I went back to the ship. I was so nervous."

"That's all right, Andy. Look on the bright side. You won't forget to send me flowers when we have our next baby."

CHAPTER

10

With slow and careful steps, Britt climbed the stairs to their second-floor apartment, Sara clasped in her arms. Andy, hanging on to Britt's suitcase in one hand, the diaper bag in the other, and a doughnut pillow circling his right forearm, followed close behind. If anyone should falter or, God forbid, fall, she knew he'd just drop what he was holding and come to the rescue. *I'm glad I gave the bouquet of white carnations to the woman in the bed close to mine—one less thing for him to hang onto.*

They made it—safe on the second floor. Andy put down his burdens, unlocked the door, and swung it wide open. He bent and scooped up his little family and carried them over the threshold. Home at last.

Sara proved to be a fussy baby—did she have colic? Britt was a nervous new mother, unsure of herself. Could Sara sense this? Drink in Britt's emotions as she nursed? Or did fate demand a payback time for the grief she gave her own mother by not being an easy baby? The old "what goes around comes around" thing. Britt persevered and gained confidence. She only fell asleep during one 2:00 a.m. feeding, and she tried hard not to resent the loss of sleep when she had to nurse Sara again at 5:00 a.m.

The first baby bath was traumatic for the young parents. Britt placed the bathing basin with its three inches of warm water on the kitchen table. Andy sat on a chair at the head of the table. With all supplies at hand, Britt undressed Sara and eased her into the tub. She happened to notice Andy's hands—they were clutching and reclutching each other. *He's wringing his hands. I never saw anyone actually do that before. Maybe I'd be doing it too if I didn't have to keep a tight hold on this slippery fish.* Sara was the calm one. After the bath, Britt wrapped Sara in a bath towel and looked at Andy, and he looked at her. Sweat beaded their faces—they were exhausted. Britt fed Sara, and she slept an hour more than usual.

Britt was learning to know Sara, to know that it was okay to let her cry and fuss for a little while, that that was what she needed before she could fall asleep. By three weeks, mother and baby were pretty much in sync. Britt found that she, herself, in order to be a good mother and wife, had to squeeze in a nap each day. When to take the nap was the question, as Sara sometimes slept only a little over an hour, and other times three hours. She learned to lie down at the very beginning of a "Sara" nap. If Sara slept for more than an hour, Britt considered that her bonus time, and she made good use of it. She had applied for a library card shortly after she'd moved into the Spring Street apartment, and now, if Sara took a long nap, she was even able to get some reading done.

By three weeks, Britt packed away her doughnut pillow, and she managed to keep to a pretty good schedule that included sleep and enjoying her baby. This changed as quickly and as dramatically as a loud clap of thunder when Andy said, "My mother and sister are coming out together for a visit. Mom will stay two weeks, and Mary six—it's her summer vacation from teaching second grade."

Britt could have killed him on the spot. "How could you? Sara doesn't even sleep through the night yet! You should have asked me first."

"Why? This is my home, the home that *you* found and moved into without even asking me. To tell the truth, I never thought I'd have to ask you for permission."

"That was different. I was forced to move—we couldn't stay there if we had a baby."

"I would have been home before Sara was born. I could have helped you move."

This sounds like payback time. "I had help—my friends helped."

"Okay, fine. I guess you didn't need me." Andy folded his arms across his chest and lowered his black eyebrows. "This is *our* home now. I can invite people over here if I want to."

"But you'll be on the ship at least half the time. I'll be stuck with your people."

"Stuck with 'my people'? They're my *mother* and *sister* for God's sake!" He lifted his arms, and his palms pressed hard on each side of his head.

"But they are strangers to me, they really are." Britt grabbed a hank of her hair and began twisting it. "Your mother is so quiet—like a closed book. I never quite know what she's thinking." Just then Sara woke up and began to cry. Britt picked her up and hugged her. *If I didn't have you, I'd run away and never come back. I'd get a divorce.* "Your sister doesn't like me. At least I get that feeling. When we were in high school together and we both happened to be in the girls' lavatory at the same time, she'd stare at me. I always imagined that she was thinking, *That's the girl that's trying to snap up my brother.*"

"That's crazy. They can help you with Sara."

"I don't *want* help with Sara. I want to take care of my child all by myself. They'll just interfere and make more work. I'll have to talk to them, feed them, and entertain them. When you're on the ship, I'll be dealing with strangers."

"They're not strangers!" Andy turned and stomped out, away from Britt.

While his mother and sister were staying with them, Andy bought wine, steak, mushrooms—things they didn't usually buy because they were too expensive. Britt felt some resentment at this, but she knew he only wanted to show them that he'd "made it." He did help with food preparation when he didn't have to be on the ship, and Britt was thankful for that. She was not a confident cook. Timing everything to be done at the same time when everything seemed to have a different preparation time and cook time was tricky. Sometimes it worked out, but more often it did not.

Sara wasn't cooperating. She was crying more and sleeping less. Could she feel Britt's anxiety? Josette, Andy's mother, never missed a chance to say, "You don't have enough milk. She's hungry; that's why she's crying."

One morning Britt woke with a hard, painful left breast, and she felt feverish. She let Sara nurse in spite of the pain, thinking that, as with a cow, she hadn't been milked enough, and that was the cause of her pain. The next day, however, she went to the Navy Hospital and saw a doctor. She had mastitis, a breast infection, and was given medication and told to take an aspirin for the pain. He asked her if she'd been under stress and if she was getting enough sleep. *Are you kidding? I'm a new mother, first time, and we have relatives staying with us. Of course I'm stressed and tired.* He told her to make an appointment for her six-week checkup and to try to put on some weight.

Britt had never felt so low. *I'm a failure. I tried to do everything right—nurse my baby so she'd get the best start in life, and now I can't nurse her because I don't want her ingesting my medication every time she nurses. I give up. I'll do what Josette wants me to. Put her on formula. Josette never nursed her babies; they always got formula. Does she think nursing is too animallike? Or does the sight of someone nursing make her jealous?* Britt headed for the library and took out a book that had a chapter on how to prepare baby formula. She sat down at a table and took notes. The librarian, an older woman, checked out her book, and when she noticed what it was about, she gave Britt further advice. She told her that she'd had three children—had nursed the first two, but her milk dried up when her father died, almost right after her last one was born. She had to turn to formula. "Be sure to put all your equipment into boiling water for ten minutes. Don't forget that the baby will need extra vitamins when you use formula." Britt thanked her, left the library, and drove to a drugstore.

She bought bottles, nipples, a bottle brush, and a canner—blue with white specks, in which to sterilize the glass bottles and other equipment used. Next stop was the grocery store. Here she bought cans of evaporated milk, a bottle of clear, light Karo syrup, pabulum, and baby vitamins. The librarian had told her that vitamins were a necessity now that Sara would not be getting all she needed from her mother's milk. Britt looked at all she'd bought. This would be a lot more complicated and time-consuming than nursing, and it wouldn't be as good for Sara. *But if I truly don't have enough milk? Maybe my mother didn't have enough either and that's why I cried so much, and maybe why I bit her once, and she bit me back—at least that's what she told me years later.*

Before Josette left for home, Sara was baptized with Mary as her sponsor. *All her life, Sara can tell people that she was baptized in the same church in which President John F. Kennedy was married. Look how good she is in spite of having to wear a white, scratchy lace gown—the same gown that Hannah and I wore. Perhaps putting her on the bottle was best after all. She's calmer.* Mary, Sara's sponsor, held her over the baptismal font as the priest poured water on her head and said, "I baptize you, Sara Joan Hughes, in the name of the Father, and of the Son, and of the Holy Spirit." Sara did not utter a peep.

Grandma Hughes, Josette, went back to the Midwest shortly after the baptism, and Sara, Mary, and Britt hung out together. One night, Britt invited her old friends from work over to the apartment for waffles. She made her mother's favorite recipe, "Elegant Waffles." The recipe called for the eggs to be separated and the whites beaten until they were stiff, and then they were folded into the batter. This made for a tender, fluffy waffle, truly elegant. She topped the waffles with strawberries and whipped cream. Everyone had a good time, including Mary, and they all loved the waffles, especially Carmela.

It was hard to get around much with a baby, but they took turns exploring the shops and boutiques on Bellevue and the galleries on Spring Street. Wherever they went, people would smile at Sara. She was a beautiful, smiley little girl, with curly hair and brown eyes. Inevitably someone would turn to Mary and say, "You have a beautiful daughter," or "You're the mother, aren't you?" It was those brown eyes. Mary had brown eyes too, while Britt's were green, like her mother's. When this happened, Britt would feel a stab of jealousy—or was it simply irritation at someone's mistake?—and say, "*I'm* her mother."

Six weeks flew by—time for Britt's post-childbirth checkup. Mary was still there, so Britt left her with Sara and went alone. The doctor said all was in order and she and her husband could now have "relations." He also said, "Don't get pregnant right away. If you want another baby, wait at least a year and gain some weight while waiting. Get your strength back."

On the way home, Britt stopped at an office supply store and bought some graph paper. She stopped at the drugstore where she bought a thermometer. She wanted to start on her rhythm method charting right away. Her book, *Catholic Marriage and Family Life*, said that she'd have to take her temperature the first thing every morning—not even Sara could come first. This would be difficult because Sara was an early riser—six o'clock. Britt would have to set her alarm for a quarter to six and take her temperature then. That's why she wanted to start right away, while Mary was still there, so that if Sara woke up even earlier than usual, Mary could pick her up.

When Britt got home, she put her purchases on the kitchen table along with her book, *Catholic Marriage and Family Life*. "Mary, come into the kitchen for a few minutes."

"Hey, I see you bought some things." She sat down and picked up the book.

"One day, Mary, when you are a wife, you'll probably need these things." Britt picked up the thermometer. "Andy and I want to space our babies' births, so we're going to use the rhythm method, as explained in that book you're holding. During the times I'm not menstruating, I have to take my temperature every morning before doing *anything* else. This is a rectal thermometer—it's more accurate than a mouth one—that's why I chose it."

"Disgusting. What's the graph paper for?"

"I'll write in all the dates in a month across the top and then all the normal temperature variations, putting 97.2 at the bottom and then increasing by .2 going up the side until I get to 99.6—a separate sheet for each month. Each day's temperature will be a dot on my graph, and then by connecting the dots, I'll be able to see clearly when my temperature dropped. The drop would mean that in a day or two I'll have my period, and it also means that I have a day or two of infertility. When I'm over my period, the next four or five days should also be an infertile time." *I used to call my period "the curse." I never will again. It's a blessing.*

Mary grimaced like Andy did when he changed a loaded diaper, "Disgusting *and* complicated. There's got to be other ways to control pregnancy and space births."

"For a Roman Catholic woman who is determined to follow the rules of the church, there is only one other way, and that is to have sex *only* when you want to have a baby. Mother Nature, however, provides an additional way that is supposed to be 98 percent effective: after a baby is born, provide *all* of the baby's nourishment at the breast—absolutely no supplemental feedings of water or formula, day or night, and little or no pacifier use until your baby is six months old. After the baby is six months old, you could become pregnant again even if you are still breastfeeding, and your chances of getting pregnant increase as the months go by and your baby starts eating solid food and nurses less."

"Those are terrible choices. I guess I'll stay single and become a career teacher. Good luck to you and Andy. You'll need it."

One of the last things Mary did before returning home was to sign her teaching contract for the upcoming school year. Britt glanced over as she signed. *She'll make $3,700. For that amount of money, I think I could get over my shyness and learn to talk to a room full of students—little students. When Sara starts school, perhaps I will go back and earn my teaching degree.*

Alone at last. The little Andy Hughes family—no company in the apartment and a baby that slept through the night—was content. It wouldn't be that way for long, because in a month Andy would be on the ship and on his way to the Norfolk Naval Shipyard in Portsmouth, Virginia, where the ship would take part in training operations for two weeks. Now they would just love each other and forget about the rocky time they'd been through.

That night as they said their prayers together and kissed good night, they reached out and held each other. Britt lifted her left leg and wrapped it around Andy, drawing his lower body into the embrace, but it could go no further. The line on the graph had not dropped, and they were both determined to follow the church-sanctioned rhythm method. One thing the hug *did* do was tell the other, in body language, that the bad feelings were gone, all was forgiven. *I was angry at Andy and briefly considered leaving him, but that was foolish—we have a baby to take care of. I can't do it alone, and I don't want to—I love Andy. Anyway, that's water under the bridge now.*

Britt took her temperature first thing in the morning every day that Andy was away, charting it every day too. The day before Andy was due to arrive back in Newport from Norfolk, the "connect the dots" line took a dive. She would be getting her period in a couple of days. *We can have "relations"—what a strange way to put it. Andy, you are one lucky guy.* She picked up his picture from the top of the dresser and kissed his smiling face.

CHAPTER

11

"The blessing" did not come when expected. Maybe it was just late—Britt's cycle had been out of commission for a while. A month went by, and then another, still no period. And Britt hated the smell of coffee. How could she be pregnant? Her temperature had dropped. She had to find out for sure. If she were pregnant, at least she could quit taking her temperature every morning—get a little more sleep. She went to the doctor the third week in October.

Every time a different doctor, but this one didn't tell her to gain weight; he just put her in the stirrups and felt around. "Yes, I do feel something. I'd say you're at least two months pregnant, maybe a bit more. I put your due date around the middle of May."

"Oh no, Sara will only be a year old. She might not even be walking. My mother said I didn't start walking until I was fifteen months old. I might actually have to tote around both children. Neither child will get enough care or attention. It's not fair. It's not right."

The doctor helped her down from the examination

table. "There is protection available, something you or your husband could consider, you know."

"Not for us there isn't. He wouldn't use anything. His aunt is a nun. The only thing we can do is use the rhythm method. I was using that, taking my temperature every morning, but I must have goofed up."

"Don't blame yourself. That method has a success rate of 60 to 85 percent. In your case, it'd be even lower because your husband is in the navy where schedules can be erratic. And I'm sure your sleeping hours aren't always regular with a three-month-old to care for. That can cause your temperature to fluctuate."

Britt was thankful for the doctor's honesty and concern, but she was disappointed—she'd tried so hard. It wasn't fair.

Andy's reaction to the news? Zilch—he just seemed to accept the inevitable, but then he didn't have to get up for night feedings, change poopy diapers, or sit up with a sick child.

Britt, wanting to get some show of emotion out of Andy, said, "Don't forget to send me flowers after this one is born— you don't want Peter Lundstrom showing you up again with another bouquet of white carnations."

"That won't happen. He's out of the picture. He was transferred to a bigger ship, a destroyer tender, a couple of months ago. I'll probably never see him again."

Christmas that year was a family affair—much different from the last one when she'd been alone. Andy bought a little tree, and Britt trimmed it with cranberry and popcorn ropes. They didn't want to buy decorations because they'd be moving again. Rumors were flying about a six-month cruise coming up. If true, Christmas decorations would be just another box to lug around. Britt broke down though and bought an angel for the top of the tree and a package of tinsel. Their first pictures to share were taken in front of this tree. They took turns holding Sara, who was so cute now with her curly light brown hair and dark brown eyes, while the other would snap a picture. Britt wished that they could have taken a real family picture by having a friend take Andy, Sara, and her all together, but both Jan and Krista were gone—such was military life.

Not long after Christmas, they got the news. Andy's ship was going into dry dock for repairs at the Chelsea Navy Yard. They'd be relocating to Chelsea, Massachusetts, across the Mystic River from the city of Boston. They would try to find an apartment in Chelsea that was close to the Naval Hospital. Britt would need prenatal care.

An apartment was hard to find. People hesitated to rent to enlisted men and their families—a repeat of the Newport experience. You took what you could get and made the best of it. The apartment had only two rooms, a kitchen and a large bedroom with a sink in it and a bath off to the side. The place stank of urine and old furniture—smells impossible to get rid of completely. The first thing Britt did when they moved in was scrape dried egg yolks off the inside walls of the refrigerator. The second thing was to scrub down the bathtub and the two sinks—the bathroom sink was responsible for the strong urine smell.

The kitchen had a sink, a stove, a Formica table and a couple of chairs, some counter and cabinet space—standard equipment. In addition, it had a tall, glass-fronted china closet. Sara would crawl by it and put her hands on the glass, leaving fingerprints. This irritated her dad to such an extent that he slapped her little fingers each time.

"Andy, what are you doing? She's just a little girl. She doesn't understand why you're slapping her fingers. You're making a mountain out of a molehill."

Andy didn't see it that way. "She has to learn to obey when she's young or she won't when she's older."

"Do you want her to think of you as a mean daddy when you're gone? Don't you want her to miss you?" Britt was angry, but she didn't want to fight. In a couple of weeks, he'd ship out and be gone for six months.

When Britt told her parents that she was pregnant again, her mother sent her a medium-sized crib. The twins, William and Owen, were now four years old, and they slept in twin beds. They put the crib, now Sara's crib, in the bedroom along with their new portable twenty-one-inch, metal—silver and blue—television set, complete with a swivel stand. A large brown chest of drawers and the double bed came with the furnished apartment and completed the room's furnishings.

They sat on the bed to watch television. One of their favorite shows was the *Garry Moore Show*. If they got tired of sitting on the bed (it was hard on the back), they put a blanket down on the floor and sat on it, which was hard on *both* the back and the bottom, but it gave Sara room to play. Sometimes they even ate their evening meal sitting on the blanket—an indoor picnic.

Britt experienced her first migraine headache one indoor picnic night. She was close to five months pregnant, sitting on the floor, eating and watching television. Soon she couldn't stand the light from the screen, pain throbbed above her right eye, and her stomach churned. She lowered her body to the floor and groaned, pressing her hand to her throbbing right temple. *Mother had migraines. I can't remember her not having them. Did she first get them when she was pregnant with me? I never realized how she suffered until now. Sometimes I thought she was even faking it to get out of her least favorite thing—meal preparation. I wish I'd been kinder and more understanding. Well, at least Hannah and I learned to cook.* She gave herself up to the waves of pain, knowing that it was one more thing she'd have to accept.

When she was feeling better, she tried to make the apartment more livable, but she did not bother with hanging pictures or sewing anything. When the ship left dry dock, it would be going to sea for six months, taking Andy away. They would be visiting ports throughout the world—Andy would get to see so much. She and Sara would fly to Britt's parental home where Sara could get acquainted with her grandparents. Her father had said, "As long as you have no more than three children, you can come home." An airline ticket was purchased and dated two weeks before Britt's delivery date. Only one ticket needed, as Sara flew free—under two years old, she qualified as a lap baby. Britt would deliver the soon-to-be-born baby in her own hometown. That was the plan.

If only they could go outside! But there was no yard. Britt and Sara were housebound. She had no friends and didn't know where to go to make any. She read Sara's books to her and played with her, but Sara took two naps a day, and what could she do then? Often she'd just stare into space, sitting on the bed as she was doing now. What happened to the "marry a sailor and see the world"? Her world had shrunk to a couple of stinky rooms. She was trapped, and she had only herself to blame. She was the one who had wanted to quit school because she couldn't decide on a major. She had wanted adventure, wanted to see the world, but she hadn't wanted to do it alone. She took those wedding vows, not even sure that she was in love, and by doing so anchored herself to a sailor—thank goodness he would not always be in the navy. She'd imagined their life would be so different. Now she was caught in a trap—the tender trap of love. Britt loved Sara, and she knew she'd love this new little life. She loved

Andy too, though sometimes he made her angry. *Enough of this wool gathering—it doesn't do any good.*

Britt hauled herself to her feet, her arms reaching behind her, palms pressing the small of her back. She arched her back. "Umm that feels good." She was so sick of being pregnant, of sharing her body with a parasite that kept getting heavier and heavier. She wanted her body to belong to her again. Sara woke up from her nap and sat up, looking at her. Britt picked her up and blew raspberry sounds into her neck wrinkles until Sara laughed. "We'll get you changed and then some lunch. What would you like, smashed peas and chocolate pudding? How does that sound, young lady?" Sara clapped her hands. "Let's get those hands washed first."

Britt waited for Andy to come home for supper. Right now he was watching a baseball game at Fenway Park—Red Sox versus the Milwaukee Braves. She envied him. He could go places and see things.

Andy bounded into the apartment, a big grin on his face. "I really got my money's worth! Before the game, they had a homerun contest between Ted Williams and Eddie Matthews! It was the greatest."

"I'm sure it was." The dishes bounced and clanged as Britt, her lips clamped together in a straight line, set the table.

Britt bent over and grabbed the handhold projections on the side of the television and tried to hoist it off its stand. Warm liquid soaked her underpants and ran down her leg. No time to time contractions. This baby was coming three weeks early.

All day Andy and Britt had been packing. They had to decide what Britt would take on the plane with her and what they'd ship back to Minnesota. Then she tried to lift the TV, and her water broke.

Andy grabbed Sara, Britt grabbed her packed suitcase, and they got in the car. Tires squealed as they careened around corners. Britt was sure they'd set a speed record by the time they reached Chelsea Navy Hospital.

A nurse whisked her off, leaving Andy and Sara to provide information at the admissions desk.

First, the enema. By now Britt was having some serious labor pains, making the enema even more pressure painful than when she had Sara. Then the shower.

"Leave me alone," she said, but the nurse would not leave her alone. She was pushed into the shower. Britt was angry, and so were her bowels—they let go in the shower, splattering the walls of the shower stall. Brit was not one bit sorry.

Next stop, delivery room. Britt's doctor injected her with what she now knew was an epidural—blessed relief.

Six hours later, on April 14, a little boy, Daniel Andrew Hughes, was born, weighing in at five pounds, ten ounces—three weeks premature.

Euphoria took over Britt's being the next morning when she held her precious little baby. *We have a daughter and a son. My body belongs to me again.* Britt undid the blanket covering her skinny little baby. She wanted to check him out, wanted to see if all body parts were as they should be. *Perfect, except for some brown stuff on one foot. Feces. What's with those swabbies? Don't they know how to swab down a little baby? This is awful.*

The hospital suggested that Britt not nurse Daniel, as the nurses on the floor were all corpsmen, and a nursing mother embarrassed them. She complied but later regretted that decision. Also, Daniel had jaundice and needed to lie under a special light until they left the hospital.

Three days later, when Daniel no longer needed the special light, Britt signed them out, absolving the hospital of any responsibility. Andy took a peek at his newborn son through the nursery window, said goodbye to Britt, and then rushed to the airport to pick up his mother-in-law, Ingrid. After he dropped her off at the apartment, he rushed to the ship and sailed away.

1 2

Britt and her mother, Ingrid, had a lot to do before their flight to Minnesota on April 23—the date Britt had planned to fly home with Sara, but this time she'd be flying home with two lap children. She wouldn't have been able to do it without her mother's help.

No bed waited for little Daniel. Not yet one year old, Sara needed her crib. Daniel, they'd thought, would be born in Minnesota. Britt thanked the powers that be for the large, old, sturdy chest of drawers in the bedroom. The deep bottom drawer would do as a baby bed. She and her mother lifted it out and put it on the kitchen table. Britt fashioned a mattress, using a folded-up quilt, and laid her baby in the drawer. In ten minutes, Daniel was sound asleep.

Somehow Britt and Ingrid got everything done by the morning of the twenty-third, and that afternoon they found themselves high in the sky on their way to Minnesota— Daniel but nine days old. The stewardess, wearing a snappy uniform topped with a side cap, or garrison cap, and high heels, said he was the youngest passenger they'd ever had.

Flying agreed with Daniel. If he fussed a bit, all Britt had to do was put her little finger in his mouth, and he sucked away and dozed. During the flight, Grandma Ingrid kept Sara busy, playing peek-a-boo with her and making her laugh by reciting nursery rhymes.

Grandma had her hands full when Britt went to the bathroom. On the way back she peeked into the kitchen—all stainless steel. When it came to mealtime, they were offered a choice of grilled tenderloins with whipped potatoes or braised chicken with rice. They chose the chicken.

As they were eating, Britt looked around at the other passengers. All were dressed up—suits, dresses. She was happy that she and her mother had worn suits and stockings—they looked good. Sara and Daniel earned their wings—metal pilot pins, a gift of the airline. Britt would give them the pins to keep when they were older, explaining what they were and how they came to get them.

Time whizzed by that summer. Britt had two children to care for, and her mother had the four-year-old twins, William and Owen. Mother and daughter helped each other and got along better as two mothers than they ever had as mother and daughter.

They soon found out that Daniel had an egg allergy, painful enough to prevent sleep for him and for his mother. Until Britt realized what was upsetting him, she spent a few nights walking the floor with him, trying to ease his stomach pain. Her mother would come up and "spell" her so Britt could get some sleep. Ingrid also accompanied Britt when she took Daniel to Dr. Karsten for his checkup, shots, and circumcision. The navy hospital could not circumcise him after his birth because he was jaundiced.

On a later visit to Dr. Karsten, Ingrid turned to Britt with a suggestion that had long been on her mind. "Britt, you should talk to the doctor about birth control while we're here."

"I've been thinking about that too, but Catholics can't use any artificial means—if they do, it's a mortal sin, which means that if they die without repenting, their souls go to hell."

"That's ridiculous. You wouldn't be killing anything—just repent and be forgiven after each time if it worries you so much."

"That wouldn't work, because you have to repent and *promise* never to repeat the sin again."

"Britt, it's not a sin to do what's best for your family—to want to be a good and responsible mother."

"I know, but ..."

"Mrs. Anderson and Britt, Dr. Karsten is ready for you now." They followed the nurse into the doctor's office, Britt relieved that the conversation with her mother was over.

She looked at Dr. Karsten and tried to get the lump out of her throat. "Um, Dr. Karsten, I-I don't want to have any more children, at least for a while. I have my hands full with the two I've got, and my life isn't very regular—my husband belongs to the US Navy, so I've been told. I never know for sure when he'll be home. That really makes it hard to follow the rhythm method."

"You're Lutheran, aren't you—like your parents?"

"No. My husband is Catholic, and I joined his church. But it won't be good for any of us if I have a baby every year. I must space them further apart. Maybe the rhythm method would work if we were out of the navy, but for now ..."

"What does your husband think of birth control other than what is allowed by your religion?"

"He wants to space our children too. He also wants me to gain some weight—be stronger."

Ingrid, who'd been listening to the conversation, said, "Her father and I are worried about her. If Andy loves her, he should be worried too. She's lost sixteen pounds!"

"We can't have that. You have two children a year apart, right?"

"Eleven months apart."

"I can fit you with a diaphragm. When you and your husband want more children, just don't use it. It's as simple as that. But are you *sure* this is what you want to do, Britt?" He reached for a package, opened it, pulled out a diaphragm, and held it out for her to see.

"It's what I *have* to do, Dr. Karsten, but how exactly do I use that thing?"

"It's easy. Look, it's just a cup that fits over the opening of the cervix. I will measure you for it because an exact fit is important. I'll give you some spermicidal gel to use with it. You'll put some in the cup and around the rim before you use it."

"I should be able to handle that."

"Of course you can," said Ingrid. "You're a smart girl, Britt."

"Dr. Karsten, how long do I leave it in?"

"Put it in an hour before intercourse. You can leave it in for up to six hours. Be sure to clean it thoroughly after you remove it." He picked up a pamphlet from his desk. "Here, keep this—the pictures and text should answer all your questions.

"Hop up on the table, and I'll measure you. I'll order it and call you when it comes in."

I can't believe how light my body felt when I hopped onto that table, but the lightness of my mind was far greater. I felt like a weight had just rolled off my shoulders.

Britt linked arms with her mother as they left Dr. Karsten's office and walked to the car. She stopped. "Mother, what about Andy? I'll have to tell him."

"He loves you. He'll want what's best for you—for all of you, and that's a healthy, loving wife and mother, not a frazzled, too skinny nervous wreck."

"Mother!"

Britt helped her mother do the cooking and baking. She'll never forget the day that her mother lined up the freshly baked bread on the kitchen counter to cool, after buttering the tops to keep the crusts soft. The counter was also just the right height for changing a diaper, and it was convenient—no having to run upstairs to their room. On this day, she changed Daniel's wet diaper on the corner to the left of the bread. As soon as she took the diaper off, air must have activated something, for a stream of urine arched high in the air and came down onto the bread loaves. Britt gasped—what to do? Urine, she'd read, is sterile, and what could be more pure than her little baby's pee? And it really wasn't that much. *Nobody will get hurt or sick. Thank goodness for the butter on top—it won't sink in.* She diapered Daniel, picked him up, and went to the drawer beside the sink. She took out a sponge and ran hot water over it. She squeezed out the excess water and wiped off the top of each loaf. *This is a case of "silence is golden."* She kept the secret, and so did Daniel.

Ironing clothes is perhaps the least liked job of most housewives—if it were not, in Britt's opinion, it should be. A Minnesota summer with no air-conditioning is brutal. Minnesota is known for its frigid winters, but the state also has high-humidity, hundred-degree days in summer—miserable. Britt endured the misery every hot, humid Tuesday when she ironed at least fifteen collared shirts. Her father and two brothers did not wear T-shirts; they wore cotton shirts with collars. In her father's case, the shirts all had long sleeves too. She developed a system by which she could iron a collared shirt in less than two minutes by the end of the summer.

Summer is a very busy time on the farm, and this was a big farm, with big men, her father and two hired hands, working it—all were close to or over six feet tall. Every time they came in to eat, Sara cried and ran to her mother. Britt spent a goodly amount of time down on her knees that summer, comforting Sara.

Grandpa Carl, Britt's father, loved little babies. Though he had a lot of work to do on the farm, after it was done and he'd eaten, he'd hold Daniel. He'd smile and talk and cluck at him. *What a picture they make. They've bonded. I wish Andy and Daniel could have had more time together before Andy's ship left. It's as important for fathers to bond with their children as it is for mothers.*

Britt acknowledged she owed her mother a lot for all the help she gave her the summer Andy was cruising the Mediterranean. She and her two children lived on the farm for six months. She had only one complaint about that time— Grandma Ingrid would feed Daniel more than he needed or wanted. She felt that she should fatten up this little preemie. In her day, a roly-poly baby was a sign of good health. Roly-poly Daniel would grow to be a husky child, wearing husky clothing. He would not like that, but he would have the will power to do something about it—he played hockey and was good at it—defenseman on the starting lineup when he was in high school. The husky child became a hunk of a man.

Andy's ship docked in Newport at the end of November. It took him two days to make it to northern Minnesota. Sara ran to him and hugged his legs. "Daddy, Daddy." Britt threw her arms around his neck and gave him a long kiss. Daniel wanted nothing to do with this stranger. He screamed as his dad lifted him up.

It was time for the Andy Hughes family to head back to Newport. This time Britt's life was too busy, too full, to spend time saying goodbye to any of her childhood haunts and farm memories, but she did find time to visit the grave of her childhood friend—Spot, black and white and whiskered no longer, but she knew her dog's spirit was somewhere.

After she'd hugged and kissed her parents and thanked them for letting her come home with two babies, they hit the road.

CHAPTER

13

Packed into the old gray Ford, the Hughes family of four started the long trip back to the navy base in Newport, Rhode Island.

"Mama, Mama." Sara's little hands had surprising strength as they tugged on the collar of Britt's jacket. "Up, up, Mama!"

"Not now, Sara. Mama's feeding Daniel. Sit down and cuddle in your blankie." Sara called her beloved, ragged blanket with the satin binding her "blankie." Sara, put off by her mother, started to cry—or rather, to whine.

Britt finished feeding Daniel, whose closed eyes and deep breathing told her he was asleep. She got a good grip on him as she struggled to turn herself around in the front passenger seat and then onto her knees. In this position, she could reach over and lay Daniel down on the backseat. They were fortunate that he hadn't yet learned how to roll over. She covered him and then held her hands out to Sara. "Up you go!" Britt clutched Sara under the arms and lifted her until her folded legs cleared the back of the front seat. Britt then turned and settled herself down on the front passenger seat with Sara on her lap. "Wow, that's quite a workout." Through it all, Sara had kept a tight hold on her blankie, and she settled down right away with her two favorite things—her mom's lap and her blankie. In five minutes, she was asleep.

"Andy, eighteen hundred miles of this—I don't know if I can stand it. I know one thing: if we make it, you better not mess with me. The size of my biceps will be huge."

"You can make it, Britt. Just take it one mile at a time."

Britt arched her eyebrows. *Easy for him to say. All he has to do is keep his hands on the steering wheel and watch the road. I have to take care of two kids in relays—both of them wanting my full attention all the time. I feel like a juggler.* She leaned her head back and took a catnap.

And so it went—mile after tiresome mile. They stopped for gas at a small town a few miles out of Chicago—twenty-eight cents a gallon, a lot on their limited budget. They needed to find a motel, get some sleep, stretch their legs, and unkink their backs. They found a motel with reasonable rates and checked into a room with a double bed. Sara was in heaven because she got to sleep between Mama and Daddy in the double bed. Of course, she had to bring her blankie with her.

For Daniel's bed, Britt took the two chairs in the room, laid them down, backs facing in and touching. She then tipped one to the right and the other to the left and moved each chair's back close in to the other chair's seat, creating a legless crib with one seat forming the headboard and the other seat the footboard. It was just enough space for little Daniel. She then folded a quilt into a makeshift mattress. She fed Daniel, rocked him by sitting on the bed and swaying her body back and forth, and laid him down on the quilt.

He drifted off to sleep. *Does he remember when he slept in a drawer when I took him home from the hospital? Probably not.*

Refreshed, they started out early the next morning after stopping at a grocery to buy milk, bread, peanut butter, bananas, and graham crackers—their version of take-out. Britt couldn't help it; she splurged and bought a package of Oreo cookies for thirty-nine cents.

Andy saw her try to smuggle the package of Oreos into the car. "What's that? It doesn't look like a necessity to me."

"It is for me—a girl needs her chocolate, don't cha know?"

"What did you get me?"

She smiled. "Peace and quiet while Sara and I are munching on our cookies. Even Daniel can work his gums on an Oreo. You can have one too, if you're good."

Andy was right. They made it. They drove through the gated entrance of the enlisted men's trailer park. This was their new home—if they could find it amongst the endless rows of green trailers, like gigantic green fruit beetles. They were all alike on the inside too.

Britt opened the front door to see a wood-paneled interior, the front of the beetle, and almost bumped her left hip on a round, cast-iron heater. To her right, a couch stretched the length of a row of windows. The couch, though it could be converted into a double bed, qualified the area to be called the living room.

A small window was opposite the door, and below it stood a table with two cushioned benches. The trio was capable of transforming into yet another bed by lowering the table to rest on the outer edge of each bench. The cushions from the benches were set on top to form the mattress—an ingenious transformation of table to extra sleeping space.

The apartment-sized stove, refrigerator, and sink completed the kitchen.

She left the front of the beetle and progressed into its midsection, which was divided straight down the middle by a narrow hall, and saw two bunk beds to the right, and to the left, a closet and a small bathroom. The narrow hall ended at the beginning of the beetle's back section, which held a not very masterful master bedroom. But it was their bedroom, and Britt was happy just to be sleeping beside Andy again after sleeping alone for the last six months.

About a week later, Britt woke up to the sound of loud crying. Daniel wanted a bottle, and he wanted it *now*. It was well past midnight, but babies don't care about the time. Britt crept out of bed, hoping Daniel's cries would not awaken Andy or Sara, sleeping in the bunk bed right above Daniel. She blinked her eyes to get them focused for the twenty or so steps to the kitchen part of their cramped trailer. Then Britt heard Andy's voice: "Oh, no, you don't! He has to learn to sleep through the night."

Darn! He woke Andy. "But he'll wake Sara up. I'll just give him a little orange juice." She stumbled to the fridge, got out the orange juice, poured some into a plastic baby bottle, and screwed on the nipple cap. Turning, Britt jumped. Andy had followed her.

"Give me that bottle. Hand it over right now." Andy's right hand reached out and grabbed. Now they both had a tight grip on the bottle.

"No!"

Daniel's cries had turned into screams, and Sara was starting to fuss. Rage boiled up inside Britt, and she squeezed the bottle as hard as she could. The cap loosened, spraying orange juice up and out into their angry faces and onto the top of the hot heater. The juice sizzled, burned, and stank. By now both kids were screaming. Andy and Britt glared at each other, still angry but shocked and speechless at what had happened.

They'd just had their first real fight.

Britt stuck a pacifier in Daniel's mouth, hoping it'd do the trick. They went back to bed. The trailer was quiet.

Britt lay awake for a while, just thinking. *In two months, we'll celebrate our third anniversary. It's not easy learning to live with another person, especially if that person is in the military and is frequently absent. I spent the six months he was at sea learning how to take care of two little ones by myself. Just when I'd figured out how to do that, he comes home and stirs things up. He was telling me how to take care of my kids!* At last she too slept.

The next morning, Britt scraped burnt orange juice off the top of the heater and realized she had been wrong. They weren't just "her kids"—they were his too. *We should be ashamed of fighting in front of our children. We have made a family, and we have to act like parents and show a united front to our children. If we have disagreements, and we will, we'll still fight but only when we are alone—no kids allowed.*

Andy stumbled in from the bedroom, dark circles under his eyes. He looked at Britt and said, "What are you doing? Oh ... we really went at it, didn't we? Here, I'll help you."

"Okay. Andy, I kind of got out of control last night. Taking care of Sara and Daniel when you were gone—you were gone a long time—I guess I started thinking of them as 'my kids,' but I know they're yours too. I'm sorry I forgot that." She leaned over the cast-iron heater they were scrubbing and gave him a kiss on the cheek.

"I shouldn't have tried to force the bottle out of your hands."

"We're both beginners when it comes to raising kids. We need to talk about how to do it. We'll learn." She walked to the refrigerator and pulled out a carton of eggs and put the small skillet on the kitchen stove, saying, "How do you want your eggs?"

"Sunny side up, as usual, and two pieces of toast."

"Coming right up." She jumped as Andy kissed the back of her neck.

For the first time, Andy and Britt had friends as a couple, and their new friends, Amy and Chuck, lived right across the alley. Like Andy and Britt, they were Midwesterners, and they also played Pinochle, one of Andy's favorite card games. Britt knew how to play, but she wasn't born with Andy's "card sense" (Andy said he'd started playing penny-ante poker when he was four). Britt's family thought card playing, with the exception of Old Maid, was a sin. Playing cards for Britt was just a means to an end—the chance to visit and talk with friends.

Christmas was just around the corner, and Britt wanted to start establishing some traditions. She'd mix those of Andy's family with those of her family. She'd not only mix them; she'd turn them upside down. Instead of Midnight Mass, Andy's family's tradition, they'd go Christmas morning. Instead of a Christmas Eve reading of the birth of Jesus and then opening gifts, her family's tradition, they'd do that after morning mass and breakfast. They would have a small tree, both families' tradition.

Food was a big part of Britt's family's Christmas. Her mother had always baked Spritz cookies and decorated them with red and green sprinkles. Britt, not having a Spritz cookies press, settled for sugar cookies sprinkled with colored sugar. She didn't even try to find lutefisk—Andy couldn't stand the smell—but she did find some *lefse*, the traditional soft Norwegian flatbread made out of flour and milk or cream, cooked on a griddle. Britt sprinkled the rounds of lefse with sugar and cinnamon and rolled them up; Andy liked lefse prepared this way.

Britt leafed through her Betty Crocker *Picture Cookbook*, looking for holiday recipes. *They all look so good.* She glanced up as Andy came in.

"Hi, hon, I'm looking for Christmas recipes. Did your family have any special Christmas foods that you loved?"

"Well, we always had a roasted goose. And I remember the sweet Christmas bread with fruit in it that my mother used to make."

"My mother made bread like that too. She called it Stollen. I think I can take one of these sweetbread recipes and just add candied mixed fruit, raisins, and nuts. That should do it. I'm glad I took bread making one year as a 4-H project, but I better make a list. We won't have a goose. That's too much. We'll make do with a small chicken."

On Christmas Eve, nine-month-old Daniel would not eat. Britt felt his forehead—he was burning up. When she took his temperature, it was 103 degrees. Christmas Eve was spent at the Newport Naval Hospital where poor little Daniel was subjected to a spinal tap—the doctor feared he might have spinal meningitis. Fortunately, he did not, but he did have pneumonia. He was put in an oxygen tent and kept in the hospital for two days. The last thing Britt and Andy heard as they left their little boy to take Sara home and put her to bed was Daniel's heartbreaking cries and screams.

It was not at all the Christmas Britt had planned, the one she hoped they'd remember, but it turned out to be memorable in its own way.

CHAPTER

14

Britt dressed Sara in her yellow, nylon snowsuit with an attached hood. Their gated trailer community had very little traffic this time of the day, and it was so beautiful outside— sun shining, birds singing. Spring was definitely on the way. Britt could see no harm in letting Sara go out for some fresh air while Daniel napped. Britt wouldn't mind getting some fresh air herself. Together they stepped out. Sara wanted to look for "her" black kitty, a stray that hung around. Sara was attracted to all animals. No kitty in sight today. They walked around the perimeter of their small yard, a yard that Andy and she planned to partially enclose as a play space for Sara and Daniel.

Daniel! *I better go and check on him. He may be awake and wondering where we are.* Britt glanced at Sara—she was fine, sitting on the ground and studying a small rock she held between her hands. Britt entered the trailer and looked at Daniel. *He's fine, still asleep, but he's kicked his blanket off. I don't want him to get cold and get a cold or, God forbid, pneumonia.* She quickly covered him up and hurried outside. *Is that a truck I hear?*

It was a truck, a back-loader garbage truck, and it was backing up and over Sara! Britt screamed and ran toward the cab of the truck, waving her arms wildly, yelling "Stop!"

One of the two men who had been picking up the garbage cans heard her. He motioned for the truck to stop, and the driver slammed on the brakes—the truck stopped ... thank God. In less than a minute, Britt's world had turned upside down.

Sara lay close to the back of a rear tire, the right side of her body snug up against the curb. Britt dashed to the neighboring trailer. "Amy, Amy, you've got to watch Daniel for me. He's sleeping in the trailer. I have to take Sara to the hospital right now."

Britt hurried to the car and jerked open the passenger side door. She ran to Sara, who lay there, not crying, not moving. Britt slid her hands under Sara and lifted her little eighteen-pound body onto the car's front seat. Sara just looked at her.

Leaving the gated, enlisted men's trailer park, Britt drove, conscious of the need for speed but also of the need to be careful. She didn't want Sara to feel the slightest bump. A traffic cop on a motorcycle stopped her car before the turn toward the hospital. The president's motorcade was crawling across the road in front of them. Britt's heart squeezed, and her insides churned—was she going to be sick? But the police must be obeyed—if she disobeyed and was arrested ... her mind couldn't go there. She braked to a stop.

Hurry up! Please, God, hurry up! Britt looked at her daughter lying on the front passenger seat of the car. Sara was wearing her yellow snowsuit, as February in Newport, Rhode Island, is cool and she'd been outside. Her brown eyes fixed on her mother. She made no sound. "It's okay, Sara. It's okay. You'll be okay."

Britt's eyes filled with tears. She looked away from Sara and out at the road, fingers tapping the steering wheel. Through blurred eyes, she watched the slow progression of President Eisenhower's motorcade. *It is taking forever! And my baby is hurt.* Britt turned her head to check on Sara. *She hasn't moved, not even her eyes. She's quiet—no sound, no sound. She just looks at me.*

Just when Britt knew she could not wait another second and remain in one piece, the policeman motioned her forward. She lowered her foot to the accelerator and went as fast as allowed to Newport Navy Hospital's emergency entrance.

"Help! Someone help! My little girl is hurt! She's in the car!" Two corpsmen ran toward them, pushing a gurney. They put Sara on the gurney and rushed into the ER. Britt followed and watched as a doctor examined Sara. A husky, scowling nurse approached.

"You young navy wives! You shouldn't have children. You don't know how to take care of them. Now you go out there and sit!"

Cringing, Britt left—not to sit but to find a telephone. She called Andy's ship, docked in Newport—about twenty minutes away by car.

"It's an emergency! My husband, Andy Hughes, is a cook in the galley. There's been an accident. Our daughter is hurt. We're at the hospital. Tell him he's got to come right away!"

She hung up the receiver and walked over to a bench in the hall outside the emergency room. In a daze, Britt sat down. Her mind was not working. A woman, probably in her sixties, holding a Bible moved toward her. Her voice was soft and caring as she said, "Can I help you?"

The woman reached out and placed her hand on Britt's

shoulder. Britt lost control and crumpled up on the bench. Harsh sobs tore at her throat. She cried as if she'd never be able to stop—until she was a sodden, tear-soaked, snotty mess. Exhausted, she lay on the bench, mute and unmoving, until Andy entered the waiting room.

He rushed to her side. "What happened? They said there'd been an accident!"

Her voice raspy low, Britt told him what happened. He held her. At that moment, they saw a priest enter the emergency room where Sara still lay. They followed behind him and stood just inside the door of the emergency room. They watched in horror and grief the anointing of their little girl with the oil used in the sacrament of Extreme Unction. Britt could barely breathe; her heart felt pierced. Only Andy kept her from falling, and she could feel the tremble in his hands.

Sara was taken to radiology. Britt and Andy sat on the bench in the hall, clinging to each other, waiting without words for the results of Sara's x-rays.

A doctor approached. They stood, holding hands. The doctor said, "She has two cracked ribs. She'll be fine, but we want to keep her overnight just to be sure."

They could breathe again. She was going to live; she was going to be fine! The roadside curb must have protected her from serious, even fatal harm. Dizzy with relief, Britt clutched Andy's arm for support as they made their way to Sara's hospital room.

They hurried to her bed, a hospital crib. Britt spoke first. "Sara, you will be fine, but you have to stay here tonight. Mama will come and get you in the morning." She didn't dare give her a hug, but she kissed her sweet forehead and ran her fingers through her curly hair. Not even two years old, Sara seemed to understand. Even now, she shed no tears. *Thank you, thank you, God.*

Andy, with tears in his eyes, grabbed her foot and gave it a gentle shake and said, "You'll be home tomorrow, Sara."

Britt picked Sara up the next day and brought her home, trying to avoid even the smallest bump on the way. She scrutinized Sara's every move for the next few days. Britt's heart ached whenever she looked at the tape covering her little daughter's ribs. Sara didn't seem to be hurting, and she healed fast. She was soon her old self, lugging her blankie around. One thing had changed—she did not want to let her mother out of her sight.

Britt never told her parents about the accident. She knew she'd disappointed them when she'd dropped out of college and married so young—and to a Catholic fellow at that! She didn't want to give them further proof of her imperfection, her inability to keep her child safe. Britt was afraid that their judgment would be the same as that of the navy nurse in the emergency room. She wouldn't be able to stand that.

When Britt was certain that Sara was healthy and strong, she sat down to think things over. "All things happen for a purpose." This was what she been taught. If so, what purpose was served by Sara, an innocent child, getting hurt? *Sara, you taught me that it's impossible to watch two children at the same time if they are not in the same place. Above all, you taught me what it really means to be a mother. Biology made me a mother when I birthed you, my first child. But our drive to the emergency room of the Navy Hospital, when you fixed your gaze on mine as we waited for President Eisenhower's motorcade to pass, deepened my perception of motherhood. Your gaze, so full of trust, rocked me to my core. Your look said that motherhood was more than birthing and loving; it* was responsibility. *I had failed you when I left you outside while I checked on your brother. From now on, I will be more responsible—I embrace responsibility. Yes, Sara, you can trust me. I now know that giving birth is only the beginning of motherhood.*

CHAPTER

15

All was quiet in the Hughes trailer. Sara and Daniel lay in their bunk beds, sleeping soundly as only the young and healthy can sleep. Mr. and Mrs. Hughes were also in bed, lying on their backs, soaking up the quiet. Their upside-down world had turned right side up again. Andy reached out in the darkness with his left hand and touched Britt's thigh. She turned toward him, putting her arms around his neck and kissing him. Andy returned the kiss with interest—a slow, soul kiss.

Britt pulled him closer. "Shh!—we have to be quiet." Then she bent her left knee and lifted it to rest on his right thigh.

Andy sprang into action. His deep kisses stirred her, made her stomach ache, and she couldn't keep track of his hands—they were everywhere. They needed each other after the scare they'd had over Sara. They needed to celebrate the health of their children and their love for each other.

Later, spent and satisfied, Andy slept with one arm across Britt's stomach. She was tired too, but she didn't want to sleep yet; she wanted to bask in the warm glow of their lovemaking. *We needed this, this coming together. We were so scared when we saw the priest go into the emergency room to give Sara the sacrament of Extreme Unction, or last rites. Seeing that made me want to die—but she's okay—we all came through it okay. I will be a better mother now, so the experience served its purpose. But was that the only purpose? Or was there another lesson? If that priest knew that I was using a diaphragm to prevent pregnancy, would he have damned me to hell as Pastor Thomas did on his one visit to me in the hospital after I was hurt in our car accident? He said I would go to hell for marrying a Roman Catholic. Was that a sin? Are we sinning now? The priest and the pope would say that we are. They might even say that the "accident" to Sara was a warning to us, a warning that we were committing a mortal sin and we, especially me—for I let my mother talk me into getting the diaphragm—would be punished in one way or another.* Britt tossed and turned, mulling over the questions in her mind. By three o'clock in the morning, she'd made a decision, and then she slept.

When Britt got up in the morning, she looked at her face in the mirror. The circles under her eyes revealed her lack of sleep, but she was not lacking in resolve. After Andy went back to the ship, she would destroy the diaphragm—the Hughes family didn't need any more "accidents." With the long, tiring trip back to Newport from her parents' home, followed by moving into the green trailer, she hadn't had time to tell Andy about it. Destroying it now meant that she'd never have to tell him. She still wanted to space her children farther apart but not if it meant she would be punished *through her children.* Britt would give the rhythm method another chance.

She removed the diaphragm from its container and

placed it on the wooden breadboard. She went to the knife block, picked up the big butcher knife, tested its sharpness by running her thumb lightly over the cutting edge, and with her lips set in a grim line, jaws clamped, and tears streaking her face, she positioned the knife over the diaphragm. *You will no longer tempt me!* She sliced through the center of it. *You will no longer jinx this family!* She lifted the knife twice more and sliced through each of the halves on the breadboard; the diaphragm was now in four pieces. *That should do it.* She put the pieces in a brown paper bag, gave the top of the bag a couple of hard twists, and threw it in the garbage. *Good riddance.*

It bothered them that the weather was beautiful but their children could only enjoy it when both parents were home—no more one person trying to keep track of two children. It was hard because Andy was gone a lot. The solution? Build a fence. Andy purchased a bundle of laths at the lumber yard, and he made a large "play pen." It started at the front of the trailer, extended back twenty feet, and then ran parallel with the trailer for fifteen feet before making a ninety-degree turn and running fifteen feet to where Andy attached it to the trailer—a three-sided play area.

Inside the play area, they put a large wooden fruit basket filled with toys for outside—trucks, shovels, a couple of pails. But sand was needed, so they bought a plastic wading pool and filled it with sand. This was great until the black kitty discovered it and used it for her own business. They had to dump out the sand, but they kept the pool for future use as a kiddie pool on warm days. Britt usually went out with them. She'd bring something to sit on and some reading material. If she had to run in and stir a pot or something, she could look out of the top glass on their front door and see the entire play area. It made things easier for all.

Andy's four-year navy hitch was up in the fall of 1957. Looking back, it had gone pretty fast. Two children were born to Andy and Britt—Sara, two and a half years ago in Newport Naval Hospital, and Daniel, almost a year and a half ago in Chelsea Naval Hospital. The bill for their deliveries was less than eight dollars apiece. When Andy had shipped out on his first six-month cruise, Britt was busy working in a Newport law office. When he had to leave on another six-month cruise, she was the mother of two children, and she had taken them and gone home to her parents. (In the first three years of their marriage, Britt had only lived with Andy a year and a half.) His ship schedule when in port was the usual—seven twenty-four-hour days on ship out of every fourteen days. They were lonely during the absences, but they were always busy. No wonder the time flew.

Some things would be missed. They would miss the commissary with its nine cents per quart of milk. They would really miss the low cost of care in the naval hospitals. (Their third child would be born in a civilian hospital in June 1958. He would not be paid for in full until he started first grade.) And they would miss their friends, Amy and Chuck, but as with most friends made in the military, they disappeared into their own lives.

They would not miss Andy's sea duty. They welcomed the chance to have a more stable married life. Andy would be using the GI Bill for education. He wanted to go to Moler's Barber College in Minneapolis. It was not to be because he'd have to wait for the spring classes, so he chose Lee's Barber College in St. Paul—he could get in there shortly after Christmas. A barber could support his family and still keep his hands clean; ever since childhood, he hated getting his hands dirty.

The old gray Ford wasn't what she used to be—part of the flooring in front of the passenger seat had rusted through.

Britt could see the road streaming backward under them as they travelled. Something had to be done. She bought a large kitchen metal "hot pad"—the padding underneath it was asbestos. It was meant to be a place on which to put hot dishes when they came out of the oven, but it covered the hole in the car floor and then some. With a floor mat on top, nobody would even know that a portion of the floor was rusted out.

The car had some rust, but it still was a reliable friend that could pull her weight and more besides. Andy bought a carrier for the top of the car and put the plastic swimming pool on top loaded with towels, bedding, and some kitchen supplies. He filled in the cracks with miscellaneous clothing items, threw a tarp over all of it, and strapped the load down securely. The car was a two-door, so they didn't have to worry about kids falling out—just falling down off the backseat.

Somewhere, Andy saw and bought a contraption that could turn the entire backseat of a car into one big area—a playpen. The contraption consisted of two panels of steel that telescoped into each other, so the length was adjustable to fit the width of the backseat. The top ends of two large hangers had "crooks" like a shepherd's staff that fit over the backs of the front seats. The back of the horizontal steel panels rested on the backseat. The whole thing formed a sturdy floor, and when covered with a quilt, it was a play, eat, and sleeping space.

Under that sturdy floor, an amazing amount of stuff could be stored to be used during the trip—pajamas, clothes, diapers, and a cooler for milk and juice. The diapers presented a problem. Soiled diapers had to be stored until they could be rinsed in a gas station or motel bathroom. For storage, a chamber pot with cover was also stashed under the sturdy backseat floor. Clothing separated the cooler from the chamber pot.

On the road—first stop Niagara Falls, a romantic place for honeymooners, which Britt and Andy definitely were not, for both were continually holding on to the hand of a child. Britt wasn't positive yet, but she was probably carrying a third child "under her heart." At least that had a romantic ring to it.

At night, beautiful colored lights behind the falls, in fuchsia, blue, purple, aqua, and green, turned Niagara Falls into a vertical rainbow. Judging from the voiced "oohs" and "aahs," every member of the Hughes family was enchanted. By day, the awesome natural beauty of the falls and the roar of the rushing, falling water—a sound that was hardly noticed when the night lights were on—made Britt want to sing her father's favorite hymn, "How Great Thou Art."

After spending time at Niagara Falls, they drove to St. Catharine, in Canada's province of Ontario, and stayed the night at an inn. No one had trouble falling asleep. Early the next morning after a breakfast of pancakes and eggs with orange juice, they left for Brantford, Ontario, the home of Andy's aunt Amelia and uncle Russell and their two sons, Alain and Denis. Andy had never visited them, and it would have been a shame not to visit now when they were so close. But just dropping in on them? This worried Britt.

It was needless worry. Andy's aunt and uncle were thrilled to see Josie and Phil's "boy," Andy, and his little wife and children, of course—so thrilled that they invited the neighbors to come over. It turned into a party. After Britt fed the children, they went right to sleep. The sight of so many strangers had squelched any desire to make a fuss about bedtime.

Andy, a natural athlete, was excited about the fact that both Alain and Denis were hockey players. He must have talked with them about the game for a good half hour before Uncle Russell got out his fiddle and began to play. He was good. No one could stay seated when Uncle Russell played "Turkey in the Straw" or "Sally Goodin." Everyone had a ball, especially Andy and Britt. They hadn't felt such freedom to just enjoy for a long time.

After a good breakfast and tearful goodbyes, the Hughes family stopped for gas in London, Ontario—just in case Sara and Daniel wanted to tell their friends someday, "We've been to London." Then they were on their way to Jackson, Michigan—back in the USA. They skirted Detroit, the automobile capital of the world, because it was just too big. A good night's sleep at a motel in Jackson refreshed them, and while Britt put some diapers in a nearby Laundromat, Andy ordered breakfast and started feeding Sara and Daniel. On the road again. They decided to stop in Kalamazoo for a while because the name intrigued them. The drive there was gorgeous. Autumn in Michigan is ablaze with color—red, gold, yellow—the leaves of all the various deciduous trees trying to outdo each other in beauty.

Kalamazoo. They stopped at a gas station for cleaning up and gassing up, and Andy asked if there was a park nearby. There was, so next stop was a grocery store for chips, dip, bread, cheese, and milk. It was a fine picnic and nice stretching break for all. Andy most of all needed the rest—he had to drive through Chicago and on to Dubuque before the kids got too sleepy. The next day, they left Dubuque and drove the one hundred and eighty miles to Interstate 35W. They turned north, and then it was just about a straight shot to their hometown. All in all, the four-day journey was not too bad, thanks to pacifiers and graham crackers and stops at the Laundromat.

CHAPTER

16

The Hughes family stayed in their hometown for a week, making their headquarters out at the Anderson farm. It was inconvenient to be so far out of town, but that disadvantage was overridden by the advantages—Britt's parents and her twin brothers were so taken with Sara and Daniel that Britt and Andy could visit relatives and friends and not worry about looking for a babysitter. Andy's parents weren't too happy about this, but they had to admit that the Andersons had more room both inside their house and outside. A large backyard enclosed a swing set and a teeter-totter, and bordering the play area, a grove of trees beckoned to little explorers.

The first thing Britt and Andy did was to clean up the "playpen" backseat of their car. The playpen had turned into a pigpen—apple cores and potato chip pieces, along with soggy graham crackers, covered the quilt that was the playpen's floor. It smelled of sour milk and something worse. They hauled out the quilt, folded all the icky stuff inside it, and dumped the food leavings into the burn barrel. The quilt, sturdily sewn in the around-the-world pattern, in Britt's favorite colors—turquoise, sage green, Chinese red, and camel—came out of the washer almost as good as new.

Britt hadn't been to a doctor, but she knew she was pregnant—a fact she wasn't about to share with her mother; she didn't want to spoil her visit with her parents by starting a birth control or a religious discussion. They'd be leaving for Minneapolis soon, and she wanted their goodbyes to be as kissy and huggy as the hellos.

Using the GI Bill, Andy would attend Lee's Barber College early the next year. In the meantime, he'd try to find work. As a veteran of the Korean War, he would not receive unemployment compensation until after a waiting period ended, determined by the amount and disbursement date of his mustering out pay. Then he would be able to receive both state and federal benefits. But a family man like Andy needed money now, which meant as soon as they reached St. Paul and found a place to live, he would have to start looking for a job. He also planned to put them on the list for low-income housing while he attended school. With all this in mind, they packed up the old gray Ford for yet another trip—this one a bit over three hundred and fifty miles. They reinstalled the playpen for Sara and Daniel's comfort.

Saying goodbye was still hard, even though this time they weren't going to be as far away. The warm kisses and hugs left Britt's mother in tears. Britt was almost afraid she wouldn't hand over little Daniel. *Are those tears real? Is she really sad? Or does she think she's supposed to cry at goodbyes? But she cries for the least little things, even when she's happy. Dad—my father, the stoic—has always hated that.*

They stopped in town to say goodbye to Andy's folks. Andy's mother served coffee and cookies (Britt nibbled on a cookie and asked for water). She hugged and kissed Britt and Andy goodbye, telling her son that she was happy that the navy didn't own him anymore. Josette then got down on her knees to give Sara a monster hug. Britt handed Daniel over to her, and he got a loving goodbye from his Grandma Hughes.

Andy's father said little and barely noticed his first two grandchildren. He did hug Andy before they left and told him, "Don't ever let your wife work." When Andy told her later what his father had said, she didn't know what to say to Andy. *Why, if his mother hadn't worked, they'd have starved!*

They found a second-floor apartment they could afford, above a family with two children just a little older than Sara and Daniel. The oldest, a girl, swore like a muleskinner. Sara was impressed and began to follow suit. Britt didn't know what to do, so she ignored it. That must have been the right thing, because when Sara got no attention for her blue language, it just died out.

Though they now had an apartment, which had not been easy to find, the next step was to find a job. Andy would find that jobs were even harder to find—the country was going through a rollback. But before Andy even tried to find a job, he applied for the GI Bill so he would have money for education. He also signed up for low-income housing. It would take him at least nine months (1500 hours) to earn an apprentice license from Lee's Barber College. Upon earning his apprentice license, the college would help him find employment.

Andy was eager to start, but he'd have to wait until he started to receive the monthly sum of $110, plus $175 a month for family expenses. A veteran was supposed to pay his school tuition and buy school supplies with the $110 and then provide for his family on the $175. In the meantime, he needed to work to support the family.

He couldn't find a job at first. When he did find one, it was with a furnace company that sent him around supposedly checking furnaces to see if they were ready for winter. If they were fine, he was supposed to tell the homeowner that such and such was needed. He quit the job that was really a customer rip-off.

Britt took one look at his face when he got home and knew something was wrong. She followed him into the bedroom. Andy lay on the bed facedown—not moving, not talking.

"What's wrong? Was it a bad day?"

Andy turned to lie on his side and faced her. She'd never seen him so down—he looked on the verge of tears, and his face seemed to sag. When he spoke, his voice was low. "I quit. I just couldn't do it."

"Do what?"

"Tell lies to old people, to poor people. Tell them their furnace needed repair when it didn't. They could be my grandparents or my relatives. I know we need the money, but it wasn't right."

"You'll find another job, Andy. Times are tough, but you're a married man—the kind of worker most people want. When a boss finds out how dependable and hardworking you are, he won't want to ever let you go." Britt cradled his head in her lap, stroking his forward and pushing back a black, wavy hank of hair.

After a good night's sleep and oatmeal with raisins and some salted peanuts thrown in while it cooked, Andy hit the streets again. Britt knew that it would crush him if he couldn't find a job good enough to support his family. She knew he'd be a good worker, and with Christmas coming, she was sure he'd find something that paid enough for them to live on until he started school and received the GI Bill.

That night when he came home, he didn't drag himself into the bedroom and collapse with depression. Instead, when Britt opened the door, he swept her into his arms and gave her a mushy kiss. "I'm working for Montgomery Ward!

And we can get a discount on kids' clothes and Christmas presents."

"That's wonderful, Andy. How much is the pay?"

"One hundred dollars a week. I'm working in the stock room. They're getting a lot of merchandise in now for the Christmas rush."

"Oh, Andy, I'm so glad—we can live on that." She put her arms around him. "I'm so proud of you."

It looked to be a merry Christmas after all. Though no relatives would be there with them at Christmas, the four of them together with no six-month cruises in the future for Andy was enough to make for a joyful, thankful holiday. Andy picked up a nice little tree and some decorations. Britt made Christmas cookies with help from Sara and Daniel. They wanted to be a lot of help, but it ended in a pushing and shoving contest to see who could get the closest to Mom and who could put colored sugar on the most cookies. Britt washed the red and green colors from their hands and faces and read them a story. Daniel went to sleep before the story was done. Sara, though sleepy, resisted sleep, so Britt set the kitchen timer for twenty minutes—the time when she could get up. Britt went into the kitchen and completed the cookie baking. She looked in on Sara. *Yes, sound asleep. Nap time for me too—pregnancy really tires a body out.*

Christmas day was cold but beautiful. The trees covered with frost looked like flocked Christmas trees. The sun shone on them and set them to sparkling, outdoing any decorated Christmas tree—breathtaking. The Hughes family members were on their way to Christmas morning Mass. Entering the church to the sound of Christmas carols brought back memories to Britt. She remembered the Christmases in the little rural Lutheran church, one in particular. She had to sing "Away in the Manger" in front of the church at a Christmas

Eve service when she was only five years old. She shook with fear, but she did it. Her parents glowed with pride. Their pride was almost worth her fear. She'd worn her light blue Christmas sweater. After that frightening performance, she never wore light blue again if she could help it.

As soon as they reached home, Andy made breakfast, French toast and bacon, while Britt unwrapped the bundled children and got them washed up for the table. Andy was a good cook, and for that Britt was grateful. Her father never cooked, washed a dish, changed a diaper, or even disciplined. He was a farmer—he did farm things. He had a wife for everything else. Britt was glad that Andy was not like that.

Daniel ate almost nothing. He rubbed his eyes and whined. His forehead felt hot. Britt put him to bed and started to read him a story. He moved, and she looked over at his body. His limbs jerked, and his eyes rolled back, and she could see only the whites of his eyes. *What is the matter with him? I've never seen anything like this before.*

"Andy, come quick! Something's the matter with Daniel."

Andy looked, ran to the phone, and called the police. "You've got to come. My little boy is sick and acting funny. I don't know what to do." The policeman, an older man with a kind face, came at once and told the frightened parents to put their boy in a tub of cold water and keep him there to lower his temperature—that's what he did whenever his children ran a high fever. Britt did that as fast as she could. While she laved the body of her little boy with cold water, Andy talked to the policeman.

"Thank you, Officer, for helping us. We'd never seen a kid act like that."

"Why did you call the police? People don't usually call us when a child is sick."

"I just got out of the navy, and we're new in Minneapolis.

I didn't know who else to call." The policeman shook Andy's hand as he left and wished him a merry Christmas.

And it was a merry Christmas in spite of their scare, because after Daniel's fever broke, he slept. When he woke up, he had a runny nose, but that was all. They were merry—the parents were slap-happy with relief, and Sara got a Betsy Wetsy doll that made her merry. Daniel, when he woke up, was just happy to cuddle his new teddy bear as Britt held him tight.

Daniel's illness proved to be a harbinger of things to come, at least for Britt. She came down with the flu in February. Andy had not yet received his education and living expenses money, nor had they heard from low-income housing. He was working full-time at Montgomery Ward. They were getting by and even saving some. When Britt got sick, Andy didn't know what to do. She tried to shrug it off, to ignore her headache and her chills and fever. She thought she had toughed it out. She was feeling so good that she washed clothes and even hung some outside to dry. Big mistake.

Britt could barely get out of bed the next day. By now she was five months pregnant and usually ate a big breakfast, but that morning she couldn't even eat dry toast. She managed to fix bowls of dry cereal for Sara, almost three years old, and Daniel, almost two, but that was all. She shuffled to the couch, making it there by holding onto the kitchen door jamb, then the back of the plush chair, and finally the arm of the couch, and then she collapsed onto the couch itself. Britt may have slept, she didn't know, but she did know that she had to go to the bathroom. She slid off the couch to the floor and crawled fifteen feet to the bathroom. She almost passed out as she hauled herself onto the toilet seat, but she did her job and crawled back to the blessed couch.

It must have been about noon when she noticed that Sara

and Daniel were in the living room. Sara had a bowl and a full carton of eggs.

"Mama, I'm making lunch for you. Scrambled eggs. I know you like them." She cracked an egg and emptied its contents into the bowl. A large piece of eggshell followed.

Daniel leaned over the open egg carton and picked one up. He stared at it and then at the floor. The floor in the living room was made up of alternating tiles of white and black. Daniel had made his decision. He had been watching as Sara had cracked open her egg, so now he cracked open his and dumped its contents in the middle of a twelve-inch by twelve-inch black tile. He grabbed another egg and chose another black tile, and so on, until Sara grabbed his hand to stop him. "No! No!" Daniel screamed and tried to pull away. They fell on the eggs.

Britt saw all this, but she didn't care—she couldn't move. If she moved, she felt dizzy, and her head throbbed. She could see that no one was hurt, and nothing else concerned her. She let them fight and roll in the slippery, gooey eggs.

Andy came home. The house was a mess. Britt watched him make a beeline for the telephone. In a fever-induced haze, she heard him place a long-distance call to her parents. "Ingrid, we've got to have help. Britt is really sick. I can't stay home—I have to work. Can you come right away?" He paused for an answer and then hung up the phone and approached the couch where Britt lay, being careful not to slip on the broken eggs.

"Is my mother coming?"

"No. She has to care for your twin brothers. Hannah is coming. She graduated from college this month and has just started looking for a job, but so far nothing."

Andy helped Britt into the bedroom and got her settled. Though she was in the bedroom now, she could hear him get the mop and scrub bucket and fill the bucket with water. He was going to clean up the broken-egg mess from the tile floor in the living room—bless him. She dozed off.

Hannah took the night train to the Twin Cities so that she'd arrive before Andy left in the morning. He had to be there to let her in and give her instructions about how to care for Britt and the children.

A knock on the door—Andy rushed and opened it for Hannah. "Come in, come in!" He held out his arms and engulfed her in a bear hug.

"Wow! That's quite a greeting, brother-in-law. Britt must be *really* sick. What do I need to know?"

"Most important, make sure she drinks lots of fluids so she doesn't become dehydrated. She's in bed now, and she should stay there—you'll have to help her to the bathroom though. She gets weak and dizzy."

"What about the kids?" Hannah surveyed toys strewn all over, but at least the space in front of the couch was clear and clean.

"Sara's potty trained. She'll eat anything or nothing—it depends on her mood. It's no big deal. Daniel goes pee in the little twelve-ounce empty juice can sitting on the back of the toilet. He likes to see it fill up, but you will have to help him because he still wears a diaper. He refuses to do the big job in the potty, so he's stuck with a diaper. Food for them? Whatever you eat. Both kids, if you're lucky, will nap after the noon lunch. Read one of their little books to them—oh, and lie between them so they won't fight. Daniel will probably go to sleep. Sara does most of the time, but if she doesn't, let her get up, and she can color. She knows where the crayons and the color book are. I'll be home at five thirty. Now I have to go. Bye and *thank you!*" And he was gone.

Hannah sat down but only for a few seconds. Sara and

Daniel were going at it. Sara was building a tower with blocks, and Daniel was knocking it down almost as fast as his sister was putting it up. Sara threw a block at him. "Stop it right now, you kids! Somebody's going to get hurt. Come with me into the kitchen, and we'll make peanut butter sandwiches. I haven't even had my breakfast." She took each one by the hand. They didn't know her yet, so they put up no resistance.

And so it went for seven long days. Britt started to feel better. She sat up and even managed to keep soup down. Hannah opened the door to check on her, and Britt beckoned for her to come in. She patted the edge of the bed, where she wanted Hannah to sit. "Hannah, I can *never* thank you enough for coming here to help us. You saved my life." She smiled at Hannah and squeezed her hand.

"Britt, I don't see how you manage. I can pick up the toys and turn around, and they're all over the floor again. They spill something at every meal. Sometimes I think Sara and Daniel don't like each other—always teasing, or whining, or crying. We weren't like that. We were friends—still are. I always tried to copy what you did but not anymore! Not after seeing how things are here—I don't think I'll even marry, let alone have children. They're so competitive."

"They'll grow out of most of that behavior. We've probably moved them around too much, and they're so close in age. That's not good."

"As a friend and your sister, Britt, how could you let yourself get pregnant again? Are you nuts?" Hannah shook her head, lips pressed together.

"Oh, Hannah, I've tried so hard to follow the church-sanctioned rhythm method, but it doesn't work for me. I'm beginning to think that it is a church plot to keep its members producing little Catholics in order to have more members than the Protestants. It's cynical, I know, but that's what I'm starting to believe." Britt hid her face in her hands;

she didn't want Hannah to see her tears or the despair deep in her eyes.

"Don't cry, Britt. I'd like to hug you, but I don't want to catch your flu—I have to go looking for a job as soon as I leave here. I'll pray for you—a Protestant prayer. I do love you, even if I sometimes think you do foolish things." She smiled and patted Britt on the back.

Britt was well on her way to health again when Hannah left. She was thankful that her family, Andy, Sara, Daniel, and Hannah, did not catch her flu.

CHAPTER

17

Hannah went home after her stint as nanny while Britt had the flu. She told their mother that Britt was pregnant. At first Britt was angry at her sister, but that didn't last long. It was a secret that could never be kept for long anyway—her middle was getting pretty big. She'd be a mother again in June. Easter Sunday was on April 6 this year, and it was already the middle of March. She'd better get herself down to confession so that she could go to Holy Communion with Andy on Easter Sunday.

Britt crept into the quiet, solemn church on a Saturday afternoon. All she could hear were the restless squeaks of impatient people sitting in pews and cracks of knees bending as people got up and then knelt again. She waited until it was her turn, and then Britt entered and knelt in the dimly lit confessional. It was a claustrophobic place the size of a public phone booth, paneled in dark brown walnut—gloomy as could be.

"Bless me, Father, for I have sinned. It's been over a month since my last confession, and I accuse myself of being impatient with my children. I've yelled at them. I've also resented the way my husband can leave the house but I always have to stay home. Father, I am expecting my third child in June, the third baby in a little over three years. I've been sick with the flu, too sick to take care of my children. May we use condoms to prevent my getting pregnant for at least a year after this baby? I need to get my strength back. Is there some kind of dispensation for that?"

"No, my child, condoms are not allowed for any reason because they prevent the possibility of sperm and egg being able to unite."

"But, Father, that's exactly what I want for a while."

"No, you don't. It would be a mortal sin, putting you in danger of eternal damnation. Other than abstinence, only the rhythm method of birth control is allowed by the Catholic church."

"The rhythm method! I've tried it and tried it. It doesn't work for us."

"Try again, and pray that it works this time. If it doesn't, have you considered that your thirteenth child might be the one to support you, to care for you, in your old age? Now, for your penance, say one Act of Contrition, one Our Father, and three Hail Mary's. Go in peace."

Britt stumbled out of the confessional. Despair filled her mind, and her stomach clenched. *Thirteen children! I've had two single births in a year, and we'll soon have another baby. He's minimizing childbirth and childcare. In fact he's saying that it might be to my advantage that after I have this baby, I should have ten more. Does he really feel that way?*

She sank down onto a pew's kneeler, her elbows on the back of the pew in front, hands cradling her head as tears seeped out of the corners of her eyes. *Did he give me any penance? I don't know; I couldn't hear anything after the "thirteenth child" bit. Doomed, that's what I am. I'll go crazy long before I reach that number of children. It's not fair! My grandmother delivered thirteen children, yes, thirteen! She wanted children—she just didn't want so many. A farm wife was expected to produce farm hands. She died of pneumonia in her sixties. She and her eight daughters did not get along, and her sons were busy with farming and their families. They had little time for her. I do not want to end up like her, angry, bitter, and alone.*

The rhythm method? Give me a break. I've had far more intimate moments with my thermometer than with my husband, and in spite of strictly observing the so-called safe days, I keep getting pregnant. The rhythm method is a method that—at least in my case—produces, not prevents. Now I know why it's referred to in the secular world as "Vatican roulette."

Andy quit his job at Montgomery Ward when he started Barber College. Since it was after the Christmas rush, the store was okay with his leaving, but they said that he was a good employee, and if he wanted to come back, he'd be able to work for them again. Somehow the Hughes family managed to live on the $385 a month the GI Bill allowed.

Andy would come home from his barbering classes with a smile on his face, and Sara would run to him, hug him around the legs, and he'd lift her high in the air. When it was Daniel's turn to be lifted, he demanded to be swung around a bit too.

Britt was happy to see him happy. They were sitting around the supper table one night after a good meal, just relaxing, enjoying the last of their apple pie, when she asked him what it was about the school that he liked so much.

"The school reminds me of one of my favorite places to be when I was growing up—Mr. Monaghan's barbershop. Mr. Monaghan always let us kids come in there and read the comic books. If the talk got interesting, I'd just keep my face buried in a comic book, but I listened to the men talk—it was actually gossip. I learned a lot about life in that barbershop."

"I remember Mr. Monaghan's shop too. Haircuts were a buck—children for half that. Men coming in from the fields, dirty and tired, were able to get a shave for a quarter, and then for fifteen cents more, a hot shower. Mr. Monaghan only charged for the use of a bath towel. I know this because my dad would get his haircuts on Saturday nights, and he saw men making use of the barbershop to clean up for a Saturday night on the town. He thought that was a smart move on Mr. Monaghan's part, providing a service like that."

"Yeah, he's a good guy and a good businessman."

"You never cut a class, because going there reminds you of your favorite place—I can understand that. But haven't you *ever* had a bad school day?"

"No, I'd never cut classes—I like 'em, and I'm paying for them. But one day I cut a little slice off the top of a customer's ear. That was bad. It took about a quart of septic powder to get it to stop bleeding. That only happened once, though—that was enough." He carried his dishes over to the sink and turned around. "Remember the first time I tried to give Daniel a haircut? He squirmed and yelled so much I had to put him on the floor and sit on him before I was able to finish."

"It was about this time of the day too, after supper. Daniel really slept well that night."

With Andy so busy, Britt wished she could help by getting a job and making some money, but she was needed at home—two children and one on the way. Britt hauled out her little Singer sewing machine and helped in the only way she could—she sewed. Easter was coming, and they all wanted to look good in church on Easter Sunday. First she sewed a dress for Sara in turquoise, with a big bow in the back and in front, a wide, white Peter Pan collar to set off Sara's olive skin, curly brown hair, and deep brown eyes. She'd look like a living doll. For Daniel she sewed a medium gray vest and lined it with turquoise material left over from Sara's dress. With a white shirt and a little black bow tie and black trousers, he'd be one handsome guy. Her children were lucky—they looked like their father. And for their father, she made a regular tie, using one of his old ties that he never wore and ripping it up to get the pattern. The new tie was royal blue with a diagonal red stripe, his favorite colors. For her? Well, she was still living in a maternity tent for now, but she'd wear her best tent.

The night before Easter, she and Andy filled a small, straw Easter basket for each child, with a little chocolate bunny, some jelly beans, and a yellow marshmallow chick. A filled basket was put at the foot of each child's bed—a morning surprise.

The morning surprise destroyed Sara and Daniel's breakfast appetite, so they didn't mind that breakfast was skipped. Britt and Andy couldn't have breakfast because they were fasting in order to be able to go to Holy Communion—besides that, they had to leave home early in order to find seats. The church filled up fast for Easter Sunday Mass.

They entered the church and found seats near the front. Britt looked around and saw beautiful white lilies, symbols of purity, flanking both sides of the altar. The organ music touched her spiritual core, as it always did. Sara and Daniel may have been affected by the music too, as they behaved like little angels.

When it came time for Communion, Britt struggled inwardly. *I didn't do my penance. What the priest said about having thirteen children upset me so much I didn't remember what he said I should do for penance. If I don't go, what will*

Andy think? What will my children think? I have to go. I don't want to add any confusion to their lives. My being confused is enough. When Andy came back from Communion, Britt hoisted herself to her feet and got into the Communion line. *I do believe in God, even if I don't believe the Catholic church is right about everything.* She knelt at the altar and accepted the wafer the priest held out to her.

By the middle of May, they were able to move into low-income housing. McDonough Homes was practically brand-new, and it was wonderful. They had so much room—three bedrooms and a bathroom upstairs and a large living room and kitchen, with a real pantry, downstairs. They even had a basement for the washer, the dryer, and for storage. If they wanted to paint a room, they could. Britt had only one complaint—no bathroom downstairs. It was hard enough to teach little ones to use the bathroom, but when it was upstairs, it was doubly difficult. Sara adapted. She knew when she had to go and made it upstairs in time, but Daniel was still learning. Britt solved half the problem by keeping an empty can in the pantry for him. He had fun standing up, "just like Daddy," and peeing into a twelve-ounce juice can. Britt didn't mind taking the can upstairs and emptying it. It was a win-win for her—fewer clothes to wash and good exercise. With Sara, she did a lot of walking before she delivered. With Daniel, fewer walks, and with this one-to-be, hardly any exercise until now. Climbing stairs was good for her.

Eight months before the birth of their third child, the Soviet Union had launched Sputnik, a shiny beach-ball-sized satellite with four trailing antennas. Its "beep-beep" could be picked up by amateur radio operators around the world. With that launch, the world entered the Space Age, changing the thinking of people and governments. The United States was astonished and fearful; no one knew what Sputnik was capable of doing as it streaked across the sky. It jolted the United States out of recession. Money for math and science courses was forked over without complaint. The newest and best equipment filled school laboratories and classrooms. The United States was in a contest with Russia. The first attempts exploded—newspapers called them "Flopniks," but these failures made the nation even more determined to succeed. The National Aeronautics and Space Administration (NASA) was created in 1958 to bring the military into the effort.

Anthony, or "Tony" as Britt and Andy always called him, came into the world, into the Space Age, the same year that NASA was created. Tony arrived in St. Paul's Bethesda Hospital on June 15. Labor pains had started around noon on a Sunday, and Tony arrived just in time for Britt to have dinner. He was a big baby, twenty-two inches long and weighing in at nine pounds eleven ounces. It was an easy birth with very little anesthetic. Britt figured it was probably because two others had paved the way.

Later that night, she ran a fever. The hospital refused to release Britt or Tony until her temperature remained normal for twenty-four hours. It took a week. The hospital was installing oxygen pipes at the time. No quiet zone in this hospital. It would have failed the white-glove test too; dust swirled in the air. At least Britt had no worries about Sara and Daniel, aged three and two, because her sister, Hannah, still jobless, again came to the rescue and stayed until the hospital released Britt and Tony. God bless Hannah.

Tony must have absorbed the energy vibrating around our globe, for he would prove to be a very active child. Even in the womb, he had pushed against Britt's pelvic bones while at the same time punching or kicking her in the ribs. The last month of her pregnancy with him, Britt could use her bulge as a resting place for her dinner plate.

Thirty-five days after Tony would celebrate his eleventh birthday, the United States would put two humans on the moon, Neil Armstrong and Buzz Aldrin; they walked on the moon, the first ever to do so. Our nation's pride was redeemed.

That fall, Andy took the board apprentice examination, passed, and got his apprentice license. He could now work under the supervision of a master barber and be paid for it. As an apprentice, he needed to accumulate fifteen hundred hours of experience in one year, after which he could again go before the board and take the master (registered) barber examination. Passing that examination would enable him to supervise apprentice barbers and to own his own shop if he so desired. He did.

Andy chose to go back to the Hughes' hometown and work under the supervision of Mr. Monaghan, the barber who owned his favorite place of refuge and reading material as a child.

18

Immediate necessities all packed and loaded into the old gray Ford with the covered-up hole in the floor, the Hughes family traveled north back to Great Prairie, their old hometown where Andy would be Mr. Monaghan's apprentice. He was happy, proud of what he'd accomplished, and looking forward to what he hoped to accomplish in a year—master barber. Someday he would own his own shop.

Britt had mixed feelings. She was proud of her husband, happy that he'd completed school and would be earning money. Her parents would let them stay with them until Andy and Britt found a place of their own in town. Then Andy and his brother, Luke, the one who spilled the ham on the floor so many years ago, would drive back to St. Paul in Britt's father's grain truck, with a three-sided box, to pick up the rest of their belongings. Britt looked down at Tony, asleep in her arms. *Another fresh start—I hope it's a good one. I've had a baby in each place we've lived—Sara in Newport, Daniel in Chelsea, Tony in St. Paul. Now we're going to settle, for a while at least, in our hometown. Will I have another baby here? I've missed a period. Am I already pregnant?*

While packing up to move, she realized that she was late. It could be the anxiety of another move, but then when she didn't want her morning coffee, she began to panic. She'd rush to the bathroom, closing and locking the door, flipping the lid down on the toilet and just sit, her heart pounding. *Thank God, some peace and quiet! I thought I'd lose it for a while there with all the chaos of packing. I need to calm down and quit all this worrying.* She got up, unbuttoned and unzipped her jeans, and pulled them and her panties down. For the eighth time that day, she checked for blood—nothing. She even felt inside herself just in case some blood was just starting to come down. *Oh, no, I can't be pregnant ... how late am I? God, you know I can't take another pregnancy. Please, please, let my period start. What will I tell Andy? He's a hard worker, but an apprentice barber doesn't make very much. He can only do what Mr. Monaghan lets him do. How can I lay this on him? I want him to enjoy being home. He never wants to be like his father who did a poor job of supporting his family. He worries that having too big a family will be just too much.*

They found an apartment right away—the only apartment to be had in that small town. But what an apartment! Britt immediately thought of the movie *Beyond the Forest*, in which Bette Davis said, "What a dump!" It was a dump, and it sat in the middle of a collection of farm machinery, farm machinery dealers, and a grain elevator or two. The dump was an old, white, two-story house converted into small apartments.

The makeshift closet off the kitchen held all their clothes. At the other end of this shotgun arrangement was the children's bedroom. It was so small that only one foot separated Tony's crib from the bunk beds, stacked, where his sister and brother slept. Between the kitchen and the children's bedroom was the living room by day and master bedroom by night. When the hide-a-bed was opened, transforming the living room into a bedroom, it almost touched their Zenith television set—the set that Britt had tried to lift, which resulted in her water breaking and Daniel coming three weeks before his due date.

Sardines in a can, that's what we are. But sardines are lucky—they're dead. That was not the worst of it. Down the hall was *the* bathroom, serving fourteen people—six adults and eight children. Sometimes when Britt entered it, provided she could even *gain* entry, she was confronted by a sink with little specks and some balls the size of popcorn—feces. Britt's mother never came to see her in that apartment. Britt didn't think that she was still upset about Britt turning Catholic. Perhaps she was just too busy, or maybe she thought, *She's made her bed; now she has to lie in it.* Her father came to see her once but didn't come a second time. Perhaps he couldn't stand to see his daughter living in such a hole. And then he got the mumps! Almost sixty years old, and he had the mumps. Of course he couldn't expose Britt and the children to that.

Britt made an appointment with the doctor; she must be three months along now. It was quite a hassle to go to a doctor because now the nearest one was twenty-five miles away. Dr. Karsten, who had fitted her for a diaphragm after she'd had Daniel, was now living in Minneapolis. Andy would have to take half a day off and babysit while she drove to the doctor's office. Britt rather liked that. It was peaceful driving.

Dr. Arnold, a graying, pudgy, comfortable doctor, put Britt at ease. She could talk to him. He helped her get up onto the examining table, putting her feet in the customary stirrups.

"Yes, you are pregnant—about three months along I'd say ... should be born in August." He helped her down from the examining table. "Are you eating all that you should? You should gain some weight." He turned, his back to Britt, as she put on her panties and straightened her skirt.

"Sometimes I just don't have any appetite for anything. We live in such a small place it seems that I'm constantly breaking up fights."

"I know you have three little ones, but can't somebody help you out once in a while?"

"Would you believe it, my fifty-nine-year-old father has the mumps, and besides my mother has eight-year-old twin boys to take care of. They keep her running. My mother-in law works, and I wouldn't want Andy's father to sit—I don't think he cares much for children. Besides, he's away from home a lot. My husband works every day. No, it's my responsibility."

"Try to rest and to eat more. You're eating for two now." He reached into a cabinet and took out two brown bottles. "The little bottle is iron. Take one a day—you look too pale. The other bottle contains prenatal vitamins. Take one a day of those too. That's it. Make an appointment for next month on your way out."

"Dr. Arnold, I don't want to get pregnant for a long time after I have this one. Andy and I are like rabbits the way we keep having babies. Do you have a pill to halt this baby production?"

"I sure do." He held out his hand, palm up. On it sat a little white pill. "Aspirin. Just hold it between your knees and keep it there every time your husband gets frisky."

Britt felt her face flush with rage. She'd be crying if she weren't so angry. Without a word, she turned on her heel and left.

When she reached their apartment house, she parked on the street in front, sat for a while, and then got out of the car. Andy, carrying Tony and with Sara and Daniel trailing behind him, came toward her. *I'm glad he put their coats on—it's cold.* Britt held out her arms, and Andy walked into them, hugging her with his left arm. Tony put a sticky arm around her neck. "Mama." Sara and Daniel wanted in on this, so each grabbed one of Andy's legs and hugged it.

"Andy, I need to go upstairs to our apartment—alone—for a while. Could you please keep them out here with you for a little while?"

"Sure." He removed his and Tony's arms, and she left. "Come on, kids, let's go for a little ride."

Brit threw herself down on the hide-a-bed and cried. The crying soon turned into howling, and she pounded the throw pillow and then threw it across the room. Her tears threatened to dissolve her. She wished they would. Her sobs turned into hiccups, and she curled into ball of sodden misery. Andy tiptoed in, carrying Tony and with the other two close behind him—all had their eyes open wide as they stared at their mother. Andy touched her shoulder.

"We could hear you. You almost set the neighborhood dogs to howling."

Britt sat up, face blotched and eyes swollen, and said, "There'll be no more tears. Come into the kitchen and keep me company while I fix all of us something to eat."

Next visit, Britt was a mess, a nervous wreck. Dr. Arnold felt her stomach and listened to the baby's heart. "Things are progressing nicely." He gave her more vitamins, looked at her face, at her expression, and added a prescription for antidepressants. *I must look awful. Does he know I've thought of suicide? But I couldn't do it. I don't want anyone else to raise my children—but if I were to crack, what kind of a mother would I be? Andy would be better off without me popping out a baby every year or so.* Britt walked out, but she heard Dr. Arnold say, "Make an appointment at the desk." On the way home, she stopped at the drugstore and filled the prescription.

Britt skipped a visit, so the next time she saw Dr. Arnold, she was in her sixth month. The antidepressants had helped her—the rage in her stomach that always gave way to depression had lessened. Maybe the baby kicked it out. Yes, she felt the little one kicking, and that helped her the most. She didn't want to die anymore. Britt wanted to see the person inside her, to nourish and raise this little person.

Labor pains started a little after eight in the evening. Andy and Britt were watching the *Ed Sullivan Show,* one of their favorites. Herding the three kids and pregnant wife into the old gray Ford, Andy gunned the engine and took off for the hospital twenty-five miles away. August weather in northern Minnesota can be frying-pan hot, and it stays hot into the night, so their car windows were all the way down in front and half down in the back—didn't want to lose anyone on the way. The faster he drove, but not exceeding the speed limit, of course, the cooler the car. Andy dropped Britt off and then drove back home to babysit and await news of yet another baby's birth.

Amy Hughes came into the world at 9:52 p.m., on August 22, 1960. She weighed in at six pounds, eight ounces. It wasn't an easy entrance for either of them. When the nurse checked Britt's birth canal for the extent of cervical dilation, she found that the baby was ready to come, but the face was in the "up" position in the birth canal.

"Dr. Arnold, the baby's head is down but in the faceup position. Are you going to deliver it that way?"

"I could, but the baby won't be able to flex the head on exit, and labor will be harder and longer for the mother." He shook his head and said, "Too bad—only one in every five hundred babies nestles down faceup. If I don't turn the baby, I might even end up doing a C-section."

"I hope not. That would mean a longer recovery time for the mother, and she has three more little ones at home."

"There's no getting around it. I'll have to turn the baby to a facedown position. It's going to hurt, but it will be better for both of them."

Britt heard all this, but she figured she'd be out of it before the real pain struck. She had discussed anesthesia with Dr. Arnold. She told him that ether made her sick. Britt had had her appendix out when she was thirteen, so she knew this. Dr. Arnold said he'd give her some gas instead—he called it "laughing gas." That name struck Britt as being completely inappropriate, considering the situation. But by the time Britt was in the delivery room, the anesthetist had gone home.

The doctor began to turn the baby, and it hurt. Britt screamed. *Am I being gutted like a deer?* She was given a couple whiffs of ether—it didn't help much. She wanted to get up and run away, but she was strapped down. Britt screamed and screamed—it hurt so much. Mrs. Strid, the delivery nurse, started slapping her, first on one side of her face and then the other, whipping Britt's head around. The baby turned, thank God! And Amy slipped into the world.

The next morning, the nurse, *not* Mrs. Strid, for which Britt was thankful, brought Amy in so mother and child could get acquainted. A wealth of straight, brown hair framed beautiful, dark blue eyes (they later turned green like Britt's). Amy, named after Britt's Newport friend, the one who watched Daniel when she took Sara to the hospital, was alert and latched onto the breast with gusto. Britt looked down at her new baby. She was responsible for the lives she'd brought into the world, and because of that, she made a decision. *If I get pregnant again, I'm going on the pill as soon as the baby is born. I've read about it, and the FDA approved it in 1960. Pastor Thomas, when he visited me in the hospital after the snowplow hit our car six years ago, said that I was bound for hell because I'd married a Catholic. According to him, hell was my destiny. But I don't want to be living there now, nor do I want my family to live in squalor. I'll raise my children the best I know how, and I'll help Andy support the family and realize his dreams. As my mother said so many times, "God helps those who help themselves."*

Four days later, Andy brought them home—back to the dump. But a little white crib was waiting for Amy, snugged up against the TV set. Two months later, they moved to a more spacious ground-floor apartment, with a bathroom for them alone. Britt never forgot one incident that occurred in the old dump before they left it.

I had gone to the bathroom, and when I reentered our apartment, there was Daniel, sitting on the folded-up hide-a-bed, with Amy on his lap. She was maybe two weeks old. How in the world did Daniel get her out of her little crib? Had she been crying, and he had become concerned? But he was only four years old! A quote from Shakespeare helped me deal: "All's well that ends well." And it certainly looked as if it had ended well. Daniel looked pleased with himself, and Amy was content.

Amy was an easy baby; as long as she was fed and kept clean and dry, she was at peace with the world. "Dada" was her first word—she was twelve months old. Two months later, she came out with "Mama." Another month, and she said her first four-word sentence: "Mommy, wait for me!"

CHAPTER

19

Unlike Tony, who grew impatient with nursing when he was four months old, preferring the faster squirt of a bottle to his mother's breast, Amy loved to nurse. Britt would try to sneak in a bottle of milk now and then, but Amy would get all red-faced and angry, turning her head from side to side and refusing to suck. That meant it would be awhile before Britt could start taking her temperature and graphing it to determine her fertile period. She was giving the rhythm method one last chance. Scuttlebutt had it that a woman could not get pregnant as long as she was nursing. Britt did not trust this—she'd heard of too many women who had been "caught" by believing this. Britt and Andy needed to talk.

The week before her six-weeks checkup with Dr. Arnold— the checkup that tells a woman if she's all healed up inside and can now have sex with her husband, Britt and Andy had that talk.

"Andy, my checkup with Dr. Arnold is in a week, but don't get any ideas. I have to start taking my temperature again, for a couple of months before we do anything." She put on her green full-length robe over her nightgown.

"I know. We waited when you nursed Tony. It wasn't easy, that's for sure." He walked over and gave her a swift hug. "You just keep covering from head to toe as you did just now, and we can make it."

"But this time it will be longer. Amy simply will not accept the bottle! It might be an eight-month wait. That's an awfully long time." She slid her bare feet into her slippers and sat down on the bed, patting a place beside her for Andy. "I could probably force her to take the bottle—her survival instinct wouldn't let her starve. But that would be so mean. And breast milk is the best."

"She shouldn't be deprived because of us." He looked her square in the eyes. "I can take it if you can."

"Wait. I should tell you something else. I decided that if the rhythm method fails again, I'm going to go on the pill after the next baby." Britt looked down at her hands, clenching and unclenching, in her lap. "We can't keep having child after child—I know I can't, and you must be worried too."

"What's this pill you're talking about?"

"There's a pill, approved by the FDA in 1957, for use by doctors for severe menstrual disorders. You'd be surprised, or maybe not, by the number of women who now have severe menstrual disorders." She folded her hands and squeezed them between her knees to keep them quiet. "I'm tempted to try and convince a doctor that *I* have severe menstrual disorders, but no doctor would believe I've even had a period. I just hope the FDA approves it for birth control by the time I want it."

"I won't object to your using it, *if* you get pregnant again. Barbers never get rich. If I can't support my family, I'll feel—I'll feel like a failure." He turned his head and looked everywhere but at her. He stuck out his hand. "Like I said, if you can do it, I can. Shake on it?"

As the weeks went by, tension mounted in the Hughes household. Britt was glad that he was working hard and brushing up on all he'd learned in barber college so that he'd be ready to take the examination for master barber in November. He usually came home tired, a good thing in their situation. If he wasn't tired, he'd go to his parents' house, a block and a half away, and play some cards—penny-ante poker was their favorite. Sometimes he and his brother would hang out on the golf course, but then cold weather and snow came, putting the kibosh on that, so they went hunting: rabbits, ducks, geese, and then deer. After those seasons were over, they went ice-fishing—drilling a hole on a frozen lake and putting down a baited fish line.

If he had to stay home, he was quiet and withdrawn, treating Britt like a stranger and disciplining the children for the least little thing. It wasn't easy for Britt either. A sexually frustrated husband is hard to live with. Though she wasn't needy like Andy, she felt guilty because she knew she was denying him, even though he'd agreed—they'd even shaken hands—on the self-imposed celibacy.

After they reached the four-month mark, the tension in the home was affecting the children too, turning them into little monsters. They fought with each other and whined and cried—even Amy was irritable. *This is not how marriage is supposed to be. I know we don't live in the Garden of Eden, but we don't have to live in hell either.*

In the Garden of Eden, God gave only two commands to his newly created, naked humans: "be fruitful and multiply" and "don't eat fruit from the Tree of Knowledge of Good and Evil." Andy and I have certainly obeyed the first command, the one about multiplying. Anymore multiplying right now could ruin our marriage, could cause a permanent division. Enough arithmetic—I never liked that subject much.

The other command of God, "don't eat from the Tree of Knowledge of Good and Evil" was disobeyed. Truth-tellers sprouted from the earth like weeds—all proclaiming to know what was good and what was evil. All their truths were different, but all said their definitions were the only true ones. Britt's definition of good was that which made her family happier and closer together.

"Andy, you were saying that your shipmates had some ideas about how to make lack of sex more bearable in a marriage. What were they? This celibacy between married people is wrong. Tell me about those ideas."

Andy's face reddened as he said, "Really? Are you sure? I'll show you tonight after the kids are asleep." He wiped his sweaty hands on his jean-clad thighs.

That night, and other nights when needed until Amy would go on the bottle, they made love without intercourse.

Naked, as were Adam and Eve, they caressed and massaged each other. They hadn't realized how starved they were for skin-on-skin contact. Her nakedness, seeing all of her, aroused him. Her breasts, nursing breasts, were full, and he tasted them. She pressed against him and with her hand, relieved him. She welcomed his soft groans of relief.

He became concerned about her pleasure on another night. The guys on the ship told him that girls loved it when guys went "down" on them. Britt found this hard to wrap her mind around, but if the fruit of the Tree of Knowledge hadn't been eaten, no one would have thought this was wrong. She gave in. He tasted her sweetness and could hold back no longer—the excitement was too great. Britt found it was exciting too, but whenever it threatened to become too exciting, she could hear her mother's voice: "If it starts to feel good, stop!" She preferred hugging, kissing, and caressing.

Andy liked kissing too; he loved her mouth. He coaxed her to take his hardness into his mouth. Sometimes she would but not often. She didn't like it—it activated her gag reflex.

They made it through to the eighth month with their marriage intact, a fat and happy breastfed Amy and older children who didn't fight, whine, or cry as much.

In November, Andy took his exam and became a master barber. He could now own a barbershop, if he so chose. He could also be an instructor, a mentor, to an apprentice barber. Then he heard that Robert Stenshol, a barber in Rillstead, fifty miles from Great Prairie, was getting ready to retire soon. He wanted a master barber to work with him for a while until he sold his shop in the fall, at which time he and his wife would move to the Southwest. Andy went to see him, and they struck a deal whereby Andy could buy the business for a down payment of $2,000 and an additional payment of $2,500, paid off in amounts of twenty-five dollars a month until it was all paid up, provided that, after working in the shop for three months, Andy still wanted to buy it.

Andy rented a room in Rillstead, and slept there at night—the commute would have been too long. He barbered Tuesday through Saturday, leaving for Great Prairie after work on Saturday, and driving back to Rillstead Monday night. The three months went by fast. It was time for Andy to make a decision, but first he had to talk it over with Britt. They had their talk on a cold February Monday, Andy's day off, as they lingered over their morning coffee.

"My three months with Mr. Stenshol are up. We have to decide whether to buy his shop or not. If I don't buy it, he'll try and find another buyer." Andy poured himself another cup of coffee.

"It's your dream to own your own shop, but is this a good shop? Would you have enough business?" Britt looked at Andy, her eyebrows lowered—she looked worried, and her hands, tearing a paper napkin to shreds, proved it.

"I've kept track of my customers—*my* customers, the ones that choose me, and quite a few of them do. If I owned the shop, they all would. I'd make more than I made at Montgomery Ward, and we managed okay with my salary then. And I'll grow the business ..."

"Whoa! You're jumping the gun. We don't have enough money."

"I know, but if I let this opportunity slip through my fingers, I may never get another chance to have my own place." He got up, put his cup in the sink, and started pacing back and forth across the kitchen floor. "Do you think your father would lend us enough for the down payment?"

"Go talk to him. He likes you." Britt rose to clear away the breakfast dishes.

"I'll do it today—right now. No sense putting it off." He went to the coat closet, grabbed his storm coat and cap with the ear flaps, and headed out the door.

Andy drove to Great Prairie and found his father-in-law in his potato house, sorting potatoes for a shipment to go out the next day.

"Carl, I need to talk to you. Let's go to the pool hall. I'll buy you a cup of coffee and a piece of apple pie."

Carl smiled. He never could turn down apple pie. They set off walking the two blocks. They talked about the weather, about the latest snowfall—six inches—and how cold it was, minus ten degrees. Though Carl was a taller and heavier man, their strides matched, and they soon reached the pool hall.

Two other men were there—that's all. The pool hall never had much business on a Monday. Carl and Andy went to the back and sat in a booth. "Pop," the owner and only waiter of the pool hall, came over for their order.

"This is on me," Andy said. "Two coffees—bring sugar and cream—and two pieces of apple pie." He rested his forearms on the table, hands folded, and got down to business.

"I have a chance to get my own barbershop," Andy cleared his throat, "but the barber, who is retiring, wants two thousand dollars down, and I'm broke. I'm asking you to loan us the down payment."

Carl looked him in the eye for a long minute. Andy looked right back. Pop came with their coffee and pie, breaking the stare-down.

"You do need to settle down," Carl said. "It's not good for children to be moving around like gypsies, not good for my daughter either. She needs to be in her own house. What's that barber in Rillstead—Stenshol, isn't it?—asking for his place?" Carl quit eating and put his elbows on the table and folded his hands in front of his chin.

"Two thousand dollars down and twenty-five dollars a month until I've paid him a total of $4,500."

"Is it worth the price?"

"We've been very busy—I've been busy. I've got men and boys who wait for me to cut their hair. It's worth the price."

"Two thousand it is."

"Yes, sir."

"Here's the deal. When you've paid off all you owe and the shop is yours, then it's my turn. Twenty dollars each month." Carl held out his hand, and Andy shook it. "Now let's finish our pie. Can't let that go to waste."

Mr. Stenshol had told Andy of a place for rent not far from the shop. Andy could walk to work, and Britt could have the use of the old gray Ford in case she needed it. With young children, you never knew when an emergency might crop up. Britt was thankful that the apartment was on the ground floor. It had only two bedrooms, but they could partition the bigger bedroom with screens to make two small bedrooms. She'd use the same technique they'd used in country school when constructing a stage for the Christmas program—hung sheets on wires. And soon—how exciting!—they'd be house-hunting in Rillstead.

Rillstead was settled by homesteaders who were attracted by the small stream (rill) that coursed through the valley and by the depth of the fertile topsoil. Small at first, it grew quickly, especially after the addition of a railroad. In the fifties, the population was about fifty thousand, and it boasted of an agricultural college and a university. Two hospitals, Bethesda and St. Francis, took care of Rillstead's sick. Public and private schools dotted the suburbs. Catholic high schools separated the girls from the boys. Several churches—most people could find their preferred denomination—were quite evenly balanced by barrooms and cocktail lounges. Shopping was superb. Two large department stores dominated the downtown area—one actually had an elevator! It was a city on the move.

Britt knew this place. She had attended two years of college here before she married Andy. Frustrated at not being able to settle on a major, she opted for marriage to Andy and a chance to see the world. That was her vision, but it didn't pan out. Her world ended up consisting mainly of cleaning up messes—dirty dishes and diapers, dusting, spit-ups, and scrubbing, and the ever present snotty noses—all within four walls.

Britt had met Jesse at the university. They'd gone out a

couple of times, and then he'd joined the army. He wrote to her, telling her where he was and asking her to write to him. She didn't write to him. She was already married. Britt thought of him from time to time—sometimes while bending over the diaper pail. *What would my life have been like if I hadn't married, and instead I'd answered Jesse's letter? Or if I'd finished college—became a nutritionist or a dress designer? Ridiculous. Wishful thinking is wasteful thinking.*

Eight months after Amy quit the breast, Britt was again pregnant—she would give birth to her fifth child in Rillstead. *This is where we're making our home. This is where I'll have our last baby.*

CHAPTER

20

Andy worked five days a week, but Sundays and Mondays—barbers had Mondays off—they looked for a house.

Britt wanted a house on a tree-lined street, close to a grade school, a park, and a library. She did not want to spend her days chauffeuring children around. Cherry Street was promising, and a house there would also be close to a hockey arena; that would keep the boys busy when they were older. It would have to be a traditional looking house so that early American furniture would look good in it. She liked her mother's Tel City maple furniture. Britt would make lots of throw pillows—not fancy ones, just comfortable ones. She felt about throw pillows the way others might feel about comfort food. The pillows must be soft, colorful, and inviting, the kind that, after a punch or two, would fit your head like an old, soft and floppy hat.

Sidewalks, extensive sidewalks, were another must. She wanted her children to enjoy roller-skating, riding their trikes, and just walking around the neighborhood. She and Hannah had learned to roller skate in a dim, dank basement, and the floor had a few cracks in it. Their skates were fastened to their shoes with clamps tightened by a roller skate key. The skating also created concrete dust. It got boring pretty fast—just going around and around. Soon they used their skates as cars or trucks for their clothespin dolls.

A fenced-in backyard was also on the must-have list. Britt would never, never forget Sara's narrow escape. She could have died but for the roadside curb that prevented the garbage truck from squashing her flat.

They found their home, one built in the 1920s. It was on Cherry Street, within walking distance of a school, a library, and a park. It had sidewalks in all directions, and it had a small, fenced-in backyard. A gable jutted from the north and another from the south roof area. Virginia creeper crawled up the west side of the house, turning bright red in the fall, according to the neighbors. Warm gray stucco with windows framed in red, it also sported a full-length screened porch on the front of the one-and-a-half-story house or bungalow—a place where children could safely play.

To enter the front door, they had to come in the front porch door and walk across the width of the porch to reach the front door. Entering the front door, they understood why the house was listed as a fixer-upper. The large, rectangular living/dining room's ceiling was wallpapered in a faded maroon, and long strips of it hung down as much as three feet. But the windows were lovely, arranged in threes on each side of the front door, and in twos on the east and the west. The top half of all the windows in the house had framed "lights." With twenty-four windows in the house, heat would be expensive at nineteen cents a gallon, but they'd have plenty of light to brighten the dark, cold, cloudy winter days—priceless. First floor also had a half bath next to a kitchen with built-in cabinets and it had a small bedroom—the master bedroom.

Upstairs were two more bedrooms, a large one on the east in which the boys would sleep and an even larger one with an "ell"—for the girls. A bathroom with a claw-footed tub was across from the boys' room, and a little farther down the hall, a storage area with a slanted ceiling. It would just fit the Hughes family.

A full basement was under it all. Going down to the basement, which they could do immediately upon coming in the back door, was a journey into the dark unknown. First you'd come face-to-face with an asbestos-clad, many-tentacled monster. It was the furnace, and it took up a large part of the basement. In the northwest corner stood the fuel oil tank, cradled in its steel rack. A northeast room had built-in shelves for canned goods and preserves. To the southeast was a workbench with a window above it. The southwest corner was the domain of the washer and dryer—a clothes chute on the second floor dumped its load in front of the washer.

The walls were plastered, with very few cracks under the layers of wallpaper—no sheetrock in this house. All doors closed without any sticking, evidence that there was no settling in this house either. Walnut-stained woodwork was in terrific shape throughout the house. This was definitely a fixer-upper worth fixing.

Before Andy could apply for the GI Bill housing loan, the house had to be inspected. An inspector came out and said that if a jack post was put in the basement, between the workbench and the food storage room for added support of the upstairs floor, the house would pass. That was done, the papers sent in, and the loan came through. It was a twenty-year loan in the amount of $10,500. Every month, for twenty years, Andy made a payment of eighty-five dollars. (A local bank soon took over the loan from the federal government.)

The Hughes family moved into their new home on June 12, 1962.

So much to do, and a baby was due at any time. Pressure! Britt felt she had to get things cleaned and set up fast. All the kitchen cupboards had to be scrubbed before the dishes, utensils, pots, and pans could be put away. Beds had to be made and floors scrubbed. Run to the post office and change the address. Connect the telephone and the TV. Arrange for regular milk delivery—important with four children in the house. There seemed no end to all that needed doing. Britt was worn out.

The June weather was hot and sticky, so Andy put a picnic table out on the screened-in porch. The kids loved it. They ate out there, and they played out there even when it rained, and they were safe from mosquitoes. (Minnesotans sometimes joke that the mosquito is the state bird.)

Five days into their new home, with Britt on her hands and knees, scrubbing the upstairs hallway, she felt a contraction, then another. By six at night, the contractions were five minutes apart and Andy was home from work. Six in the car and a baby on the way, they sped the six blocks to St. Francis Hospital.

In the labor room, the nurse jabbed Britt with a hypodermic needle with something in it to relax her. And that it did! The contractions stopped, and she fell asleep and slept for twelve hours—a much-needed rest.

The next morning, Dr. Evans, an obstetrician, came in to see Britt. "After breakfast, you get up and walk, and you keep walking up and down this hall. We've got to get those contractions started again." So she spent most of her day walking, and it worked—the contractions began again.

The birth was easy. It just took three good pushes before they plopped a baby on Britt's stomach. The baby was covered with whitish stuff—like a waxed parsnip. Britt could see bluish pink skin through the wax. This was another sight she'd never seen in the four previous births. The baby cried, and Britt laughed.

The little one weighed in at seven pounds, nine and one-half ounces, and was nineteen and one-half inches long—a nice healthy baby girl with brown hair. Once she was cleaned up, the nurse let Britt hold her. Britt looked at the tiny red face and smiled. "Hello, Laura."

Coming home a few days later to a home that they owned was wonderful. Laura slept in her parents' room, in the same little white crib that had originally been her uncle Owen's. Later that summer, the family went on a day trip to Park Rapids where they fed the deer in Deer Town. When they returned, they found a litter of newborn kittens in Laura's crib, nuzzling their gray mother, Fluffy, searching for dinner.

Laura was a good baby—no colic, no allergies, and she slept through the night when she was three months old. Britt and Andy now had a total of five healthy children all born in different places with different doctors in attendance—one for each finger of a hand; one might call it a handful. And what do you call five children in seven years? According to Britt, "Too much to handle."

At her six-weeks checkup with the doctor, she asked him to write her a prescription for the pill. After three months of nursing, she put Laura on the bottle and then filled the prescription, grateful that after FDA approval two years ago, it was now available more widely for birth control.

Britt's father, along with the hired man and twins, William and Owen, almost ten years old, started the repair of this fixer-upper. They installed a new roof on the garage. Armed with a box of tools, they took off the old shake shingles, laid down heavy black tar paper on the roof, and then they nailed down new shingles of heavy asphalt in a gray that matched the stucco of the house. First big project done.

Britt did most of the second big project—though Andy, Sara, and Daniel pitched in when it suited them—the removal of seven layers of wallpaper off the living/dining room walls. Wallpaper had to be removed from the ceiling too, but thank goodness the ceiling had only one layer to remove. Under the wallpaper was a powdery substance, calcimine. Britt learned that it was a wash or covering for walls containing zinc and glue. She learned firsthand that it was quite a challenge to remove. It had to be soaked and then scrubbed off with soap and water. It was a drippy mess. Eventually wallpaper was removed from all walls that had it, and then the rooms were painted. A tedious, horrible job—it took more than a year—but the outcome was worth it. Things were shaping up.

The Hughes family spent a quarter of a century in their Cherry Street house. In 1971, the front porch was removed. The children didn't need a porch to play in anymore, and the screens were getting tattered. They wanted a more direct entrance into the house—always entering the porch first was a nuisance. They utilized all the space where the covered front porch had been to construct a den, a foyer, and a side entrance from the west with a Gainsborough blue front door that opened onto the foyer. The beautiful living room windows were now the windows of the den.

Though gone, memories of the old front porch linger on. It was the place where you could bed down in your sleeping bag on a hot, sticky August night and get a little breeze.

Amy had a slumber party out there when she was nine. Unbeknownst to her parents, she and five little "nudies" streaked to the streetlight one-fourth of a block away.

Britt well remembers two-year-old Laura toddling out there to see what that moving yellow thing was. It was a goldfish in a bowl. Someone had taken it out there—to give the fish some sun?—and set it on a wide sill. Laura picked it up and dropped it. Water and glass shards flew, and a piece of glass grazed Laura's forehead. It bled a lot—head wounds do. Britt wrapped a dishtowel around Laura's head, carried her to the car, and off they sped to the hospital five blocks away. It wasn't as bad as it looked, but Laura still carries a small scar right below her hairline. The fate of the fish? No one knows. There were bad times, of course, but more good times, and there were never any boring times.

A baby robin, just starting to get feathers, fell out of his nest. Sara picked him up, put him on the porch, rounded up all the neighbor kids, and set them to work digging for worms. They kept the worm supply coming, until one day the robin flew away.

Those things all happened on the porch, but the house itself witnessed many more events, both bad and good.

Of the bad times, the following stand out: two broken bones (Tony broke his jaw slipping on ice and landing on the concrete back steps, and Laura broke her elbow falling off a horse); numerous cuts and bruises; poison ivy; measles and chicken pox; fights and squabbles—often between Daniel and Tony but also between children and parents over the amount of an allowance, who does the dishes, curfew times, proper skirt length, and which TV program to watch.

Of the good times, these stand out: bringing a new baby (Laura) into a new home and witnessing her first smile, her first step, and her first word ("Dada"); birthday parties—two for every child, one when a child turned six, and the other when a child became a teenager; five bicycles—the nine-year-old birthday gift; trick or treating—sometimes with a snowsuit worn over the costume; dressing up for the prom and having your picture taken before you went out the door;

two graduation receptions—all of the children graduated from high school, but only two had receptions because the idea of a reception after graduation was just becoming an "in" thing; Easter baskets; and Christmas with the grandparents.

These memories seeped into every corner of the house on Cherry Street, where life was not always a bowl of cherries, but at times, it most definitely was.

CHAPTER

2 1

Andy's shop was doing well. He enjoyed being a barber and talking to his customers. He even enjoyed sweeping hair off the floor—hair of all colors and textures; it was a sign of his success. He worked in his clean shop with his clean hands and felt good about himself.

In 1964, the year that Laura turned two, the Hughes family started camping. It seemed to them an economical and family friendly way of enjoying Minnesota's many parks and excellent camping facilities.

Andy bought a big tent, one with two side rooms for sleeping. Britt sewed seven "fart sacks" to use in the sleeping bags—a top and a bottom sheet rolled into one, easy to remove and wash. She also made each one a "ditty" bag that had a drawstring closure. The ditty bags were for dirty clothes. They bought a secondhand, homemade camp kitchen. It fit right in the trunk and carried dishes, silverware, a couple pans, and a few utensils. Add a Coleman stove, which they did, and they were all set to enjoy Minnesota's many lakes and state parks.

Being a barber and having Monday off was an advantage. They would drive into a park before noon, scope everything out, especially the campsite, maybe do some fishing or rent a boat, and then when the Sunday people started to leave their campsites, they'd move into a vacated one, usually a site that was close to a beach and close to the restrooms. Mondays the entire park was almost theirs alone. It was the ideal mini-vacation for a family with an ample number of kids.

The first year they camped, Sara was nine and spent her time catching tadpoles, snakes, frogs, minnows, anything she could, and searching for interesting stones and shells. She wanted to earn a brown Camp Fire Girls bead, the Outdoors and Environment bead. She went fishing with her brothers—Daniel, eight years old, and Tony, six—if they let her. Sara and Daniel, only eleven months apart, were very competitive. Sara thought she should have her way because she was older. Daniel thought he should have his way because that's the way the world worked—boys were the bosses. Needless to say, they fought a lot.

Daniel fished most often with his brother, Tony, who usually caught the biggest fish; failing that, he'd catch the most fish. *Why are some people luckier at catching fish than others? I'm one of the unlucky ones, so I don't even bother.* Though both could swim, they had to wear their bright orange life jackets when fishing or boating. Sometimes Sara, the boys, and their dad got up early, rented a boat, and fished for hours, all wearing life jackets—Andy had to set a good example. Britt, Amy, and Laura would sleep late and take their time rolling out of the sleeping bags. They lay, looking up at the tent ceiling as birds walked overhead. Tiring of that, it was time for breakfast and then the beach.

Amy was four, and she kept her eye on her little sister. Britt was Laura's mother, but Amy was her second mother. They filled their buckets and built sand castles with moats around them. They walked along the water's edge looking for pretty stones and shells—not easy for Laura. At two years old, she'd stumble at times and come home with Amy leading her by the hand and her bottom leaking lake water and scratchy with sand. Britt, sitting on a beach towel trying to get a little tan, kept her eye on them. *They are even closer than Hannah and I were. Lucky girls!*

When Daniel was twelve, the camp-outs stopped. Most Minnesota and North Dakota parks have poison ivy, and Daniel was very susceptible. The other children and Britt were allergic to poison ivy too but not to the extent that Daniel was. Andy never got poison ivy. The last year they camped, Daniel picked up such a bad case of poison ivy that he had to be hospitalized. The doctor told Britt and Andy that the steroids he had to give Daniel should not be used often. He suggested that they quit camping. Daniel never said anything. He was more of a doer than a talker, but he may have been relieved—not only because he'd now escape the itchy poison ivy rash but because he'd also escape sleeping in a tent, a claustrophobic experience for him.

On the whole, camping had been a lot of fun, but it was time to give it up, not only because of Daniel but because other activities were starting to fill the children's lives.

The children were developing their own characters, their own personalities, with no duplicates. Britt had often wished that they would have come with instructions, maybe a guidebook. But they grew so fast! She probably wouldn't have had time to read a guidebook on each one anyway. She had trouble keeping up with their baby books, presents given by Grandma Anderson after the birth of each one.

A fine day in 1971, school was out for the summer, and Britt sat at the kitchen table, enjoying an extra cup of breakfast coffee in peaceful solitude. The others had left the house—Andy for the barber shop and the children for park board summer activities. The sun shone down on Britt, and the birds sang to her—"God's in His heaven; all's right with the world." She took another sip of coffee, luxuriating.

The back door banged shut, and Sara burst into the kitchen. "Mom, I'm a Treasurette!" She ran over and hugged her mother, beaming with pleasure.

Britt looked at her. *She's glowing—I can't believe she's so grown up ... already taller than I.* Boys had crushes on her—they couldn't resist her dark brown eyes and long dark hair, which she often ironed so it would be straight and not curly. At sixteen, she could date, but she wasn't much interested. Just three years ago she was dancing on the coffee table to Beatles' songs. Three Dog Night was her favorite rock band, and she had dreams of becoming a veterinarian someday. "What's a Treasurette?"

"We're the group that wears short skirts, carry pompoms, except me—I carry a drum. I'm the drummer."

"When does this happen?"

"Halftime at football games and in the gym at pep rallies—whenever the school wants us to. We practice in the summer."

"I see. What about your paper route?" Sara had taken a paper route, joining her brothers in this endeavor two years ago. She wanted to earn money to buy a miniature dachshund from her uncle Luke, whose female dachshund had regular litters.

"I'm only doing the Sunday paper from now on. Mr. Swanson said it's okay if I cut down. And I told him that I was quitting at the end of this summer." She tossed her head—a defiant gesture ... *for me or for Mr. Swanson?*

Daniel, fifteen, was into Boy Scouts. He also had a paper route and dreamed of becoming either a fireman or a policeman—or maybe a priest? He and Tony both liked the television show *Combat*, a one-hour WWII drama series. It featured American infantrymen engaging in violent battles across war-torn Europe. Britt caught one of the dramas, decided that it was too violent, and wouldn't let them watch it anymore. That stirred up a battle in their Cherry Street house, but Britt stuck to her guns. One of Daniel's favorite songs at this time was SSGT Barry Sadler's "Ballad of the Green Berets."

Daniel liked Sister Karen, his ninth-grade teacher. It proved to be a boon to the family. He found out that she liked chocolate cake, so he baked her one. He also found out that he liked "mixing things up" in the kitchen, and he went on to do more cooking and baking. In a pinch, he could rustle up some grub for the family when Britt had to be late getting home. He was also the one who gathered up the dirty clothes for his mother to sort and wash.

Tony's all-consuming interest was sports, just like his father, a true chip off the old block. He also, like his father, could talk to anyone. The winter he was four, he strapped on a pair of skates and took off over the ice. (Hockey would become his favorite sport, eventually earning him a college scholarship.) When he was five, he was playing tee ball and hitting it way out there. (Later he would go on to play third base on Rillstead High's baseball team.) When it came to athletics, he was a natural.

He was no slouch at the clever comeback. One day Britt was scolding him for forgetting to take out the garbage, *again*. She went on and on. Tony looked at her and said, "Shut up," and, looking down at the floor where Sara's little dog stood, looking up at them, said, "Minnie." (The dog was a miniature dachshund; hence the name "Minnie.") Britt's mouth opened, her eyebrows went up, but she was speechless—she feared she'd start laughing.

Amy cared for people. Her emotional IQ was off the charts. She babysat to earn spending money; she had a way with little ones. With a smile to warm your heart, she seemed happy and easygoing, but she had a boiling point. *I was up on a ladder in the kitchen, changing the circular fluorescent light; Amy, two years old, sat on the floor to the left of the ladder. She started crying, but I ignored her—I wanted to get the light changed* now. *Fear of heights made me dread another trip up the ladder. She began to get really angry—or was she scared by seeing me at the top of the ladder, near the ceiling? Anyway, she was red-faced and screaming before I got the lamp plugged in. I climbed down and picked her up—her diaper was soaked. It took a long time to get her quieted down again.* Britt was glad to see that she was not only smiles and giggles—she had an iron will and would, even as early as age two, express it. She would not let the world crush her.

If they had had a gymnastic program when she was in school, she would have become an outstanding gymnast. Her flexibility was amazing. She would use her athletic gifts in high school as head cheerleader of the Rillstead hockey team.

Laura, the baby, was taught by everybody, especially her sister Amy. Maybe that's why she was so smart; she picked things up quickly. She broke her elbow falling off a horse when she was nine and in the sixth grade. Time for the cast to come off, and she had a left arm that she could draw into her body, but she could not straighten it out past a ninety-degree angle. All were disappointed, but Laura was devastated. She spent at least an hour every day after school, with Britt beside her, trying to get her elbow to let her forearm bend down. They had to do more. Britt knew the swim coach at the college and, with Laura in tow, "Exhibit A," went to speak to him.

"Coach Wilson, my daughter broke her elbow falling off a horse. It's healed, but it won't straighten. Laura, show him your arm." Laura, wordless but with her large brown eyes speaking volumes, looked up at Coach Wilson and showed him her bent left arm.

He put his large hand around her elbow. "Does it hurt?"

Laura shook her head, not taking her eyes off the coach.

Britt, watching, swallowed hard and said, "Would there be any time after school when we could use your swimming pool for a little while?" She almost folded her hands in prayer, waiting for him to answer.

He looked at the swimming schedule. "I see there is a spot—six to six forty-five. Would that do?" He looked up, pen poised to write.

"We'll make it do. Oh, thank you so much."

She watched as he wrote Laura's name in the time slot and smiled with relief and gratitude.

The swimming really did work wonders. So what if dinner had to be a heated-up Hamburger Helper casserole? Failing that, Daniel could throw something together. The arm straightened out after a couple of months or so, and that was the main thing. It not only straightened; it became her strongest arm.

The advantage to having five children close in age is that no one child can get away with anything that he or she shouldn't do. For example, when Tony saw smoke coming out of Sara's window, he reacted.

"Mom, Sara is smoking and blowing it out of her bedroom window!"

Tony had been a major factor—the other being the cost of cigarettes—in convincing his dad to quit smoking. Andy would light up a cigarette, and Tony, then four years old, would see or smell it and run in, his eyes big and worried.

"Daddy, I don't want you to die." Andy decided smoking wasn't worth the worry it caused his little boy.

When the miniskirt came in, Sara wanted to wear hers too short, in her mom's opinion. Before Sara left for school, Britt would check her out to see that her skirt was no more than two inches above her knee.

"Mom, Sara rolls her skirt band up when she gets to school." This time it was Daniel reporting.

And so it went—eyes alert for infractions.

The Cherry Street house wasn't the same either. The fixer-upper was fixed up and then some. Two incomes made a big difference. The monster furnace in the basement had been removed and replaced with an up-to-date, natural gas furnace complete with new ductwork. Though smaller than the old monster, it put out more heat for less money, and in a place where winter temperatures can dip to negative thirty degrees and more, this mattered. The room where the fuel tank had been was now Britt's sewing room. When they purchased new kitchen cabinets, the old ones made their way into the sewing room, so she had plenty of storage down there for her sewing supplies and books. A screened-in patio had been added to the backyard—a place for rainy day play and relaxation.

Yes, things always change. Britt thought she'd be relieved when all the children were out of diapers and were people she could talk to, but now she wasn't too sure. One of these days, they'd all be on their own. She and Andy would be alone. Change was a certainty, but it was also an unknown, and unknowns are scary.

CHAPTER

22

With all the activity—children's sports, Camp Fire Girls, Boy Scouts, and for her, cooking and housekeeping for a family of seven—Britt didn't have time to put her finger on who or what was causing her feeling, best expressed by Peggy Lee as she sang "Is That All There Is?" She felt restless, unfulfilled, and lonely. She also felt resentment.

Resentment festered, but resentment for what? For the fifteen loads of clothes she had to wash each week? For garbage that was supposed to be taken out but wasn't? Perhaps it was resentment against Andy, who had time for softball and golfing in the summer, and ice fishing and card playing in the winter. One friend had an icehouse he'd pull onto a frozen lake. It had a little stove, and they'd fish, eat hot dogs cooked in a coffee can on the stove, watch their fish lines hanging down the holes drilled with an auger, and play cards. Always he could fit in some card playing—a life to envy.

Yes, Britt envied him, and she resented his freedom. She also missed him. It was no wonder that they were growing apart. She wasn't a person who liked to have people around all the time. In fact, she needed alone time and had relished it in the past, but this was ridiculous. It put her in mind of another popular song, "Isn't It Lonely Together?" And it was. She missed talking to her best friend. But had she ever really had that?

Her first-ever date with a boy was a disaster. She had such a crush on that guy! He'd come into study hall, and her hand would shake so much she'd have to quit writing. The day of the date, she was a nervous wreck, worrying about what to talk about. She even read the newspaper to find interesting, discussable subjects. Came the big date, and every subject she brought up fell flat and sounded dumb. In desperation, she told him even dumber stuff, such as what she ate for breakfast (oatmeal). He never asked her out again. And she knew it was because she was boring.

When Andy asked her out, she determined not to make that mistake. She'd talk as little as possible. She and Andy double dated with Hannah and her boyfriend—he had a car, Andy didn't. When she talked, it was usually to Hannah—pretty rude, she now realized. She and Andy did a lot of hugging and kissing, making out. He didn't seem to mind the lack of conversation, for he kept dating her. They never went too far. How could they? Her sister was in the front seat, and besides, Britt never got carried away. She was doing what she thought would keep Andy interested but not *too* interested. Britt really liked him. She didn't fear him as she did other boys, but now she knew they should have talked—should have gotten to know more about each other than just the physical.

Would they have continued dating if she'd insisted on talking? But she wouldn't do that—she was afraid to talk. Afraid that she'd say dumb things. But just suppose they had talked and all he wanted to talk about was sports, about which she knew next to nothing, and she wanted to talk about the latest book she read, and he didn't like to read books. He liked western music, she now knew, while she liked classical. They both liked soft rock, though. They both liked movies, but he wanted violence, action, in his movies. She liked more dialogue and little if any violence. A little romance was good too, but too much embarrassed her. He liked crowds of people and noise, while she liked small groups or, better yet, one-on-one. She liked being alone to read and think. He hated dancing; she loved it. Britt could go on and on about all they found out after they were married.

But they shared the same values. Family came first. Children had to be cared for and loved. Vows made were vows kept. Don't lie, cheat, or steal. As both were Depression babies, they learned from their parents to be frugal—don't spend money you don't have. Their values were almost identical.

Values shared but not their worlds. Britt's world was child care and housework. When she did have some spare time, she read books. Andy spent most of his time in his barbershop, often not coming home until around seven in the evening. Their worlds overlapped only when they were with their children. Almost everything Andy and Britt did was for their children—to support them, encourage them, feed and clothe them. They never seemed to have any free time together.

In order to have some time with other adults, Britt learned to play Bridge but dropped it because she didn't like going out at night; she lost too much sleep over the game. When she got home after a night of Bridge, she'd go to bed and replay her hands, wondering what would have happened if she played each hand a different way. A night without much sleep made for a difficult day.

When Andy had any time to spare, he turned to sports,

either watching or participating. Sports were it for him. This was something Britt didn't understand. She'd been brought up to believe that sports were frivolous. We were put on this earth to work; that was our purpose and the way we got our exercise. Work and worship ruled. It wasn't that Britt believed all that her parents believed. When Andy played softball, she and the children went to his games. When their boys played hockey, Andy and Britt went to their games. Britt even learned the rules of the game and enjoyed watching but not entirely. There was always a fear tickling the back of her mind—the possibility that they might get hurt, but she also knew that the game was good for them. Excellent exercise for a healthy body, it kept them occupied and out of trouble.

Andy felt their separation too. He admitted as much to Britt one day when out of the blue he said, "I wish we could communicate better." This surprised Britt. He was missing her too, and maybe wondering what he could do to bridge the gulf between them. He began to be more affectionate; perhaps he thought all that was needed was more sex—the usual male answer to whatever was making a woman moody: "Oh, her? All she needs is to get laid."

Andy's barbershop had a loft above it. To get away from the children and let them spend some private time, get some peace and quiet, Andy would take her up there to make love when he felt the need, and it was also part of his plan to get back to their former closeness. If they couldn't talk, maybe their bodies could. *What we're doing is not making love; it's just sex. "Never say no to your husband," said my mother in her short birds and bees talk. I don't, Mother, but these loft sessions serve only to raise my level of resentment— just another thing to fit into my busy schedule, and I'm always so tired! If he worked as hard as I did, he wouldn't be so needy so often.* Andy couldn't figure out why she was so tired. He made the evening meal for her on Mondays, and that was supposed to be his day off.

His idea that more sex would bring them closer together was doomed from the start. No matter how often they had sex, Britt was still lonely. She and Andy thought of sex in different ways.

Growing up on a farm, Britt knew what sex was. It was a barnyard thing—something animals did to have babies. The babies were needed to increase the wealth of the farm. Sex was a necessity for animals, and it was also a necessity for humans.

The church Britt went to as a child, established by her paternal grandfather, did not allow for any kind of birth control. America was a big country with lots of land. People were needed to work this land to make it profitable, and children were assets. Her grandfather did his best by siring fifteen children, two of whom died in infancy. The more children, the more land her grandfather bought. Her grandmother objected to both more children and more land, but she was overruled.

Sex is a sin if it was sex because of lust. Lust made it dirty and disgusting—an animal act. Britt's Grandma Solvig, her father's mother, was a stern, mean woman. Britt will never forget what happened when she was about seven years old and her grandmother was babysitting at her house. "Gramma, there's two dogs in the front yard, and they're stuck together."

Her grandmother, who'd put the big kettle on the stove so she'd have lots of hot water to boil stains out of some white clothes, went to the door, opened it, and looked out. She then marched to the stove, picked up the steaming kettle, and poured the hot water on the dogs. The dogs yelped, pulled apart, and ran away.

Britt started to cry. "Granma, you hurt them—you hurt them!"

"Those dirty dogs! They deserved it. Stop your crying right now or I'll give you something to cry about."

Britt quit crying, but she hated her grandmother at that moment—hated yet feared her too. Now when she and Andy had sex, she wanted it to end as fast as possible. If she felt the least ripple of excitement, of desire, in her stomach or lower down, she shut it down. *Lust is wrong—it's dirty.* Logic told her that was foolish, but she couldn't get the image of those poor dogs with her grandmother pouring hot water on them out of her head whenever she began to feel—lusty? Logic did not trump emotion. Come to think of it, Andy must have learned too that there was something shameful about sex.

"At bedtime when we were little," Andy had told Britt, "Mama would listen to us say our prayers, the Our Father first, followed by the Act of Contrition, and then we 'God blessed' every member of our family. She then tucked us in and said, 'Keep your hands on top of the covers, boys,' to Luke and me before she went downstairs."

"Didn't you ever ask her why?" Britt said. "Your bedroom must have been as freezing cold as Hannah's and mine."

"It was. If we brought up a glass of water with us in the winter, sometimes it really would freeze solid. I did ask her why she said that once, telling her that my fingers might freeze off. She patted me on the head and said, 'Good boys keep their hands on top of the covers when they sleep. You two are good boys; that's why.' She smiled and went downstairs. When we heard the door to the stairs close, we put our hands under the covers to keep them warm."

Their mother wasn't around to watch those hands when they played outside, and though they may have felt guilt, they could not resist entering their "equipment" into competition with other boys. In grade school, boys have harmless contests to see who can pee the farthest or, at other times, who can pee the highest. Perhaps they even imagine they are firemen, putting out a raging fire with their "hoses." Then puberty strikes, and the game becomes a contest to see who can come the fastest. In later life, when they want to be good lovers and satisfy their partner, they come too fast. They are victims of premature ejaculation, and will lose the good lover contest, the contest they most want to win. In the old days, this didn't really matter, as women were supposed to lie still and think of other things, not about what was going on above them.

Things changed with the publication of Pomeroy's *Sexual Behavior in the Human Female* (1953). This report, expanded upon in women's magazines, turned America's beliefs about sex and women upside down. It revealed that women were sexier than anyone had thought and that they deserved to experience the big O for orgasm. It was up to her partner to see that she got the big O. Women, however, tended to have slower fuses than did men, so good lovers had to take their time. A man who couldn't restrain himself would end up feeling that he'd let the woman down. *Oh, oh, this report is going to be trouble—I hope Andy never gets wind of what's in it. I know he'd never read it.*

A woman who loves her man and doesn't want a crabby husband who thinks of himself as a loser learns to fake it, especially if she is one of those women who is the opposite of a "hot tomato," as Britt was. The result was that Andy felt good about himself, and she was pleased that he was happy. It was no sacrifice for her, as you can't miss what you've never had. It really was a win-win.

Britt didn't have to fake it all the time, just when she was tired or when she could see that Andy was tired. She didn't want to take forever if he had to be up early the next day.

Saturday morning, and Britt was busy cleaning the downstairs part of their Cherry Street bungalow. She dusted the top of the double dresser and lifted the little jewelry box sitting there. On a whim, she decided to check its contents. Not much in there: the pearls her mother had given her for high school graduation, the green cut-glass and silver necklace that Andy had given her on their anniversary, a gold-plated wristwatch, assorted clip-on earrings, and an ID bracelet. She picked up the ID bracelet and looked at it dangling from her hand.

It was a gold ID bracelet—small and quite ordinary, measuring almost seven and one-half inches long from one end of the safety catch to the other. The ID plate in the middle of the flat, omega gold chain, was a slightly curved gold bar, one and one-eighth inches long and one-fourth inch wide. The face of the slim gold bar bore three Greek letters: ΦΥΟ. *When and where did I get the bracelet and why?* She turned it over and saw that her name was engraved on the back in a flowing script, *Britt Anderson.*

Britt sat down on the bed and tried to think back thirteen years to 1952, the time when she was a student at the university in Rillstead.

When Britt first entered the university, enrollment stood close to four thousand. This was before she attended the Minnesota School of Business, before marriage to Andy and life in Newport and then in Boston, before living in St. Paul where Andy attended Lee's Barber College, before they moved back to their hometown where Andy finished his barber apprenticeship with the local barber, and before he owned his barbershop in Rillstead where they bought the house that Britt was now cleaning. She had given birth to a baby in each place that they lived—five babies. So much had happened in thirteen years.

The bracelet must have been given to me at the university. The Greek letters on the front make that the most likely place. I do remember going to an Honors Day the end of the second semester of my sophomore year.

Many were called up to the front of the ballroom. Scholarships and fellowships were awarded and prizes given to the deserving. I was among those called to the front. Being the shy, introverted student that I was back then, going up to the front of the room was accomplished in a fear-filled daze— after my name was called, I heard nothing—I shut down. But that must be where the ID bracelet came from. Britt ran to get her old college catalog and found the following entry on page 42: An engraved identification bracelet is given each year to the second-semester sophomore girl who ranks highest in all her university work.

Wow! I ranked highest! I never knew that. If I had really listened to what the presenter of awards said, I would have known the reason for the ID bracelet that day. Had I realized what it meant, would I have dropped out of the "U," gone to a "quickie" six-month business school, and married Andy? I guess I'll never know. I do know that it's fruitless to consider what-ifs.

But it is not fruitless to consider "What now?" We have a permanent address, after having had so many different addresses before we bought our house. I could start something and not be uprooted in the middle of it. Britt was ripe for a change, tired of the endless cycle of housework. She'd wash clothes on Monday, iron on Tuesday, bake on Wednesday, sew and maybe have coffee with a friend on Thursday, clean the upstairs on Friday and the downstairs on Saturday. Then there was always church on Sunday. That was actually the most stressful day. It meant getting five children and herself ready for church while Andy was urging them to hurry. He always wanted to be a little early. And there was more.

They were a household of seven people that had to be fed every day. That meant weekly trips to buy groceries and daily meal preparation followed by cleanup duties after every meal. Britt felt like a beast of burden tethered by a long rope to a well pump. With each circling of the pump, water would come out to nourish the life of those around her, but her life was being ground down by the endless cycle of repetitive, boring tasks. *Maybe the ID bracelet is telling me that I could do more with my life, that I could go back to school and develop a side of me that I've neglected for far too long. Mother always said, "When a task is once begun, never leave it till it's done." I started college but left after five semesters. Maybe now I can finish what I started.*

Andy and Britt discussed what she wanted to do. Britt started the discussion. "I want to go back to school—finish what I started. I could get a job when I graduate—help out with finances."

"We can't afford it. We have five kids to feed and clothe. You *have* a job, and that's it."

"I need more in my life. For one thing, I need to get out and be with adults. I need to use my brain. I'm afraid it's going to rust out."

"That's silly. Read books."

"I could get a student loan. I really want to do this."

Andy hit her with an ultimatum. "Fine. But if you go, you have to get a job when you're done. You have to use your education, and you have to pay back your loan, plus do the mother-of-the-house stuff."

"Yes, sir."

Monday, Britt got in the car and drove across the city to the university. Barbers in Rillstead all took Mondays off, so Andy was child caregiver that day. She signed up for a three-credit correspondence course, Survey of English Literature. Britt was on her way to becoming a high school English teacher. She had chosen English as her major because that offered the most correspondence courses. She would not attend the university until Laura started first grade.

The prospect of becoming a teacher scared her to death. When she couldn't get out of a college class in public speaking, she took it in summer school. Summer school classes were smaller, and the teachers were more laid back in the summer. It was still torture. She could hardly breathe whenever she was called on to give a speech; that made it difficult to talk. Her knee caps took to jumping up and down—she was sure the other students noticed this. It's a wonder she could hang on to her note cards with her shaking, sweaty hands. Her speech topic on one occasion was euthanasia, and she clearly said "youth in Asia" and almost started giggling out of nervousness. If, as a teacher, this happened, she'd lose control of her students.

She did not want to be a teacher—she'd be more suited to research, shut away in a lab somewhere. Now, however, if she were to earn a degree, it had to be in teaching. No other jobs were as stable or paid women as much as teaching did. Teaching also meant that Britt would have the same vacation schedule as her children. *I can just quit this nonsense and be a stay-at-home wife and mother. I have plenty to do at home. But I need to get out. I need to learn things, and I need to talk with people who want to learn. I also want to help Andy with expenses—he worries so. I have to do it. Desperate times call for desperate measures.*

Britt's father gave a huge and unexpected boost to her dreams. Britt, Andy, and the children were at the Anderson farm for Sunday dinner. During some table talk, Britt mentioned that she might return to college. Her father's eyebrows shot up, but he said nothing at dinner. Later he took her aside and said, "I bought war bonds for your college education. If you are going back, I want you to have them."

Britt's heart did a flip. She loved him so much at that

moment. "Oh, Dad, I won't let you down a second time." She hugged him tight.

It was 1968. Britt was in summer school, finishing up her bachelor of science degree. As a student, she could take advantage of couple counseling for free. Though she was very busy and had college friends, there was still, in the back of Britt's mind, the matter of her and Andy's alienation from each other. Andy, being a sucker for anything free, just might go. It was worth a try.

She chose an evening to bring up the subject after he'd had a good day and a good meal. "The college offers free couples counseling for students—*free!*"

Andy, who'd had his head buried in the sports page of the newspaper, thrust the paper aside and looked up—a look of pained annoyance. She could tell he was trying to be patient. "I don't know why you want to do that, but if you really want to, I'll go once to see what it's all about."

They entered a small, cozy room at the college. Two chairs sat in front of a desk with papers laid out upon it. They sat down—Britt sat to Andy's left. She looked around—all earth colors, beige walls except for the accent wall in back of the desk. It was painted in a pale jade green. Britt looked to her left. Three windows, close together were situated high up on that wall—so high that no curtains or shades were needed, but they let in the light. Turning to her right and leaning forward to look past Andy, she saw a rather large pastoral painting—cows grazing the grass on rolling hills, with a farmstead nestled into a little hollow, protected from high winds—a white house, red barn, with a silo standing sentry. The picture's horizontal lines gave a feeling of peace.

The counselor, a Miss Hooper, was a young, red-haired woman. She entered, and Britt and Andy stood, and they exchanged introductions. *She's so young. What can she know about marriage and children?* Miss Hooper walked to the desk, sat down in her chair, and motioned for Britt and Andy to sit down.

"Mr. and Mrs. Hughes, how can I help you?" She looked from one to the other.

Britt shifted in her chair, uncrossed her legs, and planted them firmly on the floor. "We've lost touch with each other. We used to be best friends, but now we're drifting apart. I'm lonely just having the children to talk to. They don't really converse; it's just Mama this and Mama that all day long."

Miss Hooper turned to look at Andy. "Mr. Hughes—may I call you Andy?" Seeing his nod, she continued. "Do you feel that you and your wife are drifting apart?"

"Our marriage is fine. It's fine."

Britt glanced sideways at Andy. He sat stone-faced, his jaws clamped shut. She could see he was determined to keep them that way. She turned to face Miss Hooper.

"Mrs. Hughes—may I call you Britt?" After a nod from Britt, she said, "You mentioned children. How many and what ages?"

"Three girls and two boys, ranging in age from six to thirteen."

"I can understand that you are very busy and have been for the last thirteen years. They will grow up and need less care, you know. Do you get enough sleep?" She looked down at the papers on her desk, shuffled a few, and waited for Britt's answer.

"I do now. I'm like my dad, a good sleeper. I just miss my husband. We share so few interests." *This is going nowhere, and Andy's not going to help any.*

They went only once more. The second visit was just a repeat of the first. Wasted time. Britt sensed that the counselor felt sorry for this poor guy who was obviously dragged by his wife into something he didn't want to do. *All right, Andy. If this is the marriage you want, I can accept that. I can do what's expected of me—take care of the housework and children and give you sex when you need it. Some day when we get a chance to catch our breaths, we can look at our marriage and decide what to do, either separate or stay together. We did love each other once. We went together for four years; there must have been some attraction that kept us together. Maybe we can find it again.*

By the time Laura entered first grade, Britt had racked up twenty credits of correspondence, all that were available in her major at the correspondence school. It was time for her to head off for regular college and teachers she could see. She was able to get all her classes fitted into a Monday, Wednesday, and Friday class schedule, leaving her two weekdays and the weekend at home for study and catching up on housework.

It was hard being a full-time student again. In some classes, part of the grade was based on class participation. This really stressed Britt out. For thirteen years she had been housebound. In fact, when she joined the Ladies Auxiliary in Rillstead and had to stand and tell them her name—just her name!—Britt's kneecaps jumped up and down, and she had trouble breathing. The old anxiety attack. Now she would have to answer questions in a class full of young, smart college kids. Sitting in a political science class one morning, Britt was struck with a blinding migraine. She rushed to the ladies' room and threw up and spent the rest of the day on the brown leather, mission style couch that the university had thoughtfully provided. Britt slept and recovered enough to drive home. Thank goodness she never had a migraine hit her in class like that again.

There were other times when it became almost too hard, but the ID bracelet was a reminder that she had the ability. It said to her, "You can do this." (Britt never wore the ID bracelet. She didn't want to show off; that'd be against her Scandinavian nature. Besides, she'd feel terrible if she lost it.)

Anxiety lessened when Britt got used to being a student again. In a year, including a summer school, she had fulfilled all the requirements for graduation, including six weeks of practice teaching. Graduation day was a proud day not only for her but also for her husband and children, her parents, her sister, Hannah, and her twin brothers. One of them, Owen, took Britt's picture while she was walking back to her seat, clutching her diploma. Britt had finished what she started—she had graduated.

Britt was fortunate to enter the teaching profession the same year (1969) that the United States put a man on the moon. The Russian Sputnik—launched October 4, 1957—had made education the national goal; America strove to become the best and the brightest. If teachers needed certain supplies to help them teach, they had but to ask. Superintendent Torval Johnson, a balding, middle-aged man, interviewed Britt. They sat across from each other—he behind a huge walnut desk. His suit was charcoal gray, and he even wore a vest, but his tie betrayed him. It was red with orange polka dots—this was a man who could laugh and joke and could feel compassion in spite of the three-piece, charcoal gray suit. His piercing black eyes, behind black-rimmed glasses, fastened on Britt, but she was not afraid, just a bit nervous, having never been interviewed before. She must have done okay; she was hired to teach junior high language arts, in spite of the fact that she could not coach hockey—she really was asked that in the interview, but she knew he was joking.

Britt's first year of teaching became her definition of hell for the rest of her life. It was an even worse time than the eight months of celibacy she and Andy had agreed to after Amy was born.

CHAPTER

2 3

It was a gorgeous summer, the summer of '72, so people said. Britt didn't know, for she slept through it. Her first year of teaching had been difficult, and she was worn to a frazzle.

Britt tried dragging herself out of bed in the morning, but then, realizing that her family could do without her, she slept in. Often noon came and went, but she slept on. She'd forget to eat; she'd gained some weight eating the school's lunches, and she wanted to lose it, but she forced herself to get up and make an evening meal for her family. She wished they weren't so tired of Hamburger Helper—it was an easy meal. She wandered out to the screened-in patio and did a little work on an oil painting. She painted with oils because if she didn't feel like painting, she could just cover her palette with a plastic bag and put it in the freezer. Mixing her paints with oil of cloves also helped keep it from drying out. Her painting consisted of copying pictures that spoke to her—pictures of children and flowers. She had painted very little this summer.

The evening meal was never fancy—Hamburger Helper,

macaroni and cheese, hot dogs and beans, always with a salad, sometimes just soup and salad. They really didn't care too much what they ate—at least they didn't complain. They were too busy talking about sports as they ate: hockey in the winter, baseball, tennis, and golf in the summer. That's about all Britt can remember about that summer until the evening they had Hamburger Helper, the tuna one, the one Andy didn't like, just once too often.

Andy looked at his family seated at the dining room table or, as in the case of Sara and Tony, out of their chairs and poised to leave, and he said, "Enough! It's time we had a family meeting."

His commanding tone stopped Sara in her tracks as she was making her way into the kitchen with her dirty dishes. It did the same with Tony, who was on his way upstairs, leaving his dirty dishes still on the table. They came back and sat down.

"What's the matter, Dad?" Tony said as he drummed his fingers on the table. "I gotta go to baseball practice."

"Later, Tony. We've got to find out what's wrong with your mother—too much Hamburger Helper—something's bothering her. She's not herself."

Amy, who'd been discussing with Laura their plans for the evening, stuck out her tongue and pretended to gag and said, "I hate Hamburger Helper."

Daniel's eyebrows lowered as he studied his mother with squinty eyes. Britt had been picking at her food, and now she just sat, busy pushing down the cuticles of her fingernails.

Sara, frowning, looked at her mother. "Yes, Mom—what *is* the matter with you? You never get excited about anything— you never laugh, you just sleep."

Britt lifted her head and, looking at her oldest daughter, said, "Nothing is the matter. I'm just really tired."

"You know why you're tired, Mom?" Laura decided to

share her thoughts on the matter even though she was the youngest. "It's because you don't eat—you don't eat your vegetables. You always tell me I have to eat my vegetables,"

Andy nodded. "She's right—you're too skinny, Britt. You've got to eat more."

"But I'm not hungry. I'll eat when I'm hungry."

"I could bake a cake for you—chocolate cakes are my specialty." It sounded a bit like a joke, but Daniel wasn't joking. He looked worried.

"I miss the good stuff you used to make: meatloaf, scalloped potatoes, cherry pie, carrot cake, and especially spaghetti." Andy scratched his head. "Why do *you* think you're always so tired?"

"I don't know. I just am. You kids are all growing up so fast," Brit looked at her children gathered around the table. "You have so many interests and are so busy. Pretty soon you won't need me at all."

With that, Britt heard a chorus of "We need you!" Amy's voice edged out the rest. "Mom, next year I'll have to learn fractions. I need you to help me with my homework."

"We all need you, Britt—the old Britt," said Andy. "You're letting us down when you shut down like this; you're like a zombie."

Her eyes filled with tears. She blinked to keep them from falling, but it only squeezed them out. "Just knowing that you care means a lot. Thank you. Maybe I'm afraid of the future—of what I see there, but shutting down won't keep it from coming, I know that. Sleeping is just hiding. I'll try to come back, but when you're in a black hole, it's hard to climb out. I will try, and I do love all of you."

Andy got up from the table and went to stand behind Britt. His hands rested on her shoulders. He bent down and kissed the top of her head. "Okay, kids, meeting's over. You're excused."

What was that noise? At six in the morning? Football players going to practice? Where had the summer gone? She'd better pull herself together.

One of the first things she did when she was back at school was to see the school nurse, a hockey mother friend, about her swollen ankles. The school nurse, Maggie, took one look at her and then hugged her. "My goodness, you feel like a bony bird. Have you been sick?"

Britt pulled up her right pants leg, slipped off her shoe, and rested her foot on a chair. "I'm all right, but I've never had such swollen ankles, and I thought maybe you'd know what's wrong." She looked up at Maggie.

"You're too skinny, for one thing. Didn't you eat this summer?"

"Not much. I was too tired, and I'd gained some weight eating at school, so I decided to slim down. Besides, most of my time was spent sleeping, so I didn't need many calories."

"Slim down! You're a stick. You probably didn't eat any fat, and that's why your ankles are swollen. Fat gives us energy; it's actually necessary for survival! Too much fat—too much of anything—is bad, but a certain amount is needed for health. Some fats are better than others, so choose the good fats. If you feel you must cut down on calories, and you don't, cut out sugar. It messes with your brain and rots your teeth. If you need to have something sweet, make your sweet honey and stay away from refined white stuff."

"Yes, ma'am."

"We both work full-time, and we're both raising a houseful of kids. We need to keep healthy and strong, ya hear? Now go and eat something that has fat in it and eat regular meals. Sermon over, but do what I say—you're my friend, and I don't want to lose you. I mean that."

When summer came around again, Britt was almost back to her normal weight, and she felt healthy and strong.

She never wanted to sleep away another summer. Time is all anyone has, and she'd wasted too much already. Britt enrolled in a summer art class. And she made a decision: when all their children had graduated from high school, she would leave Andy. They would both be free to find true partners—in Andy's case, a woman who liked sports, and in hers, a person who read books and liked discussing them. It wouldn't hurt, either, if he liked her artwork.

Andy and I were once lovers and partners. We were close, but now we are separated by a divide so wide we can't seem to cross it. Even Andy has said that he wishes we could communicate better. That surprised me—I didn't think he cared. Maybe we could become partners and even lovers again. We love our five children—all different but all composed of our intermixed genetic material. Their bodies, minds, personalities are all combined in different ways, yet those ways come from our bodies, our minds. We love them all unconditionally, so why can't we love each other?

Though love has not been constant, trust in each other has, and that is a very big thing. Love is harder, especially if one person shows it in one way and the other person shows it in another. I need words, words of encouragement and appreciation and being told that I am loved. Andy shows love by his actions. He tries to anticipate needs and fulfill them. He's a helper who enjoys the role; it makes him feel needed. He lives in the physical, which is why he thought he could bring us closer to each other again by sex.

I live in the mind, imaging things, picturing things—I love solving puzzles. Once I learned that the words, "I'll do it myself," irritated Andy as much as they had always irritated my mother, I tried to be less independent, and things got better.

Lying in bed one morning, Britt was struck with the thought that for much of her married life, she'd been living a lie. When she and Andy decided to marry, she imagined herself as being a courageous Daniel, the hero of her favorite Old Testament story. She'd go out into the world with her best friend by her side, a united front that could conquer anything. But she was not a Daniel. For one thing, she was not alone, and for another, she was not pure of heart. She didn't even know for sure if she had married for love—perhaps she married to escape. She could have been the opposite of courageous—a coward afraid to make decisions for herself and afraid to go out into the world alone. She married a Catholic, a "mackerel snapper." Her mother didn't approve, and she doubted that her father did, even though he never said so. Was she trying to hurt her strict Lutheran mother? She tried much the same tactics on Andy once. It didn't work.

Britt loved to dance, but Andy didn't; nevertheless, on one of their first dates, he took her to a dance. She wanted him to come in the hall and dance. He said she could go in, but he wanted to stay outside and talk with the guys. She didn't dare go in alone. Someone gave her a bottle of peppermint schnapps. She can't remember how much she drank, but she got sick. To this day, even the name makes her stomach queasy.

As a married woman, she lied every Sunday when she went to the Catholic church. She didn't believe that it was "the one true church," though that was what she said when she recited the Nicene Creed. Why, there were more man-made rules in this religion than she'd ever imagined: women must cover their hair, men and women had to eat fish on Friday and fast before Communion and during Lent. She didn't understand the reason for incense or for all those candles up front. The very worst rule was the one about birth control. The only acceptable method, other than abstinence, was the least reliable one.

What did she believe anyway? She believed, or would like

to believe, her father when he said, "I am the captain of my ship; I am the master of my soul." She liked that. She believed the Jewish version of the golden rule: "Do not do unto others what you do not want them to do unto you." Every time she faked an orgasm, she lied. A lie she had to live with because not to do so would cause pain. Pain, she believed, was an evil.

Life is a balancing act in which you must try to figure out what causes the least pain and go with it. We can't, like Daniel, escape the den—we all live in a den of sorts, surrounded by danger. God help us. And she did believe in God, the God she experienced as a child being comforted, loved, by a warm, enveloping presence—not an old man with a long white beard but a loving power. A power, a greatness, somewhat akin to what she felt when she stepped outside on a crisp winter night and looked up at the millions of stars. She could hardly breathe—it was so overwhelming and magnificent. She felt expanded and insignificant at the same time. All was in place, a perfectly balanced design. A design had a designer, and to her, that was God, or Yahweh, or Allah, or the Great Mystery. Britt also believed that the designer could change any elements that needed changing, a back to the drawing board, an out with the old, in with the new. At the rate humans were polluting the earth, using up its resources, she feared that humanity just might soon end up on that drawing board, or even the scrap pile to make way for a new and better design.

CHAPTER

24

Britt's second year of teaching junior high English was much better, but she welcomed the chance to escape her ninety-three students for three days in St. Paul by attending her first teaching convention. She looked up at the large banner stretched above the doors of the convention center: "MEA Convention—1971. She'd signed up by mail for a couple of workshops, and she wanted to find some new books to interest her students on Friday, the free reading day. She also wanted to look at the grammar workbooks—those she'd been using were so boring.

She entered and was confronted with rows of booths or kiosks, plugging books of all kinds and other teaching supplies. Britt looked around. *There must be thousands of people here, not counting those peddling something. When did this convention start? Let's see, almost right after the Civil War started. The first one was held in Rochester—a little more than one hundred miles from here. It's always the third weekend in October.* Britt walked over to a table piled with American literary classics, or so said the banner hanging down from the front side of the table. She made her way through the crowd and soon stood in front of it.

"Hmmm ..." *Not many of these suitable for seventh-grade readers. Too many big words or old words. I don't want to turn them off reading. Some parents would probably object to the content of this one.* She reached for Hawthorne's *The Scarlet Letter*, and her hand closed on—another hand. Britt looked up, right into a pair of bright blue eyes. *Only my dad and one other person have blue eyes that exact shade.* "Jesse!"

"Britt, Britt Anderson. I never thought I'd see you again. Are you a teacher? You said you never wanted to teach, that you were too shy to get up in front of a bunch of students."

"Yes, well, things change." *Why is he staring, and what is he thinking? Do I look okay?*

Jesse stood there, grinning at her, and then looked her up and down. "Maybe, but you don't. You still look the same, but your hair is darker now."

Britt gave him a closer look. "You used to have a crew cut. I liked it, but for a teacher, this is better—longer and a little wavy. You look like one of the romantic poets—a *starving* romantic poet." *I sound like an idiot.*

"Let's go grab a cup of coffee and talk. Where is that coffee bar? The last time I went to the MEA convention, it was downstairs." He took her arm, and they left the big convention hall with its stacks of books and other exhibits.

The coffee bar, warm and welcoming, was more than a bar. It had tables and smelled of fresh cinnamon rolls. A few people were in there, but Britt and Jesse found a table off to the side and away from the others. Jesse went up to the counter and brought back two steaming cups of coffee and two cinnamon rolls. Britt wrapped her icy finger around her cup to warm them.

"Coffee, a teacher's lifeblood. Ummm, and this is good

coffee." He swallowed, set down his cup, and looked across the table at her. "What do you teach, Britt?"

"Junior high literature and grammar."

"Wow. I hope you're getting hazardous duty pay?"

"No, but I should be. And you?"

"Freshman English at a community college in St. Cloud. Sometimes that can be hazardous too." He smiled, his disarming, little boy smile, and her stomach ached, a good ache, and for a second or two she felt lightheaded.

Britt's coffee was cool enough to drink now, and she took a big gulp to clear her head. "I got your letter. I wanted to answer it, but I didn't know what to say—how to say it. I'd dropped out of school, enrolled in a secretarial course in Minneapolis, and I married."

"Married!" Jesse's eyebrows arched up, and his eyes opened wide. "Who did you marry? Do I know him?"

"No. You never met him. He was my steady boyfriend in high school, my best friend. He still is my best friend. It—it was a very confusing time."

Jesse scratched his head. "I know what you mean. It was a mixed-up time for me too." Britt's hand was resting on the table, and Jesse reached over and laid his hand over hers. "I joined the army to prove to my father that I didn't need him. I ended up freezing my butt off in Korea—nothing like almost freezing to death to get a guy to cool down. Joining up was a mistake, but there I was. I met my wife there, a beautiful Korean girl. We have two little daughters—she's a great mother."

"And *your* mother?"

His Adam's apple bobbed up and down as he swallowed. "She died of cancer two years ago. We spend Christmas with my father. He's still a judge, but he loves his little granddaughters—they can do no wrong. Other than at Christmas time, we don't see him. He's busy judging people."

"I don't think I could have become a teacher without my father. We were visiting my parents, and I mentioned that I'd been thinking of going back to school. I said that I wanted to get a degree and a teacher's certificate. Later that day, my father took me aside and told me that he'd bought war bonds during WWII so that he'd be able to send his children to college. I still had half my bonds, he said, and he'd cash them in and give me the money. I can never thank him enough."

"What does your husband do?"

"He's a barber—owns his own shop. He's a good provider for me and our five children."

Startled, Jesse's mouth dropped open, and his eyebrows arched up as they had when she told him she was married, but his eyes opened even wider than they had before. *Five children!*

"Three girls and two boys. Our oldest is in eleventh grade, and our youngest is in fourth. For a while there, I was worried about my sanity." Britt looked down at her watch. "Oh, I have to go. I signed up for a workshop on Making Writing Fun in Junior High. My friend and roommate here, Delores—we drove up together—signed up for it too, and she'll be looking for me, but it was so *very* good to see you again." She stood up, coffee cup in hand.

Jesse stood up too and reached for her arm. "There are no workshops tonight, and everyone has to eat. I know a little place not far from here where the food is good and they have a live band playing songs of the fifties. They even have a little dance floor. Let's meet at four thirty at the table where we were both reaching for the same book. We have some catching up to do."

"Dancing to songs of the fifties! I'd love that. I can't remember the last time I danced to anything. I can't pass that up. I'll be at the book table at four thirty with my dancing shoes on."

It was three thirty, and the writing workshop, a good one, was over. Britt was in the hotel room, trying to decide what to wear. She hadn't planned on an evening out, but she knew a banquet was planned, so she did have something nice, her clingy, jersey jumpsuit, empire style to enhance what little chest she had. She loved the swirl of color—rust, peach, and forest green, and it never wrinkled. The wider legs made it look like a long, A-line skirt—dressy yet perfect for dancing. Britt slipped on her T-strap dancing shoes—the real thing, tap-dancing shoes without the taps, and oh so comfortable. On her way out, she grabbed her warm peach shawl, just in case, even though this October day was warmer than usual. In the evening, who knows? One never knew what Minnesota weather would be like.

Upon entering the Old Time Dine and Dance with its pink walls, subdued lighting, and cushy burgundy couches, Britt knew this place was trouble. It was too comfortable and intimate. A bar occupied the left rear corner of the room, and in the right rear corner, an organist sat at a Hammond organ, flanked by the other two members of the trio—saxophonist and drummer—playing the "Blue Skirt Waltz." In front of this trio, four couples were dancing on a little dance floor.

Crossing the floor, they entered another room, the dining area. It also had pink walls and subdued lighting, but here the couches had given way to small tables seating two to six diners. They found a table for two off to the side yet close to the other room and its dance floor. A waiter wearing a white jacket appeared and took their order. Music from the small band was piped in but kept low. The music caused memories to flood Britt's mind—nights of skating on a frozen pond under a full moon, afternoon baseball games in the summer with hotdogs and boxes of popcorn, and picnics in a park on a Sunday afternoon.

"Britt, your eyes are dreamy. What are you thinking?"

She looked at him and smiled. "Remember ice-skating in the moonlight on the pond not far from my dorm? You walked me back to the dorm, and the housemother, Mrs. Grey, stood at the door, scowling. She refused to let me in—it was five minutes past curfew. You put your arm around me and smiled your blue-eyed, little boy smile at her, and she let me in. I knew you were a good guy then."

"You looked frightened—I *had* to put my arm around you, and now I want to put my arm around you again. Come, let's dance."

The band began a soft rendition of "Smoke Gets in Your Eyes," and Jesse took Britt's hand to help her up, and with his arm around the back of her waist, he led her out onto the small dance floor. She turned to face him, putting her right hand in his raised left hand and then allowing her left arm to curl up and embrace his shoulder. Britt caught a whiff of his aftershave—it was spicy, like her dad's when he shaved and got dressed up in his church clothes.

Britt moved in closer. She wanted to be able to read his body, to anticipate his moves—she'd never danced with him before. They glided around the floor, listening to the music, enjoying the smoothness of the dance. Britt found that she was singing the words of the song in her head as they danced: *When your heart's on fire, you must realize, smoke gets in your eyes.*

Jesse held her closer, so close that she could feel him hard against her thigh. Her body responded. It felt like every nerve in her body was on fire; she feared she'd melt, and she didn't care.

The music ended, and they walked, his arm still around her waist, back to their table. Seconds later, their waiter appeared with their order. Britt could only nibble at her food. She was still under the spell of the dance. She hesitated to look up at him for fear he'd see the raw hunger in her eyes and that she'd recognize a similar longing in his. They were playing with fire.

Britt took a deep breath, swallowed, and looked up. "I love these old songs. This place is everything you said it would be. Thank you for bringing me here."

"You dance so well. You and your husband must go dancing a lot."

"No. He doesn't like to dance—he has trouble feeling the rhythm—but we both like the songs of the fifties. The song we just danced to is one of my favorites. What's your favorite song from that time?" *Why is it so hard to talk to him now? It was easy before we danced.* Britt looked down at her hands. They were strangling her napkin, twisting it all out of shape.

"It must be our lucky night, because they just started playing it, 'The Tennessee Waltz.' May I have this dance, oh beautiful one?"

"I'd love to, but I'm pretty tired—too much excitement for one day. I'd really rather get some sleep so I'm ready for all the doings tomorrow." *Yeah, right. Sleep with you is what I'd really rather do. I've never, never felt like this before—this ache, this yearning.* Was this the "feel good" her mother had warned her about so long ago? The time the gale wind blew down the cottonwood trees and they pretended the slanted stumps were their saddle horses? *I know one thing: I feel weak, and that's not good.*

Jesse signaled the waiter to bring the check. Britt escaped to the ladies' room. When she came out, Jesse put her shawl around her. It was getting chilly at this late hour. A taxi waited. It was a silent ride, but they sat close together, and Britt put her hand in his. *I wonder what he's thinking. He could be angry—he took me out, fed me, and then I wouldn't dance with him to his favorite song. But his eyes weren't angry—they looked worried. Perhaps he is thinking the same thoughts I am: Why now? Why, when we both have families? When we're trapped? Life is cruel. But I would never do something that would wreck two families. And it would, even if it was just once. It would be like a cancer, eating away the good in us.*

The taxi stopped, and they got out. Jesse took her arm. "I'll walk you to your door. I want to be sure you're safely behind it and that it's locked." They stopped at her room. "May I come in for a while? We've barely begun to catch up on all that's happened since college, since the baseball game. You looked so terrific, and you still do. We may never see each other again. We need to make the most of it."

That's true. But I doubt he just wants to talk. Right now he's talking and looking at me as if he wants more than just talk. I do want him, but I can't. I don't think I'd be strong enough to resist him. And if I didn't resist him, I'd become a different person—a person for whom I'd have no respect. I'd not be able to live with myself. She shook her head. "No. My roommate, Delores, is probably in there, sleeping. I wouldn't want to wake her."

"We could go to my room. It's just one flight up and to your left, and I don't have a roommate."

"No, but it's tempting. If I wasn't so tired ..."

"How about lunch tomorrow then? Meet you at the same time and place as we met before? It's our last day here, Britt."

Britt looked at him, knowing that she should say no, but she nodded. Jesse hugged her, a bit too hard and a bit too long, and kissed her cheek. She opened her door and stepped in. Delores was watching a movie. "Britt, you're missing a really good golden oldie, *Casablanca*, with Humphrey Bogart and Ingrid Bergman." She turned and looked at Britt. "You look sad. What's the matter?"

"Oh, I'm just tired. I think I'll shower and go to bed. We've got a big day again tomorrow."

Britt met Jesse the next day at the display of America literary classics as arranged. And as before, they went downstairs for coffee.

No quiet, no fresh cinnamon rolls scenting the air this time. It was the last day, and people were crowding into the coffee bar to drink coffee and say goodbye to old and new friends. They were slapping each other on the back (males) and hugging (females). Cries of "See you next year!" echoed around the room. They'd had a good time, but now they were willing and eager to get back home.

The "willing to go home" part was bittersweet. Conventions had to end, and usually people were ready to get back on schedule—back to normality. With emotions so high, around and inside Britt, she found it hard to believe normal would ever again be possible. She felt numb. For the moment, sipping coffee and looking at each other was all they could do.

Jesse shook his head, as if to break a spell. "What now, Britt? I'm not ready for us to just go away from each other."

"I've been sitting here, Jesse, just looking at you, trying to memorize your face. I won't forget you or our time together, but any *us* thoughts must end here." Britt stood up, picked up her empty cup, put it on the counter, and started to leave.

Jesse hurried after her and grabbed her arm. "Britt." He drew her to him and held her, whispering—his moist, warm breath caressed her ear. "I know, I know, but I'll miss you so much." They turned and walked out, hand in hand.

Britt skipped the banquet. She didn't feel like eating, and she knew she'd not be able to concentrate on the speakers. She'd never see Jesse again. Was it grief she was feeling? She wanted to cry, to bawl, to howl out her misery, but she wouldn't. She hated crying—she'd heard enough crying when growing up.

At home, she was distant and distracted. She went through all the ordinary, familiar motions of being a teacher and a homemaker, but she felt like a robot, one of Isaac Asimov's creations. *I wish he'd pressured me to have sex so I could be angry at him. Maybe I'd have slapped him good, and then I'd have been left feeling virtuous and good about never having to see him again. But he wouldn't do that. He was gentle and loving—a gentleman, and now I can't get him out of my mind or my heart. I wanted him, and that was wrong, but there it is. I would never destroy two families—too many people would feel pain, and causing pain is evil. Perhaps he thought the same as I do on this. If he did, that would only make him more lovable.* "Stop it, right now." She looked down and realized that she'd just poured half a box of laundry soap into the washer. "Damn!"

CHAPTER

25

Sara left for college in the fall of 1973, leaving a hollow, sad place in Britt's heart. She wanted to fulfill her dream of becoming a veterinarian and had decided that the School of Veterinary Medicine in Madison, Wisconsin, was the place for her.

So far away! I remember her going off to her first day of school. Her dad walked her to school—it was on his way to his barbershop, a walk he took every working day. She was so brave! She didn't even cry when I hugged and kissed her goodbye. Now she is brave again, going off to a new school in another state, Wisconsin. She was leaving the nest. The first to go, but it wouldn't be long before they'd all be gone. Having five children in seven years guaranteed a speedy one-by-one exit. Britt felt her throat close and her eyes burn as she struggled to hold back tears. *Andy and I will soon be all alone. What can we talk about? Our children have been everything to both of us.*

Britt struggled to breathe as panic threatened. *When they were little, they all wanted me. "Mama, Mama." Everyone wanted "Mama." At times I felt that pieces of me were being torn out—that I was losing myself. I looked forward to their growing up so that I could have some peace, some time to put myself back together again. But to be without them—to have them all gone!* She hadn't wanted that; she just didn't want them to be so gosh-darned needy! Britt feared that the time would come when no one would need her.

The upheaval in the Hughes household reflected the events taking place in the nation: the US Supreme Court overturned state bans on abortion in *Roe vs. Wade;* on March 29, the last US soldier left Vietnam; ninety million people tuned in to watch Billie Jean King beat Bobbie Riggs, 6–4, 6–4, 6–3; in October, the Arab oil embargo against nations supporting Israel caused an energy crisis; Lite beer was introduced in the United States by Miller Brewing Company.

In the next year, 1974, Daniel Hughes would graduate from high school and join the National Guard, and in the United States, upsetting events would escalate: a series of 149 tornadoes, the largest number in history, would hit thirteen states and one Canadian province, killing 315 and injuring 5,000; a package of Wrigley's chewing gum would become the first product to have its UPC (universal product code) scanned, changing the shopping experience forever; Alberta Williams King, mother of Martin Luther King Jr., would be killed in an Atlanta, Georgia, church; the Watergate scandal would grow, forcing Richard Nixon to resign the presidency; Gerald Ford would become president; Muhammad Ali would knock out George Foreman and thereby regain his heavyweight title. So much would happen, not only with Daniel but in our nation that Britt would find herself being pulled more firmly into the present.

Britt's romantic memories would fade even farther into the background in 1975, as Communists took over Saigon, causing mass evacuations of South Vietnamese and Americans;

President Gerald Ford would survive a second assassination attempt; Bill Gates would start Microsoft in Albuquerque, New Mexico; and the Weather Underground would bomb the US State Department office in Washington, DC.

Crash! Sara drops out of school, comes home, and moves in with a Vietnam vet named Zack. Tony graduates from high school and goes to southern Minnesota to join the junior hockey league, hoping to be noticed and drafted by a college hockey scout and be offered a college scholarship. Britt hardly dares breathe lest she disturb something that will cause another change. She doesn't have time for all the changes. Even her teaching has changed. Britt has to revamp her entire teaching program, for she's been assigned to teach "Writing to Persuade" and "The Great Religions as Literature" to senior high students in the fall. And Andy's life has changed, due to the Beatlemania sweeping the country. Ever since the appearance of those four longhairs on the *Ed Sullivan Show*, the livelihood of our nation's barbers, at a time when unemployment stood at 9 percent, was threatened. Britt was thankful that Amy and Laura, still in high school, were leading normal, everyday lives.

Back to Sara and Zack. Britt will never forget the first night Zack came calling. He had served his time amid the chaos and carnage in Vietnam. He wanted a wife and a home to help him forget what he'd seen and what he'd experienced. Zack wanted security.

The evening Zack knocked on the Hughes' front door, Andy opened it. His eyes narrowed as he stared at the young man standing there. What he saw was a tall, tanned, skinny guy wearing faded blue jeans, an unbuttoned khaki shirt, and sandals. His hair was long—an insult to a barber— and he wore love beads around his neck. The beads hung three-quarters of the way down his naked, almost hairless chest.

"What do you want?"

"Is Sara around?"

"What? Not for you she isn't. She's jailbait." (She wasn't.) Andy slammed the door in Zack's face.

Sara's fate, or choice, was sealed. Her father didn't like him. In fact, he forbade her to ever see him. Therefore, she would marry him.

Andy may have brought out the rebel in Sara, but so did Britt. When Sara came home, announcing that she'd dropped out of school, Britt said she could live at home but only if she got a job and paid rent. She was an adult now, after all. Sara was shocked and indignant—this was her home! One did not rent space in one's own home. She would make a home of her own with Zack.

Britt tried to reason with Sara. "Calm down. Take your time to think about what you're saying. Living with a guy without marriage is a pretty serious step, and it's against your religion. What if you get pregnant?"

"Then we'll get married." Sara lifted her chin and stared into her mother's eyes. "But that's not going to happen. We know how to prevent that."

"You're on the pill. Who gave you permission to do that?"

"I gave myself permission. I told the doctor I was engaged, and he wrote me out a prescription for the pill."

Britt had been unloading clean dishes from the dishwasher, but when Sara said that, she began putting dirty dishes in with the clean ones. She turned to face Sara.

"Sara, you're a Catholic. It's a sin to use the pill ... and you lied. You're not engaged."

"It's a sin for me to move in with Zack. It's a sin to have relations without being married. So that's already two sins— might as well make it three and prevent an innocent baby being called a bastard. This way there'll be no baby until we're ready. Mom, you're going to hate what I have to say next, but sometimes you have to think for yourself—use the brain God gave you to do what you feel, in your heart, is best for you."

Britt was speechless. *She's thinking the way I thought when I decided that I simply could not have any more children—that I'd go crazy if I did.*

Sara packed her things and moved in with Zack. Britt busied herself with preparing to teach the two completely new subjects to senior high school students in the fall.

In July, Sara shocked them all again. "Mom, Zack bought a little farm fifty miles south of here. He's moving out there, and I'm moving with him. The house and barn are in good condition, but we'll need to do fencing. We're getting married in the fall."

"What! You can't, Sara. That's only two months from now! I don't have time to plan a wedding and be prepared to teach when school opens."

"Mother, I don't need your help. I think I can plan a small wedding. Besides, according to you, I'm living in sin. Don't you want me to make it right?"

"Sara, I want you to have time to think about what you're doing. We all have visions about how things will be, but those visions don't always come true the way we thought they would."

"I love him, and he loves me. That's all there's to it."

"How do you know if it's true love and not just lust and a desire to get away—away from family the way you got away from school?"

"We're getting married this fall, and that's final. We have things to do before winter comes—wood to buy and stack for the fireplace, and we need to put up the storm windows on the house, things like that. It has to be this fall. You'll see. I can plan the wedding, and I want you to come, Mother."

Britt, tears brimming and threatening to fall, grabbed Sara and hugged her tight. "Of course I'll come, and so will your dad."

Zack and Sara took the marriage preparation classes required by the Catholic church. Banns were read by the priest in church for three consecutive Sundays. No one hearing the banns contacted the parish priest about any objection to the upcoming marriage.

It was a nice fall wedding in the Catholic church. One of Sara's friends from college was her bridesmaid, and Zack had an ex-army buddy for his best man. Sara looked lovely in her white dress with a wide, wavy-brimmed hat of lace that just suited her. (Britt loved the hat, and wished she'd worn something like that at her wedding instead of the cheap crown with veil attached. "If wishes were horses ...") Sara carried a bouquet of pink roses. Zack remembered flowers—or did Sara put them in her plans? Zack cleaned up pretty good. He wore a suit and tie, but to Andy's dismay, his hair was long. Actually, he looked a bit like John Denver. So many young men wore their hair long. Those imports from London, according to Andy, should not have been allowed to enter the country. Beatlemania had taken a big bite out of his bottom line by making long hair a must if you wanted to be "in"; Andy feared for their future.

When the priest came to the part in the wedding ceremony where he says to those assembled, "If anyone objects to this marriage, speak now or forever hold your peace," Britt felt Andy tense. He might actually stand up and object! She grabbed Andy's arm and held him down. The moment passed, and Britt glanced around. Her parents, Ingrid and Carl Anderson, were there. Sara must have invited them, and they actually came to a Catholic wedding. She then saw

Andy's mother, Josette, but no sign of Andy's father, Phillip. He must have been away on a construction job. A reception was held after the wedding at the Rillstead Country Club. The club catered a simple meal of assorted pastries, lasagna (their specialty), assorted raw vegetables with dip, and for dessert the three-tiered frosted white wedding cake with the traditional bride and groom perched on the top.

No honeymoon. The farm was calling. They'd considered buying a cow but went for goats instead—Nubian milking goats. Goat milk was easier to digest, said Zack, and Sara wanted to make feta cheese. They'd have chickens, of course, but that would have to wait until spring when they could buy some baby chicks for the hen house Zack was building. They also stocked the basement shelves with canned goods and put hay in the barn. They had it all figured out.

CHAPTER

In 1970, Carl Anderson had made a fateful decision. He bought a home in Great Prairie, a beautiful place close to the river. Proud of the deal he'd made with the owner and knowing that Ingrid wanted to live in town, he was eager to tell her all about it.

Carl opened the door to the back entrance of the house and let it slam—he didn't care; he was in a hurry, and he seldom hurried. Not bothering to take off his jacket or cap, he stepped into the kitchen. "Ingrid, sit down. I have something important to tell you."

Ingrid was up to her elbows in the kitchen sink, washing dishes. She wiped her wet hands on her apron and sat down. "Yes, Carl. What is it? Did something happen?"

"I bought us a house in town."

"You what? I didn't know you were house hunting. Where in town?"

"On the south side of town, the good side, by the river. It's beautiful."

Ingrid rose to her feet, eyes wide and brows raised in

alarm; she swallowed before she could speak. "By the river? Carl, you know I am afraid of water. I always have been. You *know* that." She blinked to hold back the tears that were beginning to fill her eyes.

Carl narrowed his eyes and looked at her, eyebrows lowered, and his lips pressed together, forming a thin line. "I know it's a childish fear of yours—something you have to conquer. It was a good deal—a very good deal. The guy who built that house is one of the best."

"I wanted to move into town when that artesian well was dug right outside this kitchen window." Ingrid went to the window and looked out. "Running, running, running, all the time the water was running—I couldn't stand it. I've had nightmares about drowning ever since we got that well—like the kind of nightmares I used to have when I was little." Ingrid wiped her eyes with a corner of her apron. "How could you, Carl?"

"I knew you wanted to live in town. I forgot about your water thing."

"My *water* thing? It's a fear, Carl, a real fear—one I've always had. I wanted a house in town to get away from that well but *never* a house by a river." Ingrid took another look out the kitchen window and shuddered. "Can't we buy another house in town—one not close to the river?"

"No. I've signed all the papers." Carl turned and stormed out of the house and made a beeline for his machine shop— his sanctuary.

Ingrid had had her eye on the big white house at the intersection of Maple and Main Street ever since the Simms family had moved out. It was close to uptown and to the grade school but not *too* close to either. When their sons married and had children, the grandchildren going to school would have a storm home if they needed one. (The old country school had closed, and rural children were now bussed into town for school.) Carl, stubborn Swede that he was, would have none of it. He wasn't ready, he'd said. Ingrid sat down, put her arms on the kitchen table to cradle her head, and she cried.

Britt's parents moved to Great Prairie and into the house by the river. The twins, William and Owen, now eighteen, moved in with them. They would be leaving for college in the fall. Carl had always had a hired man on the farm to help him, hiring more men during busy seasons, and now he let him move into the farm house with his family so he could not only work the farm with Carl, as usual, but he'd be able to keep an eye on things. In the spring, summer, and fall, Carl would drive out to the farm to work and to see to it that things were being done right. At night he'd drive the ten miles back to town. In winter, he and his men would work down in the big potato warehouse in town, sorting and shipping out carloads of potatoes. It worked out well for him. He even found time during the cold, gloomy days of winter to slip over to Pop's Tavern and play a couple hands of Smear and shoot the breeze with the other men, most of them farmers like him.

Carl liked the town place, especially after he'd planted a couple of plum trees and a line of evergreen trees by the river. He aimed to block out the view of the river from Ingrid's eyes, but she knew it was there, and she could see it in her nightmares.

As part of the fall cleanup in 1977, Carl went out to mow the grass with his power mower. It was an expensive new one, and he was proud of it—it had real power. He didn't want the snow to pile up under his evergreen trees, creating places for rodents to hide and chew on his trees' bark, injuring, maybe even killing them. Those trees meant a lot to him. Carl was now seventy-one years old. He and the mower got too close to the riverbank. Carl lost his balance but not his grip on the mower. They fell together into the river. A man who had lost all his savings in the big Depression would not let go of a mower he'd just bought. He'd hang on for dear life, and with the brute force he thought he still had, he'd wrestle it to the surface. It was hopeless. Ingrid's drowning nightmare had come true.

Britt went with her mother to pick out a casket. *How could this be? My dad was supposed to live so much longer— his uncle Amos died at ninety-nine, still selling life insurance, for goodness sake!*

What will my mother do now? She has trouble balancing a checkbook. Mother was so angry when Dad actually took the joint checkbook away from her. He found out she was sending checks to Oral Roberts to "save his life." It's a blessing that those boys were born. They will help her—they're twenty-five years old now. She can lean on them.

They walked down the rows of lined-up caskets—and stopped. They were in front of a casket. Its lid was open, displaying a forest of evergreen trees.

"This one," Ingrid told the man in charge. Britt nodded. *He can sleep under the trees he loved.* She turned and hugged her mother, who was sobbing now. Britt felt the tears running down her own cheeks and brushed them away.

The old country church, started by Carl's father, Oskar, was packed with people coming to pay their respects at Carl's funeral. Britt was glad that Pastor Thomas was no longer there; she didn't want to hear again that she was hell-bound for marrying a Catholic. Britt didn't know the new pastor, but she thought that he gave a beautiful, heartfelt eulogy, followed by the choir singing Carl's favorite song, "How

Great Thou Art." Britt couldn't hold back the tears. That song always moved her, and now more than ever. Hannah, who had flown in from California where she sold commercial real estate, sat in back of Britt. She loved that grand, old hymn too, and she learned forward and put a comforting hand on Britt's shoulder.

The pastor then said that if anyone had anything they wanted to say about Carl, they should now come forth. Britt's tears stopped, and she sat up straighter, eyes opening wide in surprise as Daniel Hughes walked to the front of the church. Britt turned to look at Andy, sitting to her right. He was looking at her, his expression of surprise mirroring hers. This was not at all like their oldest son.

Daniel and Tony had often stayed out on the Anderson farm in the summer, starting when each one reached the age of twelve, which meant that Daniel was first. He'd help his grandpa by mowing the large yard, and he'd weed the garden for his grandma. When he got a little older, his grandpa would let him drive the tractor out to a new field they were about to start work on—things like that. He also listened to his grandfather talk, and he liked to watch the slow, careful way he worked. Daniel had a lot of love and respect for his grandfather. Still, Britt could hardly believe her eyes when she saw him walk to the front and begin to speak.

"I loved my grandpa. He taught me a lot. When I was twelve years old, he let me come out to the farm and work. My first job for him was mowing the grass. When I got older, he let me do harder jobs. I made mistakes, but he never got angry. He just smiled and helped me fix it. I learned that more can be accomplished by patience than by getting mad—a valuable lesson. He expected me to do well, and that made me try my hardest to please him. Grandpa, I will miss you very much, but I know that you are now in a better place."

I can hardly believe what I just saw and heard. Daniel doesn't like to be the center of attention, and he doesn't often share his feelings, yet he just did both. I never knew the depth of his love for my dad, and I've never been prouder of Daniel than I am right now.

The Ladies Aid later served a lunch in the church's dining room. After lunch, family members and anyone else who wished walked over to the cemetery to the south of the church and witnessed the laying to rest of Carl Anderson amongst the graves of his parents and three of his siblings. As people began to leave the cemetery, Owen took his mother's arm and led her to where his wife, Nora, was waiting for them by the car. Owen had married a Great Prairie girl, and they lived in town. They'd recently purchased a home in a nice part of town but far from the river. To this house they would now bring Ingrid. They didn't want her to be alone in the house by the river—the river that had taken her husband. She would stay with them until she figured out what to do next.

Hannah joined Britt and Andy as they left the gravesite. They would drive her to the house in town, the one by the river. William was staying there, and Hannah wanted to talk to him about what he thought their mother would want to do about the house.

Britt turned to Hannah and grabbed her hand. "I can't believe he's really gone."

"I know. He wasn't old. I always felt that I could count on him to be on my side. I won't have that anymore." Hannah reached into her purse and found a handkerchief and blew her nose.

"Hannah, do you have to go back right away? You could visit with us for a while. It's been a long time." She looked over at Andy, who was nodding.

"I really wish I could, Britt. I have to get back. I'm mentoring this young guy, teaching him how to figure the value of commercial property. They'd better not give him my job after I've made a good salesman out of him. Sometimes I wish I had your job security."

They'd reached the car. Andy, gentleman that he was, opened the doors for them, and they drove to the house by the river and got out. Britt and Hannah hugged goodbye.

Lying in bed that night, Britt realized that she felt empty. She felt that a piece of her had just been removed and buried. Hannah had it right; he'd not be on their side anymore—he was gone. Andy reached out and held her hand and said, "He was a good man and a good father, Britt. It's your mother I'm thinking of. How awful for her that he would die by drowning—the kind of death she always feared."

"Oh, Andy, I know." She turned toward him. "One good thing is that he never became old and helpless. He was always so independent; he wouldn't want people taking care of him. But to not have him around at all!" Tears began to fall. "I can't believe he's gone."

Britt didn't know it, but her father was not finished with her yet.

CHAPTER

27

A cold, snowy Christmas, but it would be warm inside Sara and Zack's house. They had spent their first Christmas together, just the two of them. They'd been too busy getting their place ready for winter—hauling wood, working up the soil for a spring garden, and caulking their windows—to have guests their first Christmas. Now with the second Christmas in their country home fast approaching, they wanted to share it with family—to have a family reunion. It would only be Sara's family, because the sole member of Zack's family, his mother, lived in Florida and decided that coming to Minnesota in any winter, for any reason, would be insane. Grandma Anderson had sold the house by the river and had moved into an apartment complex, the complex in which William rented an apartment. He and his mother were going over to Owen and Nora's house for a small, quiet Christmas. Andy's parents, Phillip and Josette, weren't even in Minnesota. They were visiting relatives on the West Coast.

Andy and Britt were escorted into the living room by Zack, wearing an apron. Andy, a former navy cook and baker, approved of that garb over the khaki shirt and love beads of their first meeting. Britt's eyes surveyed the Christmas tree. It was trimmed with popcorn and cranberry ropes and lots of tinsel. At the top of the tree perched a lovely angel, looking down on them all. Britt smiled her pleasure. "Sara, that's just the way I trimmed the tree for your first Christmas! It's beautiful."

"I know, Mom. Of course I can't remember that Christmas, but you told me about it more than once, and I've seen pictures. I knew you'd be pleased." Sara put her arms around her mother in a big hug.

Daniel, no longer in the National Guard, attended the University in Rillstead, working for a degree in computer science. "Yeah, Mom. Sara saw pictures! Why didn't you take any pictures of me at my first Christmas?"

"Well, we were a little busy. We rushed you to the emergency room with a high fever on Christmas Eve. The doctor thought you might have spinal meningitis, but it was pneumonia. They put you in an oxygen tent and kept you in the tent for a couple of days. You hated that. You don't remember it, of course, but I think *something* in you remembered it because when we used to go camping, you slept with a knife under your pillow. Do you remember that?"

Daniel nodded. "I wanted to be able to cut my way out of the tent if I had to." He patted his mother on the shoulder. "Thanks for letting me keep that knife there."

Tony stepped up. He'd come up from southern Minnesota where he was involved with Junior League Hockey. "Yeah, Mom, now explain to me why I have such a small baby book."

Britt grabbed them both and hugged her two grown sons—both taller and much stronger than she was now. "Come on, you two. You're just trying to get to me. What was that song you'd play to really bug me? Oh yes, 'The Ten Commandments of Man Given to Woman' by a Prince somebody? It didn't really bother me much, but you guys had fun thinking it did, so I always acted as if it bothered me. I had fun doing that."

Amy came into the room. Sweet sixteen and popular, she enjoyed everything about school—the friends she made, most of the teachers, and cheerleading. But school couldn't last forever. What should she do next? Her parents wanted her to go to college, but she didn't know what to study. Maybe she should take a year off and try to find out what was right for her. She could go to Florida, stay with her uncle Luke and his wife, and get a job—see what life was like in the real world. Amy cleared her throat a couple of times to get everyone's attention. "Dinner's ready, and it smells really good."

They all trooped into the kitchen, picked up a plate, and served themselves before sitting down on the benches flanking the long, trestle dining table. Andy led them in the saying of grace, and then all began to enjoy the feast, and a feast it was: Zack had bagged a goose in the fall, and he had roasted it—their Christmas goose. Sara's mashed potatoes were smooth as could be, and her gravy was to die for. Amy had baked a couple of pies, one being her dad's favorite, a blueberry pie, and the other was apple. Laura's offering was an after-dinner one; they would sing Christmas carols, and she would play the accompaniment on her flute. She was the musician in the family.

They ended the night by reminiscing in front of the fireplace. Fire in a fireplace, especially on a cold night, has a hypnotic, magical effect. Watching those flickering dancing flames of red, yellow, and with sometimes a touch of blue above the wood seems to encourage either dreams or conversation. The mind relaxes its guard and imagines or remembers. In the case of the Hughes family, it was remembering.

Sara, tossing back her head of black curls (no ironing it straight anymore) started it out. "Remember the night Dad opened the door to find Zack standing there? What do you think now, Dad?"

"Uh. I might have been too quick to judge." He looked at Zack with raised eyebrows and a sheepish grin.

Then someone brought up Amy and her friends streaking to the streetlight half a block away during her sleepover birthday party, and everyone wanted to see Laura's fish bowl scar. And there was Tony's best catch ever, better than any he'd made when he played baseball. It was the day he caught Laura as she tumbled down the stairs in her baby walker. He just happened to be on his way up.

"Thanks, big brother," Laura said as she hopped up from her seat and went over and hugged him. "You may have saved my life. Now does that mean that you are forever responsible for me?" (No one ever owned up to leaving the basement gate unlatched.)

The next disclosure, about the "bear facts," lightened the mood. When Tony and Daniel were four and six years old, they divided up the bears: Yogi Bear and the Hamm's beer bear. Daniel claimed Yogi Bear for himself. He liked the bear's deep, silly voice. "Tony," he'd say, trying to sound like Yogi, "I should have Yogi 'cause he's '… smarter than the av-er-age bear!' and I'm older and smarter than you. You can have the Hamm's bear."

"No. He falls down a lot. I don't." Tony punched Daniel in the arm but not hard. Daniel was bigger; there might be consequences.

"Tony, you like to fish. Hamm's bear can fish all the time. He's always by 'sky-blue waters.'"

"Okay." They went back to watching *The Yogi Bear Show*.

Watching and listening to their children, Britt and Andy couldn't quit smiling. They were surrounded by their handful of children, and all were happy and doing well. Life was good.

It was getting late. Andy was tired. He'd worked harder and later than usual the week before Christmas, cutting hair and even shaving some men—people wanted to look their best for Christmas. Time to start for home. Britt offered to drive, an offer Andy was happy to accept. He shook Zack's hand and suggested they go hunting together next fall. Everyone thanked Sara and Zack for the good time. Sara hugged her mother and whispered in her ear, "I think I'm pregnant," before she hustled her out the door.

The cold, starless night and the deserted highway gave the effect of being just outside a lighted bubble, with the light from the headlights pulling the car toward home. Some snow had melted during the day, but now with night's chill, patches of ice clung to the paved road. It was almost midnight, and all was quiet but for the radio playing soft music. Britt turned her head to the right to check on her husband. *He's sound asleep. Good! Now I can speed up a little and get home faster.*

They were both tired. The shock of Britt's father's drowning and then the funeral, followed by Ingrid moving into town—it had been one thing after another: exhausting. *I miss Dad so much. I really thought he'd live to be one hundred. Maybe tonight I can sleep the night through.* Britt's foot pressed down on the accelerator pedal, and the car shot forward.

"Britt Lucy Anderson, slow down!"

Startled, she jerked her head to the right. Andy still slept, mouth open. *He didn't say anything; besides, he would have just said "Britt." That voice! It was my dad's voice. When he really meant business, he always called me by my full name—but he's dead!* Britt's stomach clenched, and her mind locked up, but her foot acted on its own and lifted off the accelerator—just in time. The front wheels hit an ice patch, and the car veered from one side of the road to the other, and then onto the road's right shoulder. The tires gripped some dried roadside grass, the car straightened, and Britt got it back on the road. She drove the rest of the way according to existing conditions, which meant at least ten miles an hour under the speed limit.

Britt slowed down, but now her mind unlocked and went into high gear. *My father is dead. He's gone but where? His voice boomed right above me; how could he know about the ice? No stars in the sky, but eyes in the sky? Spooky. It's as spooky as the letters written by my aunt Christina, a deaconess in the Lutheran church—a deaconess wouldn't lie. She and Hannah wrote to each other for years. When Aunt Christina died of stomach cancer, Hannah sent the letters to me for safekeeping. Hannah's job keeps her on the move, and she feared the letters might be lost. She said they were very detailed because Aunt Christina had planned to use them as the basis for a book about her father's "contract" with God. I'd written the story off as a hallucination of a man sick with the flu, but could the story be true? I need to read those letters again.*

The next day Britt sat down in the old rocking chair, her aunt Christina's letters in her lap. She picked up the first one and began to read. It gave Britt some background on the grandfather she never knew. Christina wrote:

> In 1882, my father, at the age of nine, left Hultsjö, Sweden, with his family and sailed to America. His life here would be ruled by two grand passions: hunger for education and hunger for land.

Summers he would work on his father's farm, but in the winter when farm work slacked off, he sought work close enough to a college so that he could attend night classes. He read voraciously. When he was twenty, he married my mother, Solvig, and together they had fifteen children—two dying shortly after their birth. He determined that his daughters, all seven, would not only finish high school but also go on and become either teachers or nurses. He wanted them to have a profession, to be self-sufficient.

Hunger for land, his other passion, meant he bought all he could lay his hands on, even if he really could not afford it. My mother objected, but he always managed to talk her into signing the papers. He was rich in land and rich in children. Father wanted the land for his sons; he dreamed of them farming close by some day—a cluster of Anderson farms. He was mortgaged to his eyeballs.

Disaster struck in 1919. Father became very ill, with what, I was never told, but I do know that the doctor came by horse and buggy out to the farm, which was fourteen miles from town.

As Britt read, she could picture Grandpa Ephraim, lying in the bed he shared with Grandma Solvig—the bed in which fifteen children were conceived and born. *He looks unconscious. He has a farmer's tan, yet his face looks pale and his body is so very still.*

I can see Grandpa Ephraim turn his head, moaning at the pain this causes. His gaze falls on the dark, walnut-stained dresser on the south wall. Above the dresser hangs the oval mirror with its carved walnut frame. Grandma Solvig loved that mirror. Britt's grandma was a handsome, strong woman. Ephraim had a tough time convincing her to marry him, but in the end, he'd beaten out the Frenchman, Durand, to win her as his bride.

Solvig hated cows. In fact, she never wanted to be a farm wife. Ephraim had tried his best to make her life less difficult by putting in the first indoor bathroom in the county. The toilet was gravity flushed and the tub gravity drained. So what if the tub needed hand filling? It was inside. He had also driven a team and wagon to the music store in Rillstead to buy a fine organ to grace their living room, finer even than the one in their rural church. It took him three days to complete the trip.

I can see Grandpa Ephraim close his burning eyes, only to open them again when he hears the bedroom door open. He watches as Dr. Guilfoyle and his nurse, Miss Imdahl, enter the room.

Grandpa sees Dr. Guilfoyle, a portly man with a warm personality, take off his hat and coat and put them on a chair. Miss Imdahl takes off her coat, but she leaves her starched, white nurse's cap on. Grandpa would appreciate that—he likes those caps, so professional.

He hears the doctor giving orders to the nurse: "Here's the thermometer. Put some alcohol on it and take his temperature." Dr. Guilfoyle rummages in his black doctor's bag and pulls out his stethoscope.

With the thermometer stuck in his mouth, Grandpa couldn't very well say anything to them; besides, he doesn't have the energy. But he keeps an eye on them and listens to what they say.

Thermometers needed to stay in the mouth for a full five minutes, so as the doctor and nurse wait for Ephraim's temperature to register, they talk, not knowing that their patient is listening.

"Do you think it's another case of Spanish flu, Doctor?"

"It looks like it, but I hope not. We've had nine cases of the flu in the past ten days, and eight have died. I do my best for them all, but there's no cure, no medicine." They look at each other, and their tired eyes reflect their mutual lack of hope.

Miss Imdahl takes the thermometer out of Grandpa's mouth and reads it, not realizing that the doctor is not the only one to hear her say, "It's 104.5—he's burning up!"

"Take his pulse, Miss Imdahl, while I listen to his lungs." Dr. Guilfoyle puts the stethoscope on Grandpa's chest and listens to his heart. "His lungs sound like crackling paper." He then checks his throat and ears. "His throat is red and sore, but at least his ears are all right. Help me turn him over. I want to hear if his bronchial tubes sound clear."

Grandpa groans when they turn him—every muscle in his body screams in pain. They turn him onto his back again, and again his muscles hurt when they touch him. He's dizzy, but he lies motionless, exhausted, but not too tired to listen to their conversation.

"What was his pulse, Miss Imdahl?"

"Ninety-seven."

"His symptoms are the same as the others." Grandpa sees Dr. Guilfoyle's shoulders slump in defeat and hears as he says, "There's nothing we can do here. He's dying. I need to talk with the family." Dr. Guilfoyle puts his stethoscope into his black bag along with the thermometer and shuts it with a snap.

He watches as Dr. Guilfoyle and Miss Imdahl leave, neglecting to close the bedroom door. Grandpa hears the doctor tell his wife and children that he is dead, and he hears his children cry. He begins to pray with all his might.

He later told his daughter, Aunt Christina, what he'd said in his prayer and what God said to him. She wrote it down in detail:

> In his prayer, he laid out the untenable situation like so: "I can't die. My wife and children need me. I can't leave them with the land mortgaged so much! I can't die now."
>
> His mind was a maelstrom, and then from the center came the deep, commanding voice of God. He had listened; He knew this man. God spoke, and now Ephraim listened:
> "Ephraim Emmanuel Anderson,
>> More time I giveth to thee.
>> Send thy daughters to school.
>> Pay all that thou owe; be debt-free.
>
>> Verily I say to thee,
>> Nine years l shall give to thee.
>> Work hard; use well thy time.
>> Take care of thy family."

In time he regained his former strength, and when he did, he called his family into the living room so he could tell them of his contract with God.

> (A solemn occasion calls for a solemn room, and this room was that. For years we'd celebrated Christmas in this room. It was perfect. With maroon draperies and Victorian style furniture, it was a rich but solemn room, a room that made all laughter guilty laughter.)

Aunt Christina describes Grandfather's talk with his family:

> When all had assembled, sitting on the sofa and straddling its arms, with Mother sitting in her armchair, and the leftovers decorating the floor, Father said, "I know you all remember when Dr. Guilfoyle and his nurse were here. Well, I heard the doctor tell the nurse I was dying."
>
> Not a sound was heard in that room until Father cleared his throat and went on. "I refused to accept that. My mind whirled, and I reached out to God and told him I couldn't die, that I had too much to finish on earth." He looked over at his wife. "Solvig, I just couldn't leave you to make do with all these children."
>
> There was the sound of sniffling, of a nervous shifting of seating positions. Three-year-old Flossie, the youngest, started to cry.
>
> "Now, Ephraim, you weren't really dead; Dr. Guilfoyle just thought you'd die, but you didn't. You are here, and we'll all be fine." Mother, ever clinging to the logical, could not believe a person standing in front of her could ever have been dead.
>
> "Solvig, I'm not done." Father cleared his throat again and went on. "God answered. He revealed that He would give me nine more years. In that time, I must pay off the mortgages and the bills we owe and put our daughters through school. Daughters need something to fall back on just in case. Solvig, I made a contract with God."

(I, Christina, second oldest of the children, listened carefully. I was born a sickly child, covered with eczema. Father told me that I had trouble sleeping and cried a lot. Mother, as I was to learn when I was eight years old, had wished that I would die. Father was more compassionate—many nights he walked the floor with me. I had a special place in his heart, and I adored him. When I heard him say that God had given him only nine more years to live, I could hardly bear it.)

"That does it," Father finished, "but it means that we all have a lot of work to do in nine years. Meeting adjourned."

All trooped out of the living room and soon forgot the big meeting and Father's revelation, all except me.

Christina watched her father as he worked. She saw that he had changed; no longer did he collect his wife and children to go and see the circus when it was in town, and no longer did they attend even a one-day Chautauqua. She kept close track of the years and dreaded the passage of each one. She writes in another letter:

It's now 1928. Father has given Carl, his oldest son and my brother, land for a farm. The farmhouse was in a low spot and had to be moved to higher, healthier ground. My father and my brother readied the house for moving by putting screw jacks under each corner of the structure. The house would be raised slowly until a large flatbed trailer would fit under it. Using Father's pulling tractor, the house was moved to the desired location. A concrete foundation awaited it. The house was lifted incrementally by way of the screw jacks, onto piles of wooden beams, called cribs, which were the height of the foundation. It started to rain. He hurried, and one of the jacks my father set slipped, crushing him from the chest down and causing severe internal injuries. My brother freed him and pulled him out.

Four days later, on November 28, 1928, at the age of fifty-five, my father died. His nine years were up; the contract was fulfilled.

Britt lifted her head from her reading and learned back in the rocking chair until her head rested on the chair's back and closed her eyes. *What am I to make of all this? Grandpa and God entered into a contract, and the contract was fulfilled. Was it a self-fulfilling prophecy that actually killed him? I've heard that if you believe something hard enough, it will come true because you act and speak in ways to make it come true. That's the way voodoo works, I'm told. Not only was his daughter Christina keeping track of the years going by, but so was he.*

He was a man of rock-solid faith who knew his time was soon up. He probably was in a hurry to get his son, my future father, into a home set on a firm foundation before the nine years were up. From what I'd heard about him, I knew he'd be moving fast, and to make matters worse, it was raining. He set the jack, yes, but it was obviously not set solidly enough. It slipped. When it rains in Minnesota's Red River Valley, the rich black earth becomes a sticky, slick "gumbo," as they call it. A corner of the house fell on him, crushing the lower half of his body. His son, my father, got him out. Or was it simply that his time was up: contract fulfilled, so—poof?

What I do know as surely as I'm sitting here in this old rocker with my aunt's letters in my lap is that my dead father's commanding voice prevented a possibly serious accident on a starless night on a lonely, icy rural road. Perhaps there is more to the makeup of us humans than just a collection of cells with a limited life span, after which they are recycled into who knows what. A caring voice called out to me. I don't understand how, but I accept its reality.

Britt couldn't get the content of the letters out of her mind as she went about her day's work. That night, while lying in bed, she tried to relax, to calm down, but sleep wouldn't come. Had her father really spoken to her? Maybe she just imagined it, the way she imagined her grandpa Ephraim's "death" bed. But the voice of her father, saying her name, including her middle name—it had to be him. But there would be no answer tonight—she might as well drop it.

Almost asleep, another thought struck her. *Sara said that she thought she was pregnant! If true, I will become a grandmother—that sounded so old! I'm not ready to be a "granny." I haven't thought of Jesse in weeks; now I'd better wipe him from my mind forever. It would be unseemly for a grandmother to have such thoughts.*

I'm going to have to learn how to knit!

CHAPTER

28

Britt was ashamed of herself. When she first thought of Sara having a baby, she thought of herself, that she would become a grandmother. How selfish. Sara would become a *mother*, and in so doing, creating and securing the future. Nothing is more important than the bringing forth of new life and then nurturing it. Britt and Andy were the old; now in with the new.

She decided that she'd crochet a baby blanket for the new life to come—but what color? No one knew if it would be a boy or a girl, so she scratched blue and pink off the list. Green and white then—green, the color of life, of growing things, and white for purity and innocence—the essence of a little baby.

Sara felt great during her pregnancy. No morning sickness, but she said at night she sometimes felt a little queasy, though not enough to throw up.

Britt was busy teaching and looking forward to being a grandmother, or so she told herself. One thing did bother her at night, and that was a recurring dream. The third time it happened in two months, she wrote it down:

> It was a dark and stormy night—evidently dreams don't mind using clichés. I was trying to climb down a steep, grassy hill, wearing a skirt and heels. Lightning and thunder only added to the difficulty of my descent. I turned and looked back up the hill. At its top I could just make out an iron fence, and then a flash of lightning revealed the dark figure of a man coming down the hill—was he after me? I tried to run. I stumbled, and the dark figure leaped on top of me. Screaming—pain rips through me as does the sound of thunder—a shot? The figure stops what he's doing. Another figure, male, has pulled him off me. Lightning flashes, and I see my attacker lying spread eagled in the grass—dead. Another flash, and I notice he's wearing a blue, bloodstained work shirt and denims—prison garb. I don't need a flash of lightning to let me know that I'm now pregnant.

Britt read what she'd written the next morning, trying to determine her dream's meaning. *Is my dream telling me that I'm jealous of Sara for being young and pregnant? And that I want to be young and fertile? But I don't want to be pregnant. In the dream, I felt hatred when I realized I was pregnant. So that's not it. It's just a dream, a meaningless dream.* Britt picked up her crochet hook and the ball of green yarn.

Little Mathieu Carl, Sara decided to spell her baby's first name the French way to honor Grandma Josette, was born on July 11, 1976, weighing in at six pounds, six ounces. His twenty inches of length was topped with a crop of curly black hair. July 11, being a Sunday, Andy and Britt drove to St. Luke's Hospital in the little town of Spilde to meet their little grandson. Britt held the sleeping baby, and her heart warmed—her first grandchild. She leaned down and kissed his soft forehead and smelled his sweet baby smell.

Two weeks later, in the little Catholic church in Spilde, Mathieu received the sacrament of baptism. Britt sat on the old, wooden pew with Andy beside her. She watched the sacramental water trickle down the back of little Mathieu's head—a joyous occasion, but her thoughts were not joyous and holy. Her thoughts were selfish and secular. *I'm definitely a grandma now—no getting around it, but I don't feel grandmotherly. I'm too young!*

By seven thirty that night, Andy and Britt were home. Britt felt depressed, but the weather was beautiful. She decided to go for a walk. Walking for Britt was therapeutic. If she needed to wake up, she walked; if she needed more energy, a good walk could give it; if she needed to cheer up, a walk would usually put her into a good mood, or at least a better one.

Britt wore a light jacket, not because she needed the warmth, it was July, but because at this time of night the mosquitoes were out. She walked down Cherry Street, the street that ran by their house, past the high school where she now taught, and continued on until she came to the little brook or "rill," the little waterway that gave their town its name, "Rillstead." A bridge for cars and pedestrians had been built across it years ago. It's impossible to just cross a bridge on foot without stopping to gaze down at the water, especially if it's flowing, and rains in the last two weeks insured a healthy flow of water. Britt stood at the midpoint of the bridge in the pedestrian pathway and looked down. It was hypnotic and set Britt's thoughts to wandering. *Water is, if you get right down to it, the source of life itself, whether it is physical life or spiritual life, as in today's baptism of Mathieu. I wonder if I'll ever be able to paint the flow and color of water—it would be difficult. So far I've painted mostly portraits; people's faces, their expressions, fascinate me. When I retire from teaching, I'd like to try my hand at landscapes. Painting a brook would be a challenge. Would that be a waterscape?*

Britt only saw three people as she walked home. The first one was a blond man playing Frisbee with his dog, and then she saw an older couple, holding hands, walking past the library. The woman wore a scarf, but her gray, curly hair was sticking out the sides, and she wore glasses that were in style some years back. She'd be fun to draw.

Back on Cherry Street, she approached the Smith house and glanced at her watch. It was 9:10. If Andy was watching a movie, she'd have missed some of it. Better hurry—only about a block and a half to go. She and Andy loved to watch movies, though not always the same kind. Yet that was something they shared.

A car came down the street toward her. By now Britt was almost in front of the Harrison house on the corner with the streetlight, the streetlight to which Amy and her friends streaked so long ago. The car slowed, lights went out, and it stopped at the curb. *Must be the Harrisons coming home.* Britt noticed a figure standing at the juncture of the Harrison front walkway and the main sidewalk, but being in a hurry, she didn't pay much attention.

Then the figure, a man, was standing at her left side. Britt looked closely at him. *I don't think he's a former student.* The streetlight, about fifteen or so feet away, revealed a stocky Mexican man with short, dark hair, about five foot six (about a couple of inches taller than Britt). He wore a dark jacket and pants, and he was clean-shaven with a short, muscular neck. What Britt noticed most of all were his dark brown and heavy lidded eyes. He asked, "Is this 518?"

"Five-one-eight of what street?"

"Front Street."

"You've got the wrong street; this is Cherry Street."

He swiveled around to face Britt and grabbed her upper left arm with his right hand. "Get in the car or I'm going to kill you."

This can't be happening! Britt froze. Then she felt his left hand poking something into her right side. *No way am I getting into that car.*

"No!" Britt screamed and swung at his face with her right fist. She saw him brace his feet, the left foot further toward Britt than the right. With a twist of his wrist, the "something poking" entered her left side. *I've been stabbed!* Britt bent her right arm in front of her face, and he stabbed her elbow.

He turned and walked swiftly back to the passenger side of the car. Britt started to run. *I should get his license plate number; isn't that what you're always supposed to do?* She bent down in the intersection, trying to read the number. *I can't read it—it's too far away, but if he sees me bending down trying to read it, maybe he'll think I did and get out of town—the farther the better.* Britt straightened and ran home. Entering the back door of her house, she unzipped her jacket and saw blood, wet and sticky. It had soaked her jacket and her ripped blouse. She felt no pain, but she was angry, so angry that what she wanted first of all was for her attacker to be caught. Britt ran to the kitchen wall phone and shakily dialed the police.

"I'm Britt Hughes, Andy's wife. I've been attacked." Upon hearing this, Andy, who had been watching TV, rushed to her side.

"What! Where?" She saw shock and disbelief on his face as he looked at her bloody clothes.

Andy grabbed the phone. "Hurry, she's bleeding. We live at 335 Cherry Street."

Within five minutes, Patrolmen Cliff Bradley and Robert Moreno were banging on the door. They immediately took Britt to the hospital, and Andy followed them by car.

Britt doesn't remember much about the ride to the hospital. She does remember that her clothes disappeared in favor of a hospital gown, and she never saw them again. Her ripped, bloodstained jacket and her favorite blouse were now torn and bloody evidence, locked up for good.

Andy watched as the emergency room doctor sewed Britt up. Turned out, Britt was lucky. The stab wound in her upper abdomen wasn't serious. It missed all vital organs. She thinks her jacket had something to do with that by making her look wider than she really was. The knife wound on her elbow missed any nerves and only needed a few stitches.

Lying in the hospital bed, Britt tried to relax; she still couldn't quite comprehend what had happened—it all seemed so bizarre. Reality hit when Sara and Zack, the parents of little Mathieu whose baptism day it still was for ten more minutes, entered her hospital room.

"Mom! Are you all right? Can I hug you?"

Britt didn't cry when she saw Sara, but it was a struggle not to. They hugged, being careful of her sore spots. "I'm fine, Sara, I really am. My guardian angel must have been on the alert."

The next morning, a police lieutenant took Britt's statement, a police sergeant serving as witness. After he'd asked the standard questions—name, address, birth date— he asked Britt to describe the circumstances of the assault and to describe her assailant. She was also asked to describe the car. All she could remember was that it was midsize and dark colored—either dark blue or dark green. He asked Britt the year, and she said maybe 1970s, but she didn't know.

"Can you describe to me the type of voice he used? Was it a gruff voice, loud voice, soft voice?"

"It was low and firm," said Britt, looking down and fiddling with the top sheet.

"Did he have an accent?"

"No."

"What nationality would you say he is?"

"Uh. Spanish American."

Those were the main questions. After Britt's statement was taken, seven mug shots were lined up on the hospital's bedside table. The lieutenant asked her if she could identify the person who had assaulted her. Was he one of the men pictured? Britt wouldn't choose because she wasn't sure. Later that day, eleven photos were lined up on the bedside table. Again Britt was asked to try to pick out her assailant. A couple of pictures looked similar to the man who had attacked her, but again, she wouldn't choose. She was still upset, and her elbow hurt. She needed quiet time to think.

Britt got that time at home. It took her almost a week of thinking and trying hard to remember what the man looked like. Sunday night, a week after the assault, she sat down and drew, but she just couldn't get it right. Monday morning, she got up at six thirty and started drawing again. This time she could see in her mind his heavy-lidded eyes looking at her as he asked about a house number. The streetlight highlighted the left side of his face. Britt finished the drawing, put it on the dining room table, and called the police lieutenant who had questioned her in the hospital. No answer. All that day, whenever she passed the dining room table, she looked at the picture, and each time Britt felt fear. *This is the man that hurt me.*

She ended up personally delivering the drawing to the

police station. The lieutenant and other officers recognized the likeness as being that of Juan Youcha, a repeat sex-crime offender.

With the drawing done, Britt began to relax, and her thoughts drifted to the dream she'd had a short time before she was assaulted. She remembered her anger, or was it despair? In the dream, she was pregnant. *What else was in that dream? I remember trying to go down a grassy hill in heels. I stumbled. Someone fell or jumped on top of me—a man. Now that I think of it, I'd seen a dark figure out of the corner of my eye as I started going down the hill. The weather was awful, lightning and thunder, and it was getting dark. I heard a sound; I thought it was thunder, but it must have been a gunshot. The man on top of me stopped what he was doing when someone pulled him off me and threw him to the ground. Impregnated by a rapist—I wish I'd been shot and killed too.*

Silly dream—or was it so silly? Had that dream been a warning? Was that dream the root cause of her hitting and screaming? Britt knew that when he said, "Get in the car or I'll kill you," she would choose death rather than get in that car. The dream knew how to push her buttons—knew that she feared pregnancy. The dream, in effect, scared her into acting—made her fight. Britt believed this but knew others would think she was crazy.

Our culture puts little stock in dreams, unlike the Old Testament, especially the story of Joseph, Hannah's favorite. Joseph was sold by his brothers into Egypt to be a slave. Word got around, however, about his ability to interpret dreams. The Pharaoh dreamed a strange, disturbing dream about seven fat cows grazing and seven skinny cows then joining them and eating up the fat cows. The Pharaoh sent for Joseph to tell him what it meant. Joseph said that the seven fat cows meant seven years of good harvests, but they'd be followed by seven years of famine, and they'd better stockpile food for the bad years. And that's exactly what happened, but because of Joseph, Egypt was prepared. Some dreams may be silly, but not all are.

July 11, a Sunday, a most memorable day, began with the morning baptism of a new grandchild, water trickling down the back of his head, ushering him into spiritual life. It ended with a Sunday evening assault on Britt's body, blood trickling out and staining her clothes, a baptism of blood that could have ended her physical life. She had been sitting in church a few hours earlier that day, bemoaning the fact that she was a grandma. When she mulled over the events of the day, she thought, *How shallow. I'm alive! I'm strong! And I embrace grandmotherhood.*

There was a trial, of course, the State of Minnesota, plaintiff, versus Juan Youcha, defendant. Britt, witness for the state, remembers very little about it, but she does know that Andy was not with her because he had to work. His shop was a one-chair shop, he being the one barber. Daniel, attending the university, was able to be with Britt through most of it. His presence was a great comfort. The trial ended with a guilty verdict, and the judge sentenced Mr. Youcha to thirty years in prison.

Britt's mother never asked her about that night or about the trial, and Britt never brought the subject up. She once asked her mother what "rape" was; she'd just read the word in the daily newspaper. Her mother said, "It's nothing you need to know, but I need to know what you plan to do for your 4-H project next year." Britt got the message. Many people consider sex crimes, even potential sex crimes, to be just too horrible or too shameful to talk about; her mother was one of those people.

CHAPTER

29

Britt set the patio lounger's back to a comfortable angle. She put a folded quilt on top of the vinyl strapping—she didn't want strap marks on her back. She then ran into the house and grabbed the big butcher knife and inserted it between the folds of quilt, within easy reach of her right hand. Britt was determined to catch some rays before school started. She was tired of looking fish-belly white. Shorts, tank top, sunglasses, water, a good book, and the knife for protection—yes, she had everything she needed to relax and soak up some sun.

Britt had always thought that Rillstead was a safe town with friendly people. Now she knew nothing was 100 percent safe. She remembered her youngest daughter, Laura, saying, "You have to expect the unexpected, Mom." At the time, she nodded, not wanting to fight about a statement that didn't seem to make much sense, but Laura was right.

Getting ready for bed that first night home from the hospital, she wondered if Andy would treat her as usual, or would he not even touch her, thinking she was fragile—she did have stitches. Their conversation that night was burned into her brain:

"Andy." Britt sat on the edge of the bed and waited for him to look at her. "Would you still love me even if I'd been raped?"

"Sure, you're the mother of my children, but I wouldn't *make love* to you. I'd close my eyes and see him with you, and that would shut everything down."

"I could have been killed! Would you rather have me dead than have your *space* violated by another man?"

"Stop it. You're getting too emotional. You didn't get killed, and you didn't get raped. You fought and got away— I'm proud of you."

"I saved what you consider *your special place* in me. Is that what *really* matters to you?" She could see him in her mind. His shoulders slumped, and he threw out his arms, bent at the elbows with his palms up, after she said that.

He sighed and said, "It's late. I've got to be at work early tomorrow." He climbed into bed.

Britt had removed her earrings and joined him. They had held hands and said the Lord's Prayer together as they'd done every night they'd slept together for over twenty years. They had been careful to make sure that only their hands touched until it came to the good night kiss, which was just a chicken peck. No sleeping like two spoons in a drawer that night.

Britt had tossed and turned. She had been too keyed up to sleep—happy to be at home in her own bed, safe and sound, but she'd not been happy with how things stood between her and Andy.

I could have been killed. It, the whole thing—the attack with a knife and the trial—made me realize how fragile life is. It is not something to be taken for granted. Fate, or a supreme force, has been trying to teach me this for a long time: when

a snowplow hit us from a side road and the impact rolled our
car into a ditch, when the garbage truck backed over eighteen-
month-old Sara, and now the knife attack on my body. I've been
one slow learner.

Our life together has become shabby, in the sense of being
neglected and not maintained, and it is getting shabbier. This
has to stop. The children and our struggle to provide for them,
to be there for them, have long been the be-all and the end-all
of our world—the thing we've shared, our one togetherness.
Now that is changing.

Sara started it when she married, and the other four will
follow one by one. What will Andy and I do then? Be lonely
together or lonely apart? We have a history together, a history
that has created a strong bond of trust. Love may have waned,
but trust has grown, and that's not a small thing. Can we
get the love, the caring, back? That is something we need to
find out.

Once they were best friends. Could they be so again?
Or had they grown so far apart that they couldn't even *like*
each other anymore? They had to find out, but Britt couldn't
leave now—school was starting in a couple of weeks. Maybe
the first part of October would be possible, after she'd got
her students squared away and provided that the school
administration would allow her to take a couple of weeks off.

Britt turned in detailed lesson plans to the office so her
substitute would know what to do when she was gone—if
she could be gone. She asked for two weeks off and got it.
The two weeks off started the first of October. Andy didn't
need permission. He was his own boss, but the first part
of October worked for him too. Harvest was in full swing.
Farmers just didn't have time to come into town for a haircut,
and he'd be home in plenty of time for the Thanksgiving
haircuts. Ingrid, Britt's mother, was happy to be asked to

come and live in their house and supervise the comings and goings of Amy and Laura, the only children at home now.

This could be their second—or was it third?—honeymoon. A snowplow had put the kibosh on the first one, so it probably shouldn't count. They had called the month before Andy's ship sailed away on a six-month cruise a honeymoon because they'd had such a good time seeing all that Newport had to offer. Second honeymoon, that's what this vacation would be.

Andy and Britt decided to make it a camping trip for just the two of them—they'd have to interact. They bought a new, smaller tent than the one they had when the children were small and two sleeping bags that zipped together to make one double bed. Their old camp kitchen and the Coleman stove were taken out of storage. They then set out to find adventure and each other.

Cooped up for hours in a car with Andy, eating unsalted sunflower seeds and reading to him from a book she'd borrowed from Sara (it was a novel about hunting, so she thought he'd like it), she became conscious of a smell. It was sweat. October can be crisp and cool, but it is also a sunny month, and it can get warm, especially if you are riding in a car without air-conditioning, as Britt and Andy were.

I'd forgotten how much I liked the smell of his sweat. Sounds crazy, but I've since read that the pheromones in sweat can be a sexual turn-on. I used to go to his baseball games when we were teenagers. After a strenuous game of baseball, he was irresistible. I married him, and he quit playing baseball and started using deodorant—darn!

They went up north to Winnipeg, Canada. While there, they decided to see some of the sights. Andy wanted to go to the Assiniboine Downs, the live racetrack, and try his luck betting on the horses, but he changed his mind—he didn't want to become short of money at the start of their trip. Britt wanted to see the Assiniboine Park Zoo.

"Let's go to the zoo. My parents went there when William and Owen were six years old. When my dad was looking over the llama enclosure, he bent his head to look at a baby llama, and his glasses fell off."

"Did he go to the zoo manager, or whoever, to see if he could get them back?"

"No. You know how he is—the quiet, don't-bother-anyone type. He bought new glasses when they got back home. I want to see if there's a llama wearing black-rimmed glasses." Britt started giggling at the thought.

Britt's giggles were infectious, and Andy grinned and poked her in the ribs, which only increased her giggling. "Yeah, sure—a llama with glasses. That I'd like to see. Let's go."

They saw the llamas—none were wearing glasses, but they were interesting. They saw live polar bears and even a snow leopard, the first time they had seen either species. They passed "Aunt Sally's Farm," a children's petting zoo, but didn't go in. They had left their children at home.

Leaving Winnipeg, they drove cross-country headed for Banff, Alberta. Driving through Saskatchewan, Britt saw a machine that looked like a huge prehistoric bird; it constantly bent down to drink and then looked up to swallow. It was an oil rig.

Other than the oil rig, the trip to Banff was a blur of campgrounds, with two important exceptions that Britt will explain later. Their days were spent marveling at the passing scenery. The towering pines and snowcapped mountains took their breath away—not surprising, as they were used to land as flat as a pancake. They took turns driving, so both would have time to read and later talk about the book, and they ate the ever-present unsalted sunflower seeds.

Reaching their destination, they pitched their tent at a camping area in Banff National Park. To get a really good look at the area, they rode the ski lift up to its top and gazed down at magnificent Lake Louise—a giant emerald held in place by the sharp, snowcapped peaks of the Canadian Rockies.

The next day, they walked on a glacier. Britt had expected something grander than a slab of dirty snow and ice, but at least now she could say, "I walked on a glacier!" Banff is a pretty town full of shops designed to attract tourists, and they enjoyed being touristy and looking around at all it had to offer but agreed that the surrounding natural beauty completely upstaged anything they'd seen in any of the shops. Next stop: the basin and its hot springs. Soaking in the hot water, smelling the rotten-egg odor of sulfur, relaxed all aching muscles. They emerged from the springs feeling like well-cooked egg noodles.

Their last night at the Banff campground turned out to be the first of the exceptional campground experiences mentioned earlier. They sat close together in front of their tent, holding hands and gazing into a fire. Britt welcomed its warmth in the evening chill. She began to feel toasty and then lusty! Every inch of her skin burned and zinged with desire. She turned her head and gazed at Andy's profile. He must have felt her gaze on him, because he turned his head to look into her eyes—a long look. Britt, borrowing some moves from a long-ago romance novel, stuck out the tip of her tongue and in slow motion moistened her top lip and then her bottom lip. Still gazing into his brown eyes, she lifted her right eyebrow, and before she could lower it, he grabbed her. She melted against him. They rose as one and stumbled into their tent.

Britt's hands were shaking, and she struggled to get out of her clothes—she was too hot! Andy, naked, helped her undress, and they embraced, hot skin on hot skin. They dived into their sleeping bag, kissing and touching. A dog barked, and someone yelled "Shut up, Bruno!" They'd forgotten all about the other people in the campground. Their lovemaking became more urgent—a need for speed kicked in for Andy, and soon—too soon—it was all over for him, but the touching continued for a short while, and then sleep descended on a satisfied couple.

Andy told her once that he always felt the need to hurry. As a teenager, he would masturbate. He knew the Catholic church considered masturbation a sin, but sometimes he just couldn't help it—he felt such pressure that he just had to.

Once when he and his father were sitting in a freezing cold duck blind, waiting for the ducks to fly in, he brought up the subject, hoping the white plume of his exhaled breath would partly hide his face. "Dad, is masturbation a bad sin?"

"Self-abuse," said his father, not wanting to say the other word, "is a sin, but if it came to a choice between doing that or using some girl for your own selfish purpose—which is abuse of the girl—than self-abuse is the better choice."

Andy knew his father would not want him to go to hell, so self-abuse must not be a mortal sin. But when he did it, he always felt that he should do it fast and get it over with.

The next day, after a lazy breakfast, they packed up their things and headed for home. They drove and camped, drove and camped, passing though towns with great names: Crowsnest Pass, Medicine Hat, Swift Current, Moose Jaw, Portage la Prairie, and Winnipeg, all the while getting closer to home.

As they rode along, Britt's thoughts turned back to their night of burning love. *I lusted after him. What made me feel that way? Was it the sunflower seeds we munched all the way from Minnesota to Alberta? Was it the togetherness we enjoyed while exploring Banff? We were also together in the car, no air-conditioning, and even Canada can get quite warm. Could the pheromones in his sweat have produced my sexual excitement? It could have been my hormones. I may be premenopausal. Has my brain suddenly flooded my body with super sexy hormones? Will I ever feel that way again?*

The night before they were to reach home, they camped in Winnipeg, Manitoba. That night proved to be the second exceptional experience during their campground honeymoon.

As soon as their tent was up, Andy started meal preparations on the portable camp stove. Britt sat on a picnic table with her feet on the bench, watching a neighboring camper start a fire in his fire pit. It was chilly, so she didn't mind it when the warm smoke from his fire bathed the left side of her sleeveless T-shirt and shorts-clad body. She thought over all they'd seen and done. And she wondered about her unexpected flood of passion in the Banff campground.

"Beans and hot dogs—come and get it!"

She jumped off the table. "Thank goodness. This smoke is making my eyes burn." *What are the words to that song? "When your heart's on fire, you must realize, smoke gets in your eyes." Yes, that's it.* She and Jesse had danced to that song.

Jumping off the table and turning around solved the smoke-in-eyes problem. *No smoke in my eyes now, but my heart is definitely on fire.* Britt took one look at her husband— it must have been a burning, yearning look, for they went to bed hungry that night. It's a good thing they had pitched the tent as soon as they pulled in.

Their lovemaking proved to be a replay of the night in Banff, Alberta. It was just too much for Andy to have his wife, a woman who was seldom interested in sex—it took a lot of foreplay—turn into this hot and horny babe. It blew his mind. He could not contain his excitement or himself. He came too soon again, but so what? Britt loved the closeness, the hugging and kissing, his need for her.

The final stretch of their journey was the homestretch from Winnipeg to their Minnesota home. Britt was happy to be home. She was also itchy, and she noticed small blisters popping up on her arms and legs. Her left ear itched, and when she looked in the mirror, she saw that it had swelled to almost twice its size. *It's a large, cauliflower ear like some wrestlers have, only it's red. I have poison ivy!*

Ever since she was little, she'd dreaded camping trips because of poison ivy. Britt learned to be very careful, always watching out and avoiding those plants with leaves in groups of three. *How did I fail to spot the enemy? It was the smoke at the Winnipeg campground. The camper making a fire must have been burning some old, dried poison ivy vines mixed with the wood. The smoke drifted right over to where I was sitting. Mystery solved: misery in full force. Even my scalp has itchy blisters on the left side. I can't stand it!*

The only thing that kept the misery at bay for a while was to take a ten-minute shower, as hot as she could stand it. Something about the hot water made her body produce antihistamines, or so she'd read, and it must be true. The itch stopped, and she could sleep. This went on for days. She started to think she'd never look normal again, and she dreaded the arrival of the utility bill.

School! She had to go back to school, and she looked awful. She went to see Principal Hart. He took one look at her and gave her two weeks off.

Once she was clear of poison ivy, Britt again thought about their vacation of exploration. *Why, during my marriage, have I enjoyed only two nights of overwhelming passion? A premenopausal hormone surge is the logical explanation, considering my age—forty-something. But could old "mommy tapes" have been doing a number on my brain? That day in the woods, so many years ago—I was ten, and Hannah eight years old. We were riding our broken-off and leaning over, burlap-saddled, tree-stump "broncs." Mother heard us having a good time and came out to check on us. She said that day, "Girls, if that starts to feel good, stop!" I got away twice with not stopping: once in the Banff National Park and then again in Winnipeg. Wait! Did I really get away? Was my terrible case of poison ivy my punishment for disobedience—for not stopping? Ridiculous!*

Yet it's not ridiculous if my mind now links passion and poison ivy. The punishment could serve to get my sexuality out of high speed and put me back into normal mode, which for me is a slow, dial-up sexuality.

I can understand now how people can be swept off their feet by passion. I can even understand crimes of passion, because I've experienced a lust that is a burning fire—a fire that not only blinds the eyes but invades and consumes the heart.

Britt and Andy did find out that they could again be friends. Their friendship was based on a solid foundation of shared values. They both believed in God, though with some differences in how to show it. Promises were meant to be kept, especially when they were formalized by the term "vows."

They were both born during the Great Depression. Andy's parents lost their farm, and they had to move in with relatives. Britt's parents lost all their savings. In both families, money was scarce, and Andy and Britt probably learned the meaning of frugality through the air they breathed. In particular, Andy could never really believe that he and Britt had enough money.

In marriage, their relationship was one of equality—they honored each other—but blind obedience? No. They did believe in a division of labor. A mother's job was to raise the children, and a father's was to provide for them. Together they produced and raised five children—all of whom grew up to be good people, the kind that form the backbone of a country. They did the best they could and were proud of the results.

Even when they were bringing home similar paychecks, Andy provided the necessities, and Britt provided the extra money to maintain and improve their property, to see that Laura got the braces for her teeth that she needed, and to put money aside for emergencies. Their respect for money also served to keep them together. Married people who divorced almost always ended up poorer.

They trusted each other even in the times when they didn't particularly like each other. Complete trust in another human being is a "Pearl of Great Price" (Matthew 13:46).

They weren't soul mates, the kindred spirits people talk about, but with their shared values and trust in each other, they could live together in contentment. Britt had always felt that the third human right in the Declaration of Independence, the right to pursue happiness, was too giddy, too exhausting. Much better would be the right to pursue contentment.

A contented life allows for differences. Andy would follow every sport, except tennis, which he didn't care for, and he'd golf regularly. Britt would paint, read, and become a seeker of *her* spiritual truth—a truth that rang true in her soul. She wanted to revisit that place of utter love and security that had enfolded her in a soft, orangey cocoon when she was eight years old. She had wanted to stay there forever. Perhaps meditation and prayer would get her to that place again. She could just hear what her parents would say to that! "We're put on this earth to *work*. You're just sitting around doing nothing." *Nothing, my foot! I'm listening.*

Together they would dote on their grandchildren but not to the extent that children would again become the be-all and end-all of their existence. They would care for each other, make time for each other—watch movies and go out to dinner and tell each other about what was going on in their individual lives. They could also be lovers if they'd just get the timing right—figure out how to be more in sync.

And that would be their marriage. *It sounds good to me, and I* know *Andy, and he would agree.*

EPILOGUE

The sun streams through the east window, filling the room with warmth and the people with contentment. Britt and Andy finish breakfast—waffles, Andy's specialty—and are lingering over coffee while reading the *Arizona Star*. Andy concentrates on the sports page while Britt skims the local news.

Andy seldom reads more than the sports page these days. In 1985, he read the June 7 issue of the *National Catholic Reporter* (NCR), the issue that reported on the sexual crimes of Father Gauthe and the concealment of same by clerical authorities in Father Gauthe's diocese. The account sickened Andy in body and soul. How could his Catholic church protect a pedophile, someone who preys on children? An editorial in the NCR accused the Catholic bishops in America of inaction and silence. He would not, could not, go to such a church. Every time he sees a priest, he wonders, *Is this one a pedophile? Have my boys been touched by one in a bad way?* He needs a change, needs new surroundings, in the hope that he can shut his mind up and stop thinking about the NCR report on sexual crime.

Andy decides to sell his barbershop and retire to a warm place and stay away from church—any church. "Holy" men abusing children and not even punished for it! He feels betrayed. Britt's heart aches for him; she knows what it feels like to have your trust in a belief turn to ashes. Her college textbook, *Catholic Marriage and Family Life*, gave instructions as to how to use the rhythm method, the only method of birth control allowed by the Catholic church, other than abstinence, but it kept failing them. Britt felt betrayed then, and their marriage suffered. Trust in each other kept them together; it was a constant. Complete trust shared with another human being is a rare and precious treasure beyond measure.

Andy's barbershop sells, and they put their Cherry Street house on the market. They figure they might as well; their children are grown up and living their own lives in other places. The empty nesters opt for a new nest all their own. Britt and Andy migrate to the sunny Southwest without regrets; they've been responsible parents and are proud of their adult children.

Now Andy golfs in the winter—no more blizzards with the resulting snow to shovel, no more black ice roads or temperatures dipping down to thirty below or more. He has a part-time job that he enjoys—it's his social outlet. Britt paints, gardens, and reads whatever and whenever she wants. Through the years, their love has been like Elton John's "Candle in the Wind," wavering when bad times hit but coming back stronger and brighter than ever. They are content in their love for each other; it is their one true thing. Wasn't it the Beatles that sang "Love Is All You Need"?

They keep up with the "kids" by e-mail and telephone, and now they have grandkids too, so the children are married and breeding but not like rabbits—they only have nine grandchildren among the five couples.

Laura, the daughter who urged her mother to eat her

vegetables, is now a nutritionist, and she and her husband have a darling baby girl, Rebecca.

Sara and Zack are still survivalists. They grow and sell organic vegetables on their little farm—a healthy environment for their two children, Mathieu and Chloe. After Chloe started first grade, Sara resumed her college education—a case of the nut not falling far from the tree. She made her long-ago dream come true; she is a veterinarian, caring for dogs, cats, and goats.

Daniel, who some would call a computer geek (but that's fine with him), likes his job and is good at it. And he's good in the kitchen too, cooking and baking when his wife needs help. Their active trio, two boys and one girl, keep their parents on their toes.

No, Father Felix, Tony did not become a priest. He played college hockey and went on to be the athletic director of the college. He and his wife have a daughter.

Amy is the glue that keeps the family together by informing all of what's going on and putting on reunions from time to time. She is also the loving mother of two children.

"Andy, look! Hannah, my dear sister, has been selected Architect of the Year by the Southwest School of Design—her dream came true." Britt hands the article over to Andy.

"I'll read it later, Britt. Time's a-wasting, and the fairway is calling." He goes to her and grabs her by the hands, and she stands to receive and return a big smooch.

Britt smiles as she watches him go out the door. She appreciates the time they now have for each other, time to watch movies together, time to go out to dinner and catch each other up on what's going on in their lives. Sometimes they are even lovers, but at all times, they love and care for each other.

This is their marriage. To quote Britt, "Life is good."

Printed in the United States
By Bookmasters